THE MAN WHO WAS LOVED

Kay MacCauley

THE MAN WHO WAS LOVED

TELEGRAM

British Library Cataloguing-in-Publication Data
A catalogue record for this book is available from the British Library

ISBN 1-84659-002-7
EAN 9-781846-590023

copyright © Kay MacCauley, 2006

This edition published 2006 by Telegram Books

TELEGRAM
26 Westbourne Grove
London W2 5RH
www.telegrambooks.com

Venice, 1546

For the first two hundred years or so, his favourite pastime had been to throw himself under the speeding hooves of horses. This until it was no longer exhilaration and thrill but disappointment that afterwards he came together as though nothing of them had touched him.

And now it was more than four hundred years that he had trodden this land and he had learnt, not long after the start, that what they had said was a lie. For the world had not grown more beautiful on repeated view, and any insights he had gained as to the nature of men had revealed them not better but worse.

From where he sat now, crouched against the foot of the Ponte Santa Maria dell' Orio, he watched the sun go down. Drifting veils of pink and violet, the billowing sails of a galleon, floated across the sky, deepening to crimson and a coppery magenta as they slowly travelled west. And gradually the darkness fell, blowing onto the city in waves from the direction of the Lagoon. It settled onto the inky waters of the canals and doused the gleaming spires of the buildings.

He stood up, brushing the flies from his skin. He could smell the rotting of his flesh, see it hanging in strips from his bones. Picking up the handles of his cart, he turned and began to run towards the Piazza San Marco.

His name was Lelio but people called him the Collector, because that was what he did. Gathering lovingly unto himself all that was worn out, discarded or dead.

Usually he could smell the blood of the dying, sometimes before even they were aware of what came, and so he knew enough to follow those whose low bent heads or hesitant gait promised he need not wait long.

It was this scent that, moments before, had woken him.

A sudden wind blew dust swirling up from the embankment. Lelio felt the particles heaving in and out through the disintegrating bags of his lungs. As he coughed, the dust gusted in clouds through his body and emerged through the gaps in his skin.

'Such an ugly baby,' Sister Assunta said, moving him to one side, a little more roughly than was necessary, to clear space for a fifth infant in the cot. 'Look at that nose, Sister Clara. He'll never make his living by his looks, that one.'

In later years he often wondered whether this, his first memory, was correct. After all, he would have been too young to understand her spoken words. More probably, the sadness that he remembered creeping over him had been caused by the tone of her voice, the look in her eye and those fingers, like rolls of cheap sausage meat, that had pushed him out of the way.

Sister Clara sighed. 'How many of these little ones do you think will ever have a chance to make their living at anything?'

'And you are saying there is something we should do about that? Did we ever have our proper chances? If we had, would we have chosen to end up here, day after day, looking after other people's garbage, the fruits of their fornication?'

Sister Assunta bent over him, prodded at his face and arms with distaste. Where, she wondered, had this one come from?

There had been no clues as to his origins, no tell-tale trace of his parentage. A fisherman had found him on the bank of the Lagoon at Giudecca, so tightly entangled in weeds, he said, it was as if the infant had grown there.

Some that were delivered to the Shelter bore an indication as to the place of their birth – a blotching on the skin from the dye on a workshop floor or the bitter smell of the liquor used for the preparation of animal hides. Others, wrapped in bejewelled and bloodied gowns, seeming to have about them already a dawning of the proclivity to sin that festered in the veins of their mothers. These, the offspring of courtesans, she could hardly bear to touch.

Now drawing her hand away from the child, she whispered, 'Is that what you are? The child of a whore?'

To her astonishment, the infant turned to her, its eyes limpid and open in question. 'You see?' she cried to Sister Clara. 'Even from the cradle, they have no shame. We toil to tend and care for what would have been better left to die.'

Sister Clara put her finger to her lips. 'Hush now, Sister Assunta. Those are not words for God's ears. Let us sit outside for a moment, while there is still some sun.'

He watched Sister Assunta go. The boy she had squeezed in next to him began to cough, then lay silent. He knew that this new arrival would not last long. Those who lacked the will to cry, even at the beginning, never did. Then when they died, Sister Assunta would come – it was always Sister Assunta – and she would pick them up, spit on their foreheads, remove from them any clothing, tie around their necks a bag weighed with a large stone, or some such heavy thing, and then with only slightly less care than she disposed of the remains of the bean bread and cabbage stew that

10

she and Sister Clara always used to eat for their lunch, she would slide them out of the lowest window and into the canal. This stretch, a narrow bywater through which no boats passed. Those laid to rest there remained unseen and undisturbed.

Across the room on the back wall was the hatch through which most of the infants arrived. Accessible on the outside only from the main canal and not visible from the front pavement, it ensured that deliveries could be discreet and anonymous. It provided not only an acceptable means for the disposal of those whose entry into the world was for any reason unwelcome, but also a pleasing salve to the conscience, for it was carved above the curves and curlicues of the front entrance that all infants placed into the care of the Shelter would be brought up in the ways of the Holy Redeemer Himself.

There were ten wooden troughs in the room, each equally crowded, but on entering that place from the brightness outside, any visitor might at first have thought it deserted were it not for the smell. The smell of human waste, of tears silently cried and the particular thin, sour odour found unexpectedly sometimes in the corner of rooms – the unmistakable aroma of misery.

Only gradually, as the visitor's eyes adjusted to the gloom, would they notice with surprise the shapes of the troughs, and only on moving a little closer still would they see the row of tiny bodies that each contained. Most of the infants made no noise at all. Usually, the only sound to be heard was the occasional lip-lapping of the waves, accompanied by shouts from the gondoliers as they passed.

The sacking on which he lay was sodden and stinking, and the skin on his back was rubbed raw, but it seemed now, as he lay there, that the pain it caused him diminished.

The room appeared to be growing distant and, although he was keeping perfectly still, he had the sensation of being pulled upwards. He could feel a warmth against his face and was aware of a light, quite different to that which filtered in from the windows overlooking the canal. He could hear the voices of the two Sisters in from the yard now, but there were other voices too, kind and gentle, and even though they spoke no words and were so faint as to be only part of the evening breeze from the doorway, he knew that they were calling to him. He knew that he could join them if he chose. The longing he felt to be held in that warmth made him ache. He closed his eyes.

He rose up and felt the hands touching his face and soothing the pain on his back. They pulled him closer to their embrace. They could feel he was tempted to stay. Beneath him, his body lay motionless in the trough and beyond that he could see a pale streaming of sun from the courtyard. The pink-gold light of a winter afternoon. A reminder of earthly things.

With a sigh, he tried to turn his mind from the fingers that touched him, from the voices that continued to call. He tried to descend. Aware that as he began to press himself back to his body, the hands still stretched out to him, reaching forward to grasp. He did not look at them. He pushed himself down – his torso, his limbs, his head – back into the cold, painful confines of flesh.

With all the strength he had left, he concentrated on the room around him, trying to bring it back into focus. He fixed his attention onto the figure of Sister Clara, now standing by the door, aware that if he let his mind wander, even for one instant, he might again slip away. He needed somebody to touch him, a contact to engage and grip, to tie him back into the world.

She didn't turn round. He was aware of her saying goodbye to

Sister Assunta and preparing to leave. The room began to dissolve and fade and from up above him he heard someone calling his name. The voices he had heard before began to sing, and he fought the urge to rise in response.

The shadows in the room appeared to move, assembling to make solid form, settling to wait at his side. He felt the touch of foul-smelling shreds, a dampness on his cheek.

Now the pulsing of his body slowed further and as the rattle in his throat commenced, desperately he sucked for breath, staring at Sister Clara, willing her to turn and look at him. A pressure built inside his head, swelling hot and tight, pushing against his brow with such a force that he began to weep with pain. Fearing that his face would break open, he cried out and suddenly the tension burst, splintering, sounding an agonising crack, with a reverberation so violent that his eyes seemed to come loose from their sockets.

For a moment he could see only darkness, then as his vision cleared he saw Sister Clara, looking down at him as though she were surprised to find herself standing there.

Unable to remember what had impelled her across the room, she hesitated – then picked him up. He concentrated until the look in her eyes changed from incomprehension to a slow dawning of recognition and wonderment. Tears appeared. Her shaking hand traced the shape of his face. He shivered with pleasure. Those things he always would remember, although he had no idea how, that first time, he had known what it was that he should do.

Sister Clara began to tremble. So much so that she was frightened that she might drop her child, but she could not bear to put him down. She wanted to fall to her knees and cry up her thankfulness to God, but she knew that she must remain quiet and not give any sign of what she saw.

'By the saints above,' she whispered. 'My little one.' She moistened the edge of her sleeve in her mouth and wiped at the stickiness of the sores on his back. 'I will take you home,' she said. He felt her tears on his face.

He closed his eyes. He was safe. From outside, he heard the sudden, torrential downpour of rain and the turbulence of the canal as it turned against the wind and flowed back towards the Shelter.

At the end of the Ponte San Barnabo Redentore, Lelio picked up the handles of his cart, turned it round and began to run with it back up and over the bridge.

He had been at the Shelter. He had come so quietly with the shadows that the Sisters sitting out in the courtyard, on a bench in the sun, had not even noticed he was there.

Straight away he had found the infant, smelt it out, seen its eyes already misted over, gazing inwards, away from the room. Then something in the expression on its face had drawn him to peer more closely, something that seemed familiar. A look about the eyes that was unusual for a child.

Leaning forward further, Lelio had licked its cheek before sitting back to count its breaths as they weakened, knowing when it had reached the one which should have been the finish. He had heard the deep, sweet rattle in its throat as the last of life drained away.

Savouring for a moment the thought of this gift, he had bent over the trough, been about to pick the infant up when something unexpected had happened.

The infant's breath had begun again with a convulsive shuddering that increased to such an intensity that the outlines of its form appeared to shift and change, as with the rage of the wind over water. Lelio had thought that the child's innards would surely soon break out through its skin. He had waited for it to burst. And at the instant when it cried out, it seemed that indeed it had. For one moment, the lines that kept its form to itself had gone.

But while Death had not taken him, Lelio still smelt His presence and raised his hand to the air, searching. It seemed the child was still marked for His favour.

Suddenly, the Sister had come in from the doorway, and Lelio had dropped to the floor. Reaching up, he had taken the body of the infant who lay next to the first, crawled to the edge of the room and left from there.

At the end of the bridge, Lelio laid down his cart and sat on the stones. Perhaps a wise man would have understood.

Sister Clara hurried from the Shelter with the child concealed beneath the pleatings and folds of her habit. The paving of the streets to the right of the canal was not yet complete and every passing horse or cart sent up whirling clouds of fine black dust. She drew her habit more closely over the infant's head and crossed the bridge that led to the market.

The short brilliance of the winter afternoon had already faded. Stall-holders were lighting their lamps, and the air was filled with the smells of burning oil and woodsmoke. The pink and gold in the air had thickened, darkened, now dropping in layers that swayed in waves to the west.

It was in the sunset rather than the dawn that Sister Clara felt God most present. His arrangement of the beauty of sunset perhaps a reminder that He would be there during the coming hours of darkness. There was so much that she wanted to believe.

By cutting through the middle of the market place and crossing the canal that lay beyond the church of Santa Maria dell' Orio, one came upon a narrow confusion of streets known locally as 'I Nastri'. Their name, 'The Ribbons', was an accurate description of the winding way in which they lay, but one that promised to an outsider something altogether more pleasing than the reality.

While by no means the poorest area of the city, Venice had no other district which would so trouble the senses of a stranger entering unawares. Even the officials responsible for public health no longer went there, although they still entered it onto their records that they did.

When Sister Clara walked there, the street ahead of her always emptied at her approach. Yet she knew herself watched from the shadows of basements and doorways and that, even if they did not welcome her, they would not do her any harm.

At the end of the first street beyond the canal stood a tree that had been struck by lightning. It had not fallen but remained there, its trunk cleft almost entirely in two, and the blackened stumps of its branches stretched up in supplication to the heavens.

Everywhere mounds of human and household waste, putrid, rotting, swarming with flies. The people here did not trouble to take their refuse as far as the canal. Sometimes she used to stop for a while, pausing on her way through, and stand, breathing in the fetid air, waiting. She did not know why she waited, nor why the compulsion persisted.

Whenever she was alone, unaccompanied by Sister Assunta, she always took this longer route back to the convent.

But, today, it was not until reaching the far end of the market that she realised she had taken the direct path and had passed the road that led there.

The convent of San Barnabo Redentore was situated on the next street to the San Barnabo Redentore Shelter For Foundlings. For six days of the week, the nuns from the convent devoted their services to the Shelter and other institutions in this, the district of Castello, where the Administrator, Sebastiano Finetti, had decreed that the presence of God should be felt. Both in the convent and in her place of work, Sister Clara lived surrounded by others yet in complete loneliness, as she had done since entering the order fifteen years before.

Now, as she crossed the footbridge leading to the convent, church bells all over Venice began to chime the hour, sounding reminders from every direction of who she was and the vows she had taken.

She stopped and looked up at the sky. With shaking fingers, she pulled back the pleat of her habit and looked at the infant. His eyes were closed. He was asleep.

She stared at him. How odd it was that he seemed to look quite different now. Even the shape of his eyes, which before had been those of her own beloved, seemed changed. Was it that, in the dim light of the Shelter, her own eyes had not seen clearly?

There, when she had picked him up, the urge to take him, the knowledge that she could and should, had driven out all other thought. When she looked into his eyes, she had been overcome, as before, by that same irresistible outpouring of love. For a moment, she had even sensed herself back in that room, on the bed, with the sheets unwashed, dark and stiff from the woman who had lain there before her. And she remembered the bucket in the corner, covered with a cloth.

And while she was still bleeding from his birth, they had pulled him from her arms and given him to those who waited. She had seen them watching from the doorway, impatient for her to be done. They had come from their boat to the house, to the door there, so that they could collect more speedily that for which they had paid.

But now, on the bridge, as she looked down at the infant sleeping in her arms and tried to summon back that other face and that intensity of love, she found that she could not. Then he stirred, stretched, opening his eyes, and as they met hers, there, suddenly, she felt it again. Of course it was him. His weight in her arms repaired what before had been broken.

Licking her finger, she drew the shape of a cross on his forehead. 'Marin,' she whispered. 'My son.'

On entering the convent gates, she pressed him to her so tightly that he could scarcely breathe. Yet this sensation he found intensely pleasurable. Her skin was rough, none too clean and smelt vaguely of mouldering apples and curdled milk, but to him it was the most beautiful scent imaginable.

Hurrying along the path through the courtyard with her child

20

clutched to her bosom, it seemed to Sister Clara that the stones were slippery underfoot.

Over the archway at the entrance to the main hallway hung a portrait of San Barnabo Redentore. His face was drawn, his cheeks were hollow and his eyes, sunken far back into the recesses beneath his dark and heavy brows, stared down at those who passed there. Portrayed at the age of twenty-one, he already had the face of a man bowed and wearied, worn out from the strain of redeeming those who wanted to repent and the greater effort of hauling from the mire those who would rather have remained there.

Inside the hallway was nailed a small plaque telling the history of his service and beside this another picture portraying the events at the time of his death. Blurred strokes of the artist's brush showed a procession and a throng of people pressing forward to touch him.

Both artists had dated their work. The second had been painted the year after the first.

Sister Clara lowered her head as she passed and moved quickly through the hall to the cells.

Speech, other than at mealtimes, was not permitted, and the only sound to be heard in the corridors was the subdued shuffle of softly shod feet on the stones. Stones of porphyry, stolen by crusaders from Cairo, now worn smooth by the passage of penitents and the weight of the sins that had brought them there.

When she reached her cell, Sister Clara tucked Marin into the large basket of sheets that it was her duty to stitch and darn and placed the lid in a position that allowed him air to breathe. Entry into another nun's cell was forbidden. He would be safe there – as long as he did not cry.

'Now you must always be quiet, my little one. If they find you it will be the end for us.' Her lips shaped the words without a sound. And he was quiet. As the days passed, he never cried.

For the six working days of the week, Marin lay silently in the basket, from the five o'clock call to morning assembly and prayers, until late in the afternoon when Sister Clara returned, slowly slid back the lid of the basket, then in a rush snatched him up into her arms, so fiercely that he was unable to draw breath.

Of course he never cried during the day. What reason did he have to cry?

Occasionally, Sisters of the convent would leave either due to a change in personal circumstances – a conception unlikely to be Immaculate, or because of an opportunity to live in some other way, outside. It was not unusual for this to happen but it was most unusual for a woman of Sister Clara's age to be successful in her request for employment.

'You are to see to the cleanliness of his house, to the cooking and to his comfort,' Sebastiano Finetti told her. 'In return for this you will receive your board and lodging and a salary of four ducats.' He cleared his throat. 'You should also bear in mind, Sister Clara, that you are fortunate, very fortunate indeed to have been offered this position. For a woman of your ...,' he hesitated and pronounced his next word carefully, '... countenance, you are aware, I am sure, that the choices now open to you are not so many. Perhaps it is God's will that you are able, in this way, to look after your sister's child.'

Sister Clara looked down at her feet. She had no sister but

the lie suggested a charitable nature which she knew would be commended.

And so it was arranged that Clara Sannazaro should become the housekeeper for Vittorio Matteotti.

After she had left the office, Sebastiano Finetti wiped the chair where she had sat. He pressed his face to it to make sure that it was clean. He knew why she had come to the convent, but today he had shown that, like Jesus, he could be merciful too. It pleased him to consider himself an instrument of the Divine, tuned to its pitch, strung to its will and thus prepared to send forth a note so pure and so sweet that its sound would crumble and prise the work of the Devil out from every corner where it lodged.

It had been some months now since Death had shown His face. Death teased him.

Lelio lay in his favourite place, on the mud stretch that bordered I Nastri. He spoke softly to those who lay in his cart. It remained his hope that maybe one day, unwittingly, one of them would give him an answer.

It was growing dark. Another night approached. He had noticed that it was during the night that most of the people died. Some having forgotten that another morning would come, and others from fear that it would.

He had seen that, at night, things appeared other than what they were in the day, taking deceptively greater or lesser shape. This especially in the hours between midnight and dawn when – left to itself, with no sun to obey – time was no longer fixed and could vary and move according to whim, dancing backwards and forwards to no other call but its own.

And Lelio had had much time to ponder this and to watch the way of its working because, since the day of his changing, he no longer had the ability to sleep. All this time, all these years, not even broken by the oblivion it granted.

Looking back to the beginning he would have laughed, but it was some time since there had been cause for merriment.

Before his changing in the year 1099, Lelio had lived on the island of Torcello. As a thief. That was how he lived. From other people's belongings, their salt, their fish, their clothes, their coins. Things that first belonged to them and then belonged to him.

On the day he entered the house he had been surprised to find it deserted. Filling his bag with goldware, ornaments and jewels, he made his selection at leisure.

He could not remember now whether it had been the pull of greed or gratitude that persuaded him to linger. To take from the library those parchments with the most decorative coverings and clasps, and to break off the lock from the cupboard where he had found more gold, this time strangely warm and smelling of spice. And next to it a pot of what he had thought was a vegetable broth.

He had not stopped to ask himself why any man would keep his broth with his books, or what could possibly have made it so delicious that there was need to lock it away.

He had drunk it down in gulps, even though he had not been the slightest bit hungry. Drunk it only for the pleasure of taking one more thing that belonged to another for himself.

At home that evening, in his hut on the marsh, squatting on the floor by the fire, he had wiped his hands clean of the oil from the smoke before reaching to touch parchments. Never having learnt to read, he had no idea of their meaning but enjoyed the smoothness of the vellum as he rubbed it between his fingers.

And over the following nights, now suddenly unable to sleep, he took out his papers and stroked them, admiring the patternings of the words.

During the next year, he had been slow to realise that something strange was occurring. He had always been a sickly man, prone to bouts of fever, but all at once this illness ceased completely; and as time went on, and the faces of his contemporaries grew creased and worn, and their hair turned grey and then fell out, he himself remained unchanged. His face firm, his eyes clear and his brown curly hair undiminished.

He had been a man of average looks, his features too bold for beauty, yet not altogether displeasing, and much was his pleasure on seeing that this was the way they stayed.

Moving away from that district when his appearance began to cause gossip, he then travelled from one town to another. And, for two hundred years, he enjoyed perfect health and the sport of throwing himself into the path of rapidly moving horses, carts and boats, repeatedly into the way of Death. Remaining broken only for a moment or two, before the continued beating of his heart, or the pieces in which it lay, summoned his parts back together.

Of course during this time he had his share of romance, producing a number of offspring from a number of wives. And there were many who were glad of his company, for he had become a source of never-ending good cheer.

While most grateful for this unexpected blessing, at the back of his mind was the fear that as inexplicable as the event of its arrival might come that of its sudden departure.

So to safeguard his status as far as he could, to demonstrate himself as deserving, he renounced his profession of thief and took pains to more nearly conform to the standards God had intended. He went regularly to his local church and became an expert weaver of cloth. A trade to which his dexterity was suited.

Now he grew ashamed of what he had been before. This more so when he saw its like evident in the behaviour of others. So most often he was glad to leave the place where he had been living, hoping that in the next a different air, a different soil might have proved more conducive to the flowering of man's better nature.

Only on occasion did his parting cause him sorrow, but no matter how close the bonds he had made, he knew that the length of his stay must be limited. For time, while plotting its pitiless course across the faces of those around him, left his own as ever, implausibly smooth and youthful.

And once in his mind a date had been set, he began his attempts at concealed farewell. Words to serve as apology, declaration of his fondness and unwillingess to go. Means to explain after he had gone.

But having no gift for words, he doubted that his hesitant phrases had ever been understood. And as he went without warning at night he thought on this, knowing when they woke to find him gone, they would imagine that blame lay with them.

Never did he take with him anything that would act as a

reminder. Only coins enough for his journey, and the parchments. The only link with the past he permitted.

Much of what had passed in those years was faded, forgotten, but some memories were still as fresh and as clear as if on closing his eyes he might wake there – the smell of the grass at dawn in a secluded garden in Sicily – a wife in a village near Bari with a soft downy fur on her back – a daughter born in a mountain hut in Bergamo, the most beautiful child of all.

Returning some years later to see her again, if only from afar, he had found her not in bloom but elderly, decrepit, blind. He had not counted those years correctly.

She was crouched on the step of their home, weaving wool with slow and crooked fingers. Sitting on the grass some paces away, he stayed for the whole day to watch her. Only once did she pause and raise her head as though she felt his presence. And then he longed to approach, to speak, had stepped towards her to do so, before cowardice had persuaded him that the greater kindness would be to leave.

Riding from Bergamo, travelling south, having intended to visit Milan, he had seen a carriage coming from the opposite direction, bumping rapidly over the stones. And from force of habit, springing from his horse, he had hurled himself under the wheels. The startled occupants screamed in fright and craned their heads from the windows. Raising a severed arm to wave, Lelio had laughed as the vehicle careered away, veering wildly from side to side.

He had begun to ride again, but after some minutes was surprised to find himself overcome with such tiredness that he was forced to dismount and rest. For several hours he had lain at the side of the road before crawling back to where he had met the carriage to check that no part of him remained on the ground. Searching in the grass he found nothing, but nevertheless stayed there through the night so that in the morning he might search again.

His body was numb with fatigue, his breathing laboured, and efforts to move his limbs resulted in the most terrible trembling. Such a weariness as if all this time while the world had been changing, he had been running alongside to keep pace.

As the dawn had come, a harsh light on the stones around him, he remembered other dawns far more beautiful than this – the sun's gradual rise from the marsh, mists hanging over glimmering pools before parting to reveal the day. The landscape every morning slightly different, as if painted each time afresh.

He yearned to be in Venice, the city of his birth. The people he had known there now long since dead, there was no reason why he should not return.

The year was 1299.

Lelio had entered the town of Verona on the first day of September, his journey having taken three days longer than planned. He was forced to travel so slowly, becoming dizzy after any exertion, often barely able to remain clinging to the back of his horse.

And it was in Verona, in an eating house, from a merchant who traded in cloth, that he first heard news of a plague in Venice. But having judged the man's words as exaggeration, he was unprepared for the sight that would greet him.

To prevent further spreading of infection some areas had been sealed completely, the inhabitants confined that last month, the healthy along with the sick. No exit was permitted but nobody prevented his entry.

Shops were closed and squares and marketplaces deserted. In place of the bustle he remembered, the sounds of everyday commerce, now a dreadful silence. Wooden barriers at the ends of alleys were affixed with notices warning that to pass beyond them was to die. And in the air a smell which had puzzled him then but which he recognised now as the rich, cloying sweetness of Death.

He had stopped at an inn behind the Campo di Rialto and found the innkeeper asleep in his chair with the furniture of the room piled around him. Some had already been sawn for firewood as if there was no hope that it would serve any other purpose again. Rats scuttled, undisturbed, in a corner.

Lelio had to shout into the man's ear before he woke and then to convince him that his requests for a meal and a place to stay were not trickery. As the innkeeper showed Lelio to a room at the side of the inn, they had heard the voice of a boatman below, a sonorous call filling the air, its echo repeating again and again, giving the impression that it was not one who spoke but a diligent chorus of many. '*Corpi morti*! *Corpi morti*!' The order that the dead of the plague be brought out and delivered unto him for burial.

The innkeeper spoke quickly, nervously wringing his hands. 'You require assistance to unpack, Signor?' He set Lelio's bag onto the bed and opened it. 'For longer than one night I can name a special price. I assure you that there is no cause for alarm. One need only be careful. Your meal will take me only an instant to prepare.'

As he hurried from the room, Lelio saw the livid pustule at the back of his neck.

The meal, when it came, delivered with bows and flourishes of the innkeeper's hands was spiced to such a degree that Lelio could not be sure whether the fibres he chewed had once walked or if they had grown from the ground.

Then came the sudden noise of footsteps on the stairs from the streets and at the same time the voices of a crowd growing closer. But before Lelio had time to look out from the window, the door of his room had burst open, and there had stood a young man, his eyes ablaze with fear. To meet in this way with company, clearly of equal surprise to them both. The voices of the crowd below drew nearer, grew louder and passed on in the direction of the bridge.

The young man's eyes had followed their path and, only as the noise grew fainter, did he appear to collect himself and draw breath. Gesturing towards a chair, Lelio invited him to close the door. 'If it is you that they seek, it would be safest to wait here and leave under cover of night.'

He had seen no reason for actions other than kindness. There was no harm that a murderer could do him. His purse would be poor pickings for a thief and, besides, there was something about the fellow which he had immediately found likeable. Seeing him hungrily eye the food, Lelio pushed the plate across the table towards him.

'Are you perhaps a murderer?' he asked, intending his question as a jest.

To his surprise, the young man had shrugged. 'That remains to be seen. Who is to tell what a man may do in his lifetime?'

And so it was that Lelio had met with Barnabo Mezzadri.

Vittorio Matteotti lived in the district of San Polo, in a house close to the ornamental gardens.

Clara's heart had been high and crowding with hopes for her future when Sebastiano Finetti had shown her the place on a map, stabbing at it with his pen. 'It is an area of much wordly wealth,' he said. 'But I think that you have learnt during your time here, Sister Clara, that nourishment for the soul is not a food one can buy with ducats.'

She remembered his words now as the gondola moved northwards along the Canale Grande, past the palazzi that stood on either side, gleaming gilt-tipped turrets. But past they travelled and past, manoeuvering through the fishing boats that cluttered the base of the Ponte di Rialto, then turning suddenly left into a side water, and slowing opposite a warehouse and a barge where some men were unloading a cargo of cloth.

They stood in line on the deck and the gangway, transferring bales tossed from the hold – up, down, one to the other, as lightly as ears of corn. Others ran back and forth from the warehouse, carrying in loads on their heads. Their skins were dark beneath brightly coloured coats, wrapped and tied with leather.

'There,' the gondolier said, jerking his head towards a smaller canal across from the barge. 'The one nearest the corner.' He steered the boat towards it. The house was a short distance in from the start of the canal. Its mooring posts were rusted and broken, and the window shutters unopened for so long that strands of weed had sewn themselves criss-cross over their edges.

The gondolier shuffled impatiently as she stared. 'Well,' he said, 'will you get out or not? You could stay here all day if it pleased you, but I think that the cost would be bigger than your purse.'

She flinched. The loss of her habit had resulted also in the loss of concordant courtesies. Today she was dressed in clothes she had not worn for fifteen years and aware that their fit was no longer becoming.

Clasping Marin tightly to her breast, she climbed from the boat. Every time she lied about the reason for his presence it became easier. In fact, the act of lying had ceased to trouble her at all. When she looked into his eyes, it was not only love that she felt but a gathering together of the tatters that remained from the person she had been before.

The door of the house opened before she had touched the bell-pull. Vittorio Matteotti had been watching.

Opening the door, he allowed her barely enough room to enter. He had the eyes of a drowsy reptile, his skin was so greasy that he looked to her like some poor creature, liberally fatted prior to roasting, and his throat worked constantly, even when he did not speak, as though he were always trying to swallow some particularly obstinate piece of food. His eyelids flickered as he looked at her. Without a word he beckoned her to follow.

Dark and damp, the hallway smelt as if animals had slept there. Stale and of things that had long ago died. Following him through to the stairway, she saw that his body was crooked, the upper part at an angle to his legs. He walked awkwardly, as though it caused him pain.

They climbed the stairs in silence. The passageway walls on the floor above were hung with tapestries, their golden threading black with mildew. New, they would have been the sort she had seen on unlicensed stalls in the Piazza San Marco. Sold there by stall-holders who shouted at passers-by that they could let them have for two ducats what would cost them five hundred in the Mercerie, or for one ducat what would cost them three hundred in the Ruga Speziati. As unobtrusively as she could, Clara put out her hand to touch one, wondering how long they would take her to clean.

The silence was making her uncomfortable. She spoke. 'I am very happy to be here, Signor Matteotti. Please do not be concerned about the boy. He is very good. He never cries.' Vittorio Matteotti gave no reply. 'This area is very pleasant,' she continued. 'I do not know it well but I imagine it would be enjoyable to walk along by the gardens when the weather is fine.' Immediately, she realised the carelessness of her words. Walking for him, with his body so stiff and bent, would never be enjoyable. Whatever the weather. But he did not appear to have heard her. In any case, again he gave no reply.

From the last room on the passageway, at the back of the house, she could see daylight. When they reached it, he turned and saw the puzzled expression on her face. 'Ah,' he said. 'You were talking to me. You must excuse me. I am not much used to company, and besides that I cannot hear you. I cannot hear at all. You must face me if you wish to speak so that I can read your words. Please come in and sit down.'

He observed her as she passed him, watching for the barely perceptible drawing away that he had learnt to expect from most female acquaintance. He did not see it.

She moved in a manner that, without words, bade people not to come too close; and if there were some who might still have been tempted, her expression would have persuaded them otherwise. He wondered if she knew she did this.

He dragged a chair from the window to the fireplace, turned it round and sat down with his back to the light.

The room was filled with a profusion of furniture. All manner of tables, objects for sitting, wall-brackets, cupboards, and next to the fireplace a row of three wooden stools on bronze-studded legs, which seemed to Clara too small to be of any use for anything. And along the walls – on every wall, miniatures of trees and flowers in ugly frames of paste. Everything covered in dust. More that she must clean. Clara smiled. 'I am very happy to be here, Signor Matteotti,' she said.

He nodded. He knew what she thought as she looked. The dirt. The cheap, gaudy objects. Nothing that was pleasing to the eye. He had left it that way for a purpose.

'Your room,' he said, ' if you would care to look at it, will be upstairs. You may take whichever one you wish. I sleep down on this floor. Your duties here will be to cook and clean, and also to read to me each evening from the book.' She followed the direction of his eyes to a large tattered Bible on a table by the window. 'I believe the terms have already been discussed?' he asked. Clara nodded.

The top floor had been furnished in much the same manner

as the one below, and the rooms were in a similar state of neglect. She chose the smallest. Lying awake in her cell at the convent, she had dreamt so often of having a room such as this for herself. One heavy with draping and full of carved and lacquered objects for her to place things on, in, or under. But in reality she found such abundance confusing.

She moved a low table into the corner next to the window, draped it with a veil and placed on it a small wooden cross, a Bible, a string of rosary beads and a picture of the Virgin Mother.

There was a bed in the main room overlooking the canal, and some marks on the floor in the room next to that where another might once have stood. She pulled out the lowest drawer from a chest in the larger room and put it onto the floor in hers to serve as a cot for Marin.

In another drawer she found a woman's comb and mirror set, with resin handles polished and stained to look like ivory. Everywhere, there were hooks for shoes and cupboards for clothes, all empty.

She would not ask. She would not make him sorry that she had come.

The next morning, Clara forced open all the shutters of the house, and from that day she cooked for Vittorio Matteotti and she cleaned for him, and every evening after dinner she read to him. Even though he could not hear a word, it pleased him to watch her sitting by the lamp, the candlelight playing on the folds and dimples of her face and neck, and on her roughened fingers as they turned the pages of the book. And it pleased him most of all to look at the movement of her lips as they shaped the words especially for him. She knew that his eyes were on her and as time went on she ceased to mind.

During the day, sometimes, he would secretly watch as she bustled about the corridors of his house, dusting, cleaning, tending all those things which were not hers. He wondered what it was that had stooped her shoulders so. He wondered about her life before the convent and who he was, this boy she said was her sister's son.

The child unsettled him. He did not like to look at the boy. Or more truthfully, he did not like the boy to look at him. Why, he could not explain. He watched Clara as she sat for hours – rapt, motionless, next to the boy's cot as if she drank from his gaze. It was an instinct as strong as hers to be close that made him, Vittorio, recoil.

Clara had become aware of an ebb and flow to this tide of love she felt for her child. It did not always come at her summons. To be able to immerse herself in it completely, Marin had to be there with her and looking at her. To only think of him was not enough.

Did she really believe that he was her child returned? Sometimes she did. Sometimes she did not. What she had learnt was that the workings of God were manifold, and that He did not intend that they be comprehended by man.

Whether Marin was, or whether he was not her son, she clung to the hope that the fact of his presence was a sign of forgiveness. And each morning she prayed up her gratitude as if it were. Marin heard her whispering and wondered to whom she said these things and why.

Clara was happier now than she had ever been in her life. She had her child with her, and Vittorio Matteotti was proving to be a kind man. She often found a few extra scudi in her purse at the end of the week. And on the first day that she had coins of her own to spend, she went to the Mercerie and bought a new cloth to cover the table in her room, placing the cross, the Bible, the beads and the picture on something of a more decorative design.

While Vittorio did not talk much, the silences they shared were comfortable, and the attraction she began to feel towards him came not in spite of, but rather in part because of, his physical appearance. For she had learnt that God often painted most beautifully those who had ugliness to hide.

She changed the position of the chairs in the main room so that when she sat there with Vittorio in the evenings, in the lamplight, they were close enough for it to seem that their two shadows, cast upon the opposite wall, were joined.

As the first years passed, Clara became aware of Vittorio Matteotti's affection for her and he, in turn, was surprised to realise hers for him. She had noticed soon after her arrival that his choice of the passage she was to read each evening was not one he made at random. It would always relate to something that had happened during the day – sometimes, she felt, expressing those sentiments which he could not express himself. The words he chose, though not yet of love, went so far as to indicate the possibility of its approach.

It was four years before, one evening, Vittorio's hand reached out across the space between their chairs and gently covered hers. Without a word, she moved her other hand to cover his. And from then, after her reading, they sat that way each evening. But neither of them spoke of this touch or the reason it occurred, as though to speak of it would necessitate something further.

And Clara wanted to appear as modest as she thought he would wish.

Mostly they sat in silence. Both preferred it so. Only occasionally did they speak.

One evening, Vittorio said, 'And so, my dear, were you not sorry after all that time to leave your calling? To look after your sister's child.'

Clara sighed, gathering breath in preparation for the lie. 'It was my duty, Vittorio. Her husband had died some years before, and there was nobody else to take the child. And to begin with ...' she hesitated. 'To begin with, it was not a calling of my own choice. My family were not wealthy and as is sometimes the way when it is felt that a daughter will not marry, they sent me ...'

'Ah.'

'Yes.'

'Were they close enough for you to visit?'

'I did not see them again. It was easier for them that way.'

'Ah.' He paused. So this, then, was her sadness, or some of it. He wanted to give her kindness but she did not seem a person much used to kindness. And if he offered it and she could not accept it, perhaps it would remain hanging in the air, an obstruction between them because she had seen it as pity. So he said nothing.

She sighed again. 'Time passed, and then one day I found that I did not have any tears left to cry.'

He wanted also to rub himself against her. Flesh against flesh. His against hers. He wanted to feel her calloused fingers gently touch his face. He said nothing of this either.

'I believe it was God's will that I entered the convent,' she said.

And so in all probability it had been. As she had entered those gates, He had washed her clean. God knew what lay behind discarded. It was He who had filled the spaces left by those who had gone.

It did not please her to lie to Vittorio, but sometimes what was less pleasing served best. Her history as she told it now was not a noble one, but she felt that its story of pain, inflicted by others, bore some relation to the truth. At times she had come close to believing it was. She had become accustomed to its fit.

For the passage of time could prove merciful in its power to cloud and transform, and so twist for you along its length, the past, so that it became other than what it might have been, should have been, or was.

Marin noticed that Clara prayed more frequently. He could hear the clicking of beads and her voice in regular low recital. Sometimes he pushed open the door of her room and watched, moving away as she bowed her head to finish, for her face suggested that these were not always happy occasions.

But one morning, she saw him and asked him why he sat there.

'You say my name,' he replied.

'There is never a moment when you are not in my thoughts. I have God to thank for your presence.'

'He gave me? I came from him?'

'It is God who brings all things. That I am your mother is His gift. But He also brings punishment when we do wrong. It is God who rules over us.'

'But where does He sit so that He may watch what we do?'

'God is everywhere around us. Nothing we do is secret.'

'He does not forget what He sees?'

'It is only we who try to forget.'

And for days afterwards, Marin went about the house, gripped by the fear that punishment might come for actions he could not remember.

At night, Marin used to lie in his bed, perfectly still, the better to sense the atmosphere around him. Aware that something in the house had changed, he began to question Clara more often and to listen more closely to her replies

'And it really is true that you are my mother?'

Clara's response remained always the same. 'Of course it is true but I have told you before that this must be our secret.'

He had not dared to ask her why this must be so. Yet he was certain that Clara loved him, her feelings warm on his face could not lie. This was what he held on to. Her thoughts were as necessary as the air he breathed. Even more than her touch or her kisses, he yearned to feel her thoughts. Soft things, warm things, beating like butterflies over his skin.

She gave him what he saw her withhold from Vittorio. He told himself that this would never change, and he took this thought of his own and tried to wrap it, like a blanket, around him.

He tried to push from his mind the fact that Vittorio would

hardly look at him, and when he did, half closed his eyes as if to block out what he saw.

Clara continued to spend her hours with Marin as before but sometimes, as if too often she had looked too long, and the surfeit of it now turned sour, into her mind came other things. Not just the room, the woman and her coins, but the man who had left, and more. And as time went on, more memories came. Creeping back, unbidden.

And seeing the change in her face, Marin wondered what it was in him that now frightened her.

At the age of six, Marin was a somewhat detached and dreamy child, given to frequent bouts of reverie from which Clara could rouse him only by repeatedly calling his name. Often, she found him sitting pressed, motionless, against a mooring post at the front of the house, staring at the water, his long, angular face rapt with concentration.

His features were of the type that would usually arouse interest rather than admiration. However, Clara had noticed that when they did go out, and passers-by stopped to look at him, and he looked back, their expressions told that it was not only she who found him so beautiful.

Vittorio never accompanied them on their outings. He never left the house. He had never told Clara that she should not do so, only regarded her with a look of dull surprise on the rare occasions that she did. Surprise that she would have found such a thing necessary.

One spring day Clara took Marin with her to the market, stopping on the way to watch the procession of the Tailors' Guild as it crossed through the Campo San Salviati.

Bright banners stretched tight against the wind. The most senior workers leading the way. Blue woollen cloaks, tasselled batons and steps and movement as neat and precise as the stitches that made up their clothes. Small boys in identical tabards, darting turquoise at the rear.

Marin edged his way in closer, pushing forward through the crowd. He found himself near to a girl, about his own age, who turned to smile at him. He smiled at her in return. She looked puzzled for a moment and then laughed as if he had told her a joke. He felt her stroke him even though she was not close enough for touch.

She came closer, took his hand, pulled him to the back of the procession, and following the apprentice boys, she whirled him into a dance, until he was giddy and gasping for breath. 'Now,' she said, 'run with me. Come.'

They ran through alleys and side-streets, then she stopped by the side of a canal and a row of narrow wooden houses squeezed at the end of a bridge. 'Wait here,' she said. 'I will show you to mother.' She left him and disappeared into the door of a basement.

Marin heard voices shouting – the girl's and another, angry, in a language he could not understand. He turned to run, but then they came out. An older woman was holding the girl by the arm. The woman siezed him and looked into his face, tilting her head, peering at something, he could tell, that it was not so easy for her to see.

He was frightened. But he knew that if she loved him she would do him no harm. So he looked at her, concentrating, willing, waiting for it to come. It did not. He stared back harder and smiled. Then he felt her find what she was looking for, but it was not something that made her smile in return. Instead she took him roughly by the shoulder, pushed the girl away, and with her face turned to the side so that he could not see it, she walked him back.

On reaching the square, Marin saw Clara sitting on the steps at the well. And as they approached, she raised her head, her face grimed and dusty, streaked with tears. Marin twisted from the woman's grip. He did not want to go back to Vittorio's house. But the woman caught him, turned him round and pushed him forward with her hand.

Clara ran to him and swept him up as the woman stood and watched. He wriggled free and moved to stand some paces away. When Clara turned to thank her, the woman looked embarassed, ill at ease. She touched Clara's arm, pulled her a little to one side. She opened her mouth to say something, then fell silent and looked away. When she did speak, Clara saw by her awkwardness that her words were not those she had first intended.

'It is good that he is back with his mother,' the woman said. Clara saw that she searched for more to say. 'He is a beautiful boy. Such beautiful eyes. So blue, like precious stones ... Good day to you.'

She walked slowly back across the square and into the side-street from which they had emerged. Clara stared after her. Marin's eyes were brown.

Clara went to Marin and took his hand. 'Why did you try to run away, Marin?' she asked him quietly. 'Did you think I would be angry?'

He did not reply. He was too tired to find a lie. She took hold of his hand. If she could, she would have kept him forever an infant, unable to move unless carried by her.

They began to walk back to the house in silence. He had much to occupy his mind. Today, he knew, he had learnt a truth, that there was another who lived inside him. Only now did he realise why Clara sometimes looked at him in that certain, peculiar way. And he had seen it with the girl and he had seen it with her mother. And perhaps it was because this one's face was unusually small or faint, or for some other reason quite difficult to see, that people needed to look and look before the Other was clear.

Across the street ahead of them rattled the Collector's cart, the tangled limbs of the corpses it carried rocking as it pitched its way over the stones. Behind it scuttled the Collector, running sideways like a crab.

Lying in his bed that night, Marin wondered what his name was, this Other, and he called out softly, trying a few to see – Lorenzo, Fabio, Luca. But he did not receive a reply.

And after that day Clara realised that she, like Vittorio, no longer had any desire to leave the house. And so, as it had been there before she and Marin had come, all the household's needs were delivered. The outside world thus arriving only in approved and allotted portions.

Occasionally during the day, when he did not know that she watched, Clara could see that Vittorio's thoughts travelled far away. And she wondered then if he thought of the woman who had used the comb and mirror. Perhaps she had left him for another who could buy her sackfuls of combs and mirrors, with real ivory handles, or anything else she wanted from the Mercerie. Clara composed in her mind a picture of the woman who had left and gradually, by its side, another from which her own face smiled forth.

It troubled her that Vittorio never spoke of his past, for how then was she to defeat this foe, this one with whom he walked when he did not know he was watched? How was she to know what behaviour would serve her well or ill when she knew nothing of this woman from before, of the manner of her going, or even whether she still lived?

Clara had learnt that those who were dead could prove to be the most cunning adversaries, their overthrow requiring a great degree of skill. They had on their side the army of memory, swollen tenfold by the feelings dragged to light on their death. Clara had seen this before. Damn him for his cowardice.

She had been cleaning as she thought these things. Scraping her brush along the ugly frames of paste, with a fury that raised more dust than it cleared. She dropped her brush and stopped.

And what would God say of those thoughts, and moreover, what of her intentions behind them? So much was becoming confusing. Too much trespass from the past. And along with the memories were coming more pieces of the person who had lived them. Not all of these pieces things of which she was proud or which she would have wished Vittorio to see.

But surely God would not have set Vittorio on her path if He had not meant them to be close. So she decided then that, as with Marin, their meeting was a gesture of forgiveness and a sign that her penance was done. A gift. And if that trespass from the past became too slippery underfoot, then surely Vittorio, in his goodness, would hold her firm.

One evening as Clara and Vittorio sat, hands entwined, Clara ventured to speak. Having tried in her mind first one question, then another, she chose the one she thought would draw the fullest response.

'Does it grow easier to bear your sorrow? I feel that in the past there was much happiness in this house.'

'Happiness?' Vittorio spat the word out hurriedly and with distaste, as though surprised to find it in his mouth. He looked away for a moment and when he looked back she saw that there were tears in his eyes, and the expression on his face made her ashamed.

The next evening, he gave his reply, as though their conversation had continued unbroken from the day before.

'It was the promise of happiness that was here,' he said. 'I was married. My wife is now dead.'

'I am sorry,' Clara said. 'Forgive me. I meant no intrusion. You must have loved her very much.'

'Yes,' he said.

She noticed that he did not look at her as he said this. So perhaps this one lay more quietly in her grave and would accept the passing of time and the passing of possession from one hand to another.

Vittorio tightened his hand around Clara's. And he thought of Isabella.

Isabella. Ah, Isabella. He remembered how much he had come to despise her. The foolishness of her ways, her silly snobberies and the ceaseless commotion which followed her wherever she went. He could not hear the noise she made, but was constantly aware of it nevertheless, the chaos in the air behind her.

Had he ever loved her? Had his motives, in truth, been any more honest than hers? He knew that they had not.

It had been her dream, her dearest wish, to live as muse, inspiration to one she considered an artist. It had been his to be married and thus prove wrong those who had whispered the phrase he had seen shaped on various lips ever since he was a child. 'Oh, but of course he will never marry.'

And perhaps both he and Isabella had been aware that some opportunities in life come but once and then never present themselves again.

They had met in a bookshop on the Mercerie. He had stepped in there, only for a moment, to shelter from the rain. He remembered having noticed her, standing slightly to his left, moving gradually closer as he leafed through the pages of a book. She had approached and asked him what he considered the book's literary merit and worth. He responded with the same words he had seen the owner of the shop say to a customer just minutes before.

She had been wearing a dress of pale yellow satin and carrying a tiny fan of feathers dyed to match.

'Are you a writer?' she had asked him.

'Yes, I am,' he had lied.

'Do you write poetry. I am especially fond of poetry.'

'Poetry is my passion.'

And so it had begun, his life as a poet. He who knew nothing of poetry and who, before that day, had never desired to.

He remembered that at the time he had thought she was beautiful.

Clara's memories grew more vivid. When she looked into Marin's eyes, she saw reflected there things he could not possibly have known, a blending of what was and what she had decided was not. But she loved him so much that she could not draw back. And each day more of the past unfurled before her. An ancient, filthy flag.

Frederigo Gaspari had been handsome. He had been a man of such astonishing good looks that people used to follow him in the street. But he had chosen for a wife a small, grey girl, thin and mean of spirit, whose face brought to mind the gloom of the seabed and the contents of fishermen's nets. And then he had chosen Clara. He did not like to be eclipsed.

He said that his wife did not let him love her, that she did not even allow him to look at her undressed. Clara could still hear, in her head, his words.

And he had led her to the tavern. The tavern behind the Campo di Rialto, with its rooms to let by the hour, for those seeking pleasures not available at home. Rooms as unclean as that which they witnessed.

Again and again he had said he would leave his wife, and again and again he did not. Then Clara discovered that she was with child.

At this same time, the wife took ill with fever and, for once considerate of the happiness of others, dropped dead in a heap in the hall. But her meanness returned from beyond the grave, and Frederigo cried bitterly that he saw her everywhere, just greyer, fainter than before, weeping, floating through the house, accusing.

And now he called her rose, not thorn, and her reticence virtue, not curse. And to Clara, he had sighed and wept, then eventually said yes. But they must wait he had said, until he had the funds for them to leave, so that his state of mind could be repaired and he himself back to the man she deserved. That she and their child deserved.

'But not this one,' he had said, she must understand. He had in mind those children that would come in the future. 'For we have our whole lives ahead of us to produce and love as many as you wish, my darling. I hear them now from where they are waiting.' She remembered how he had cupped his hand to his ear, as if in playful protest at their children's clamour. 'We must be ready for them,' he had said. He then suggested that she visit an acquaintance of his, somebody who could rid them of their trouble and, moreover, turn this disposal to profit.

So Clara had arranged it with the woman from Livorno. The exchange of gold coins for her child. The sum offered had been generous, with the stipulation that one ducat be deducted for each visible flaw. There had been none, so the purse she gave Frederigo was full.

And then he had gone. Like a bucket of filth thrown to the water – one moment there and the next, swallowed in on itself and vanished.

He had not left alone. She learnt that he had gone with the aunt of his wife, a woman of similar characteristics which were complemented in a similar way by the most charming amount of wealth. Clara learnt too that they had been close for some years.

When Marin was seven, a private tutor named Signor Ruscelli was appointed to come on weekday afternoons to see to his schooling. Otherwise, the activities of the world outside scarcely intruded upon their lives.

Marin continued to ask Clara whether she was his mother, and she continued to give the same answer, reminding him that this must remain their secret. The same words from both of them as if lessons learnt by rote. He wondered why giving birth to him was such a shameful thing that it must always be denied.

Vittorio spent his days in the library. He used to study from the leather-bound volumes crammed onto the shelves, picking out in the morning whichever first caught his attention. Then he would read from it passages and chapters at whim, before replacing it and on the next day choosing another. And also, he would write. He set himself the task of covering at least ten full sheets a day. Sonnets, villanelles, sestinas, meandering inarticulate over the page.

For the past fifteen years he had done this. He knew that it had been Isabella's view of him as poet and scribe that had, for her, negated deficiencies elsewhere. And so it was too, he knew, in the eyes of the world. And even perhaps in his own.

From the day they met, Isabella had referred to herself as his muse, and he came to understand very quickly that she wished him to do the same. So he did and made great efforts, in addition, to prove to her its truth. Each evening he had come to her with the writings he said she inspired. Before speaking, she used to read them slowly, running her finger along the lines on the page, in a display of careful judgment of their worth. But he knew that it was the thought of having been their inspiration, the source which had given them birth, that pleased her, rather than anything of the work itself. He understood that what had been produced, his feelings on the page, were of very little consequence.

He suspected that even in their marital bed, while he strove and laboured to please, her sighs came at the thought of their tangling translated to verse, rather than present physical pleasure from him.

The library was the only room into which her tawdry touch had not intruded, yet it was here, now that she was gone, that he thought of them most.

While she was alive, he had often imagined how he would change the decoration, every piece of it, should she ever go. But in the event, guilt had stilled his hand, and he had not been able to alter a thing.

On the day they drowned he had quarrelled with her. She had followed him into the library and would not let him alone. He remembered the incessant movement of her lips, beating at the air between them.

Instead of seeking to calm her, he had been more disagreeable, purposely, wanting only to be left in peace. And so she had left the house as he had hoped she would. But she had taken Tomaso with her. Tomaso, their son, had been seven years old.

They had been gone for a week before he learnt they were dead. Dragged up from the bottom of a canal.

Vittorio had seen their bodies before they were prepared for the grave. Glassy-eyed, festooned with weed and filth. And he knew that it was he who had done this.

Some time around his eighth birthday, or the day which Clara had named as such, Marin became aware that sometimes after being with her, he felt exhausted, not altogether present, as though something of himself was missing, or blurred, reduced to lines less distinct.

And at these times he felt the need, urgently, to pinch and pull at his flesh, his face, body, arms and legs to make sure that all of him was still there, still whole, to make sure that nothing about his shape was changed. He felt that if each part were not, in this way, separately, immediately and definitely recalled that he, Marin, might gradually grow smaller, weaken, then be gone.

He developed the habit of staring into mirrors, approaching quickly, at a run, in case a warning might have given time for a disguising of the truth. But always he saw the same reflection staring back. Perhaps he had not moved quickly enough.

And at nights, he still called out, to see if the Other replied. And he wondered if it was only from shyness that this Other did not admit he was there.

It began almost by chance, an accidental touch leading to others that were not. Then it became habit for Clara to share Vittorio's bed.

After that first night, so unlike any with Isabella, Vittorio truly felt moved to write of it. But words would not come to explain.

And Clara, with too many emotions so many-faced and varied, preferred to spill them, unexamined, as tears. She wept as she dusted.

Neither troubled the other with their thoughts.

While Clara did not show Marin any less love or affection, he became aware that he was, unexpectedly, having to share something which formerly had been entirely his. And might this share, he wondered, grow yet smaller, even eventually disappear?

His reaction was instinctive: he decided to draw to him Vittorio's love in the same way that he had always reassured himself of Clara's. By looking long and deeply enough until the separation between them was gone. For only if Vittorio loved him, too, could he be certain of a continued part in their closeness.

Another source of unease was the fact that Clara's reactions to him were changing. He could not understand why sometimes, when she held him, she cried so, apologising for events in a past of which he had no knowledge. It occurred to him that perhaps it was the Other who knew and that it was he who was to blame.

Having had no measure of normality against which to compare his own, he found the idea that he shared his body with another disagreeable, but not unreasonable. Just one of the less pleasant aspects of life, like the fever, the pox or flies.

Whatever the truth, he knew that he needed her look and her touch to survive. There was nothing that could have made him hold back.

Until this point, the relationship between Vittorio and Marin had not been a hostile one but built as it was, piece by piece, on the residue of the small jealousies between them, this was the direction into which it leant. Neither of them had learnt quite how to behave with the other. The everyday words of household commerce changed, mid-journey, from the lips of one to the ears of the other, into weapons of offence. They fought without knowing they did so.

But now Marin began to pay much closer attention to Vittorio, pushing for his attention, offering his help to tidy or rearrange the books in the library. And instead of going to his room when Clara read from the Bible each evening, Marin stayed to listen. The readings bored him as much as before, but now he sat rigidly attentive, close and sphinx-like, on the settle by Clara's side, so that Vittorio's every glance in her direction must of necessity take him in too.

It was ridiculous, Vittorio knew, to be so troubled by the eyes of a child, but he avoided him just the same. When Marin was near, and Vittorio knew that he watched him, he so often had the feeling that if he had lifted his head unexpectedly to look, it might be somebody else, not Marin, who stood there.

And although sometimes he had quickly raised his head and seen that really it was only Marin, it still seemed to him that from day to day the boy looked different. Sometimes this change was a constant thing, like the view of a pebble in a stream, distorted by the water washing over it.

One afternoon he saw on the boy's face a shadow, like a scar, the exact same shape and in exactly the place where Tomaso had also had one. In a burst of what he knew was foolishness, Vittorio had siezed Marin, rubbing at his skin, tracing with his thumbs the outline of what he thought he had seen. But now he saw nothing, and Marin had started to cry.

Later that day, alone in his room, Vittorio worried that his eyes now followed the way of his ears. He thought of Tomaso lying in his casket, and how in death his scar had appeared more livid than in life. It had stood out so strongly against the pallor of his skin that Vittorio had leant into the box to rub at it, to check that those who had prepared his body had not, as a joke, touched at it with the same paint they had used to brighten his lips.

Upstairs, Marin pressed his face to a mirror. He examined his features, pulling them this way and that, trying to see for himself what it was about them that had altered.

Neither of them mentioned the incident to Clara.

After two weeks in retreat from Vittorio, Marin was assured, from daily observation of his reflection, that nothing new or alarming emerged. Nothing which would explain Vittorio's behaviour. So he dismissed what had happened as meaningless, as only the old man's folly and perhaps a sign that he was befuddled by the games of the Other.

Redoubling his efforts, Marin engaged Vittorio's eye at every opportunity, staring, in the hope that something of what he wanted, Vittorio's love, would stare back. He stared with such intensity that at times it made him dizzy and caused Clara to ask, one evening at dinner, whether his stomach gave him pain.

Not knowing why, Vittorio drew back even more. Remaining away from the boy when he could and, when he could not, looking everywhere and all around Marin's head, anywhere except at him.

But as the weeks gradually went by, he no longer found it so easy to look away. And he found that he wanted to look, realised that he had wanted to look for some time.

And when one afternoon he did look, he discovered that he loved Marin, indeed, that he had probably done so all along. He loved him completely and without bounds, in the same way it had been with Tomaso.

And afterwards Marin became aware that the situation had suddenly changed, altered to the way he had wished it, but aware too of more of that loosening and fading of his sense of himself. As if, in him, those things that kept one person himself, and not another, were not securely enough in place.

Vittorio could not prevent himself from looking at the boy and every time he did so, it seemed that a little more of what had been shut away crept softly into the light.

Yes, he loved Marin. But from there, over the months, the

matter progressed. All the walls he had so carefully built were crumbling, and there behind them, as they fell, stood Tomaso. Tomaso in the eyes of Marin.

But was he truly there or was this some trick of the Devil? And if it was the Devil's work, was it He that Vittorio saw now or had Marin been sent as apprentice? Or was it simply that he, Vittorio, was mad? His grief, buried so long in darkness, now blossomed forth as that?

He found Marin's stare hypnotic, a bottomless well, brimful of the promise of horrors. He was there waiting, watching at every turn, around every corner at every minute of the day.

Then the pictures he saw continued, even when the boy was not there. As if a seed had been planted and, now rooted deeply, grew every day, whether tended to or not.

Vittorio watched his past advance, triumphant.

Vittorio's attention to the daily business of life grew less and refusing to change out of his nightshirt, he shuffled, muttering, through the house, each day visibly further from reprieve.

Clara pretended not to see this and she did not ask him why. Neither did she comment on his clumsiness when he dropped his cup or broke the lamp on the stairs, his hesitation before every movement as though he were mistrustful even of himself.

She laid out his clothes each morning, and each night she folded them away. And she gave him medicine to ward off fever. She had seen the way he looked at Marin.

She knew now that he was her son – sent back in retribution. Atonement in the convent had not been sufficient. He had been sent by God as the agent of His will. So this, then, was part of that. The working of His way. And of course there was now reason for her and Vittorio to be punished.

During the day Vittorio still sat in the library, but now he no longer read or wrote.

In a corner under his bed had been a box of Tomaso's toys. He had moved them to the library now where he could touch them, undisturbed. They were soldiers, made of tin, with their coats and helmets painted red. The plumes of their helmets were golden. He held them in his hands in silent prayer and waited for response.

And after some days he heard them. They spoke. He knew what he must do. He unbuttoned his nightshirt to bare his chest, slowly raised a toy to the air and as hard as he could, he struck at his heart. The plume of the helmet caught and tore. Blood came.

He took up another toy and then another, and struck again and again, until his chest and stomach were almost completely covered in a velvety patterning of bruise.

Coming to the dinner table that evening, his face was blotched and swollen, and he wore a cravat, speckled with blood, that covered his neck. Marin saw that his hands were shaking. Vittorio did not speak one word during the meal, but later Marin heard him say to Clara, 'I think you would be better sleeping alone again tonight, my dear. I think I have a touch of the fever. You said so yourself. And I fear I shall be restless.'

From his bed, Marin heard Clara walk slowly up the stairs to her own room and shut the door, and shortly afterwards he heard the door to Vittorio's room open and the uneven sliding of his feet along the tiles. The library door opened and shut. Marin waited a while, listening, then he pulled on his robe and went quietly down the stairs.

He pressed his ear to the library door, then bent down and looked through the keyhole. He saw Vittorio, the bloody spurts and trickles from his ruptured skin, colouring his fingers and the toy. And the handkerchief he held in his mouth to mute his cries of pain.

Marin pushed open the door. Vittorio saw him, paused, but then continued, more quickly, more fiercely than before. Marin ran to him and snatched the toy. He saw that next to Vittorio's feet was a box of others, similar, all stained.

Vittorio spat out the handkerchief. His mouth hung open, twitching, following the convulsive movements of his throat as he endeavoured to speak. But all that emerged was a low, dry scrape, like the dragging of coal over stones.

Then, with a lopsided move, he flung himself at Marin, knocking him to the ground and pinning him there with his weight. Grunting, gasping, he began to cry, his arms flailing wildly, striking at Marin and himself.

Closing his eyes, Marin pushed hard against Vittorio's chest, his fingers slipping on the open wounds. The blows stopped, and Vittorio sat up slowly, his hands still erratically batting the air.

Marin laid a hand on his arm. 'Please ...' he said. 'Please, stop.'

Gradually Vittorio grew still. Both of them were weeping. Vittorio wiped Marin's eyes with the handkerchief. 'Go to bed, child,' he said.

But Marin crept from the house and sat outside on the steps until dawn when the first porters arrived with carts and barrows to collect their orders from the warehouse. Narrowing his eyes until the figures of the men were a blur, he stretched out his hand and imagined the world distant, as if he need only touch it through cloth.

The next morning while Clara cleaned in another part of the house, Vittorio called Marin to the library. 'Perhaps you might sit with me for a while,' he said.

Marin sat on the chair on the far side of the desk. Vittorio turned back to the papers in front of him, arranging neat piles, then sliding them back to where they had been to begin with. He did not look at Marin.

'I would be most grateful if you did not speak to your aunt about ... about what passed here last night. It would only distress her.'

Marin replied. 'Yes.'

Vittorio paused. 'I think it is time that you prepared for your lessons now. Signor Ruscelli will be here soon.' So many other things to say, none of which would come.

Over the next days, Marin knew that Vittorio watched him. And it was a week after the events in the library that Vittorio told them that Signor Ruscelli had gone.

'Signor Ruscelli has unexpectedly been called away,' he said. 'A private business. He did not wish to discuss it before he left. But so that there shall be no break in your schooling, Marin, I shall take over your lessons myself until a suitable replacement can be found. So your tuition will resume tomorrow as usual.'

He spoke casually but Marin saw that his fingers, clenched around his drinking cup, were trembling.

'That is very kind of you, Vittorio,' Clara murmured. 'But what of your own work?'

Vittorio looked down at his hands. 'That is of no matter compared to the boy's schooling,' he said.

The next day, on their first afternoon together, Marin's lessons were grammar and composition and mathematics. Vittorio was an able teacher but his mind was not on his teaching, just as Marin's was not on that which was taught.

Before they began, Vittorio said, 'Perhaps in the past I have not taken the time to know you. Perhaps that is why ... Sometimes misunderstandings arise because there is too much of a distance between people. I would like us to be friends now.' He was aware how thin his voice sounded as he spoke. How it was squeezed from his throat and trailed out to nothing.

He was aware also of a beckoning from a place long abandoned and a response within him that was too deep to read.

When lessons were over, Marin bounded from the room with a jollity that he did not feel, and Vittorio remained in his chair until Clara found him there in the evening, sitting in darkness.

And so every weekday afternoon Marin came to the library where Vittorio, in his nightshirt, waited.

In the mornings at the breakfast table, Vittorio saw the faces of Isabella and Tomaso staring bleakly from his plate. He could smell the rotting waste that had been caught around their bodies. The pages of Marin's lesson books were the weeds in Tomaso's hair. And it was after about a month of his teaching Marin that he first asked him to speak the words.

'Would you do something for me?' Vittorio asked. 'Something that shall be our secret?'

Marin shrugged.

'Would you say something for me? Just a few words. Would you say, "I forgive you, Papa"?'

Marin repeated the words.

'Turn to me, please. Please, look at me when you speak.'

Marin repeated the words once more.

Vittorio smiled. Marin looked away.

The words became a regular part of their lesson time. Marin never questioned this. He sensed that past wrongs, whatever they were, had rendered his obedience due.

What welled up inside the house was growing too large to contain. The air was thick with unspoken feeling that roared silently for release through the stairways, rooms and halls. And at night Marin wept, sensing he was its cause. All three of them knew that something approached, but its tread was too faint to hear clearly.

It was one evening at dinner, shortly after the feast of San Giovanni, that Vittorio first mentioned the party. 'It is your birthday soon, Marin,' he said. 'This year you will be ten and nearer to manhood than boy. We should mark this occasion. Clara, my dear, you shall have a new dress and, Marin, for you a new suit. We shall have a party, a special party. ' His eyes, as he spoke, gleamed hard with excitement and anticipation. He laughed.

Clara watched him. She would have stretched out her hand had she not feared it would take him down with her, instead of pulling him upwards and free. She saw that there was no happiness in his laughter.

On the day before Marin's birthday, he and Vittorio sat in the library, working through a book of mathematics. Vittorio scolded Marin for a fault in his figures, but his words came sounding sharper than his intent.

Marin turned on him in surprise and temper. 'I thought that we were friends. I say those things. I keep the secret. But if we are not to be friends any more, maybe I will tell Aunt Clara about the words that you ask me to speak.' He pushed back his chair as if to stand.

'No!' Unable to rise to his feet as quickly, Vittorio struck out his hand to hold Marin back. The movement was violent and clumsy, and the stone on his ring caught Marin's face.

Slowly, Marin wiped the blood from his lip with his sleeve. 'I tell you now, I tell you now,' he whispered, 'that I lied. I never meant those things you made me say. I do not forgive you, and I never will. Never.' He overturned his chair, with a crash, and ran, weeping, from the room.

When Vittorio did not come to the dinner table that evening, Clara went to his bedroom, assuming that he slept. She knocked and rattled at the door, and when at last he answered, she hesitated before she pushed it open. The lamp was burning low, casting wavering shadows at the wall.

Vittorio lay at the foot of the bed, his body curled in on itself. As Clara came closer he stirred. 'Leave me, please,' he said. 'If you care for me at all, leave me now. I would like to rest by myself this evening.' She took one more step forward, then turned and left him.

She and Marin sat down to dinner alone, and they laughed and they joked and they talked of their preparations for the next day. And when they had eaten and the table was cleared, and Marin had gone upstairs to his bed, neither of them could remember a word they had said, and both were relieved that the evening was done. And that now they were apart.

Before she retired for the night, Clara put out onto the table the cake she had baked for Marin's birthday, sprinkling it with sugared rose petals which she arranged to spell out his name. When she had finished, she went to Vittorio's room and listened for a moment outside the door. Silence.

Usually, at this time, she could hear boatmen on the canal, the strident voices of lamp-carriers calling out to those who walked in the darkness, or sometimes the shouting and the rush of activity that accompanied unloadings of late shipments at the warehouse across the canal. But this evening she could hear none of those things.

The night was extraordinarily still.

When Marin came downstairs the next morning, he thought he had been the first in the house to wake. But Vittorio had come to the dining room before him. His large misshapen feet, swaying gently above the cake, had knocked the rose petals into disarray, and his face – as shiny and purple as an over-ripe plum – dangled from the noose of the cord of his robe. A dark stain had spread over the back of his night-shirt, filling the room with its pungent odour. Marin turned away to retch. He was glad of the pain in his chest, and he dug his fingers there, hard, one by one, so as to feel it more.

The sheets of notes that Vittorio had made for their lesson the morning before were still on the desk in the library. The uppermost was smudged where Vittorio's sleeve had brushed on the ink before it was fully dried.

Marin stood for some minutes, looking, staring, until the words and figures were blurred with his tears. Then he took off his shoes. He tore the papers into pieces, screwed them carefully into balls and packed them tightly into his shoes, so that when he put them back on again his toes were crushed so painfully he thought they might break when he walked. So he walked. Around the library and around the dining room collecting into a bag any small things that could be sold and one scudo that he found in the money tin in the kitchen. He took only what he judged was necessary. Nothing more. Absolutely nothing more.

An hour later, as Marin and Clara made their way across the Campo San Polo, the Marangona rang out, summoning the city's workers to the start of their day. And from every direction, out of the mists, they came. Street cleaners swinging perforated cans of water, porters rolling barrels of sweet yellow wine from the Fondamenta del Vin, or pushing or dragging wooden carts packed with fresh fish, salted sardines, or fruits and vegetables from the islands of the Lagoon.

Marin walked ahead, his eyes on the horizon, oblivious to the activity around him. Each step squashed his toes against the paper in his shoes and pain shot from his feet up his legs and into his back.

Clara followed a few steps behind. He could not look at her. Her piteous cries were like those of an animal. He could not bear to listen. Then she began to cry and pray to God for the deliverance of Vittorio's soul, but forgetting the words when she was only partly through and having to start it all over again.

Marin turned into a backstreet and towards the ferry point.

Clara followed, stumbling, her prayer now reduced to a low, desperate jumble of sound.

They took the gondola ferry to its last stop at the Riva degli Schiavoni. Standing silently, heads bowed against a sudden spattering rain, they were the only passengers on the boat as it curved a swift sweeping path to the south.

The ornaments and brightly coloured glasses that Marin had taken from the house proved to be almost worthless, and the best lodging he could find for the money they had realised was a single basement room. A black fur of mould glistened on the walls there. The door to the alley outside was broken, and sometimes pigs from a yard nearby pushed their way in. They came snuffling for food, half-blind, their eyes gummed and clouded by disease.

At the end of the first street after the canal stood a tree that had been struck by lightning, its branches charred to blackened stumps.

Recognising where they were, Clara knew that her punishment was now close to completion and she began to pray for the salvation of her soul and for the deliverance from hell of Vittorio's. She spent hours each day on her knees, on the dirt on the floor. Her prayers of petition so lengthy that they allowed her no time to sleep. Occasionally her eyes would close from exhaustion but, even then, her lips still moved. Her moanings kept Marin awake.

He heard her beseeching God not to take away her child, but

when he went to her, she looked puzzled, confused, and tried to push him away. He supposed that she looked for the Other, but that maybe he was hiding from view.

Marin stole what food he could, but Clara would not eat. When he forced the pieces into her mouth, she would only suck before spitting them out. Each day, her body took up less and less room in the tatters of the soiled dress she wore, and her attention turned more and more from him towards a world that only she could see. As she cried out for, and spoke to, Vittorio, she cradled in her arms an invisible child.

Lelio remembered Barnabo Mezzadri as a most unusual and companionable fellow and they had settled into conversation as if they had been friends for years. Talk of life and love and women but throughout all this, despite other confidences shared, Barnabo would not say why he had come that night or give any indication as to why it was the people in the street had sought him. Conversation continued and the hours passed unnoticed.

Then all at once they were interrupted by the crash of the door flung open with such a force that it broke the hinges in half. Into the room had come the innkeeper, leading a band of men who rushed at Barnabo, seizing him, holding him fast, grasping at whatever parts of his body they could. And then they had turned to Lelio.

'Do you know this man?' the innkeeper asked. 'I see you keep company together.'

The only thought in Lelio's mind was that they might take him prisoner too, leaving him to spend one thousand years, most likely more, captive in a cell. Time enough to fully contemplate his foolishness.

And so he had answered, 'No.' He told them Barnabo was a stranger and he did not move to stop them when they dragged Barnabo away.

Already ashamed, he had watched them go, listened to their passage in the street, their terrible howling and wailing as from hungry wolves preparing to devour their prey.

With the next weeks had come the first signs of winter. Damp squalling winds that blew from the north, striking a chill at the skin. And by the middle of October, a thin frosting of ice on the smaller canals at night.

It was true that the plague had abated but its demise seemed less swift than the Administration maintained. Corpses with blackened boils were still to be seen in the gutters and dumped at the ends of alleys, before officials came with shrouds to remove them.

And gradually the city resumed a normality, but for Lelio there came no restoration. He was not as he had been before.

He never saw Barnabo again, never knew what became of him or learnt the details of his crime. Endeavouring to put the matter from his mind, he moved back to the island of Torcello. His old hut was gone, that whole area now crumbled and fallen to marsh. So he had found himself another, derelict, dilapidated at the edge of the Lagoon. From there he could hear the bells of the church of Santa Fosca, marking the hours, the days and weeks. And from his doorway he could see, in shadow, beneath the surface of the water, the broken pieces of boats and houses. Sunken fragments of the past. His weariness continued and grew worse.

While Lelio did not know the cause of his lasting triumph over time, he had made no effort to learn. It was only at the onset of his present condition that he felt any need to know more and began to seek out and question men said by others to be wise.

And from among the complex answers and theories they gave him, there emerged only one which seemed to explain his symptoms. The man, in a room on the Calle della Bissa, had pulled him close to whisper it. He suggested that what Lelio had swallowed that day at the house had not been a vegetable broth but, as far as he could tell, from what now had happened, it appeared that the pot had contained the alchemist's dream. Lelio had drunk of the Elixir of Life. A proposition of seeming absurdity, yet no more absurd than the fact of his continued survival.

And as no other more probable cause was presented, it was regarding the Elixir that he made further enquiries.

One man had said that it was a food, a most nourishing food.

Also of benefit to the eyes, the teeth and the skin. And in addition that it lightened the colour of the hair so that one need no longer trouble to soak it with urine.

Another had told him that it was the essence of a rare and precious moss that grew only in shaded areas. And that for it to be effective, one had to gather it at dawn.

Yet another had confirmed that it was the alchemist's dream, the key to everlasting life, and that if indeed it existed, it would be a most wondrous thing and the attainment of its secret a miracle.

Told many different things by many different men, Lelio came to believe they were all either fools or liars because one morning he discovered that he had begun to rot. As regards this new development, the man in the Calle della Bissa had provided no answer. Suggesting only that they renew their acquaintance once the problem was solved

And then his bones had started to powder, so that when he walked he could no longer keep a straight line. And where would it end, he wondered? When he was no more than dust, blown about by the wind with each separate speck still aware that it lived?

Not finding an answer from the lips of men, Lelio turned his attention to books, and grown mistrustful of the advice of others, he pursued his task alone.

He endeavoured to learn to read, many hours of distress and struggle. But still the letters remained only indecipherable shapes.

Poring over the parchments he had taken from the house, he studied until he cried with effort, running his hands over the words and praying that they would speak. Were they the recipe for the broth? Had he taken all those that were needed? If the truth of the matter was in the parchment, he would not now be rotting. So had what he drunk been a failure or merely half-complete?

Life or death? It had come to the point where he no longer cared which. Only to be delivered safely onto one side or the other. No longer adrift, slowly decomposing in between.

It had come to seem that Death would be his most likely friend.

Marin spent his days walking. With no particular destination in mind, he walked the same streets and bridges over and over again, as though after some divinely determined distance covered, all would again be well.

Having seen so little of the world, he at first found it overwhelming. The crowds that heaved and jostled their way through the streets, alleys and marketplaces. The ceaseless bustle at the waterfront, of merchants, refugee soldiers from the mainland, beggars, and nobles with their servant boys. The street-girls who used to gather by the Ponte di Rialto – their breasts bared and tied high with lace, calling out in sing-song voices to passers-by, 'Come see! Come see!' Marin lay on the ground, out of sight, and watched them combing and oiling each other's hair, braiding and pinning it to coils, dabbing rouge to each other's lips.

But whatever the outward differences among these people around him, they all seemed to be joined in something he was not. They lived their lives in a language he did not understand; and even though they did not touch him, he felt himself buffeted from their way. To begin with, this made him fearful, but he kept his eyes cast downwards, and it appeared to him that, for most, he was not an object of interest.

There was a particular place where he used to go to sit, on the Rio de Padri della Fava. In the weeds where the canal curved, where no one else could see him, and where the small agitations of the water as it flowed made sounds that came like words. Calling out to the air and murmuring their own reply. Things he sensed he should have understood, a feeling that at one time he had.

He used to watch the water move against the current, flowing in towards him. He stretched out his hands in return, yet never so close that they touched it.

One early spring day, Marin stopped to watch a circus procession moving through the Campo Santa Maria Formosa. Dressed as angels, children threw tiny shreds of paper at the people who watched and cheered. The children were followed by dancers, acrobats and clowns, and finally by the cart that carried the freak show.

The crowd roared with delight as the cart passed by and they began to hurl rotten fruit at the people carried in its cage. Among these was a girl with a card tied round her neck which stated that she had two heads. But Marin was close enough to see that she only properly had one. The second, disappointingly, a growth coming out from her neck, onto which had been painted a face with tendrils of hair stuck round it. A lemon struck her real face. The girl crouched down against the bars of the cage and cried.

Next to her stood a man who sang in a sweet, pure soprano. His features were Eastern, and suggested blood from Mongolia or maybe Kazakhstan. He wore a tunic fashioned in the top half as a woman's dress, but cut so short over his legs that the reason for his voice was clear.

Marin watched for a minute or two, then turned and walked slowly back through the square, and into the alley leading to the canal. He was hungry and thinking of fat, spicy rolls of sausage meat. He imagined them in his mouth.

So deep was he in his thoughts that he was not aware of the men until they were almost upon him. Shouting, running, the cracking of whips against stone.

He half-turned, instinctively, moving to be out of their way. But he moved in the wrong direction and one of those running collided with him and fell. It was the eunuch from the freak show.

The two men pursuing pushed Marin against the wall of the alley, closed in around the eunuch and began to strike him, repeatedly, the man beneath their whips forgotten as they became lost in the pleasurable repetition, the rhythm, their faces rapt in contemplation of the cadence of their blows.

The eunuch convulsed in time to their strokes but he did not utter a sound.

Then the taller man said, 'Enough. He will not be any use to us, dead.'

As they tied a sack over the eunuch's head, his eyes met Marin's, just briefly. Then the men dragged him by the feet, back towards the marketplace, a trail of his blood marking their path on the dirt.

On his way back home, Marin saw the Collector moving at great speed along the Calle dei Orbi. He was running towards the horizon, in such a hurry that bodies were spilling from their pile on his cart and rolling onto the ground.

Marin arrived back at the room to find Clara lying loosely crumpled on the straw. She was cold. She was still. She did not breathe. He moved away from her and sat in the opposite corner of the room. For the whole night he sat there waiting, to see whether she might move and whether he might have been mistaken.

At dawn, when he saw that she remained exactly as before, he fetched water from the well in the square and, wetting his hands, rubbed at her face to clean it. He wanted to rearrange her hair, to comb it, but it began to come out, falling from between his fingers. He tried to pat it back into place. He kissed her face and left her.

He pushed a note under the door of the nearest church, next to the convent of San Barnabo Redentore, telling the nuns where to find Clara's body and asking them to take care of her.

Later that day, crouched in the shadows, he watched as they brought out her body, wrapped it in cloth and wheeled it away on a barrow. Their song, a soft requiem, still echoed when they had gone.

Slowly, Marin walked to his place by the water. Stretching out his hands, he saw it gather itself and swell, move to touch his fingers, pushing forward over the bank and reaching. For a moment he could not breathe. He felt that he was drowning. Closing his eyes, he leant in towards it, longing, then suddenly he was fearful and, the instant before it touched him, quickly drew back. He heard the water recede.

He opened his eyes and surrounding him on the bank he saw fish and weeds in places where the water had not been. He picked up a piece of weed, smelt it and pressed it to his face.

Then in the glimmer of the sun on the surface of the canal, as it flowed back into itself, he saw a face. So beautiful that he knew he would never forget it.

Lelio did not know what it was that lately had made him so nervous. He did not know whether it was excitement or fear. He sensed that Death was all around him, even though for so long he had not seen Him anywhere near.

But some minutes ago, he thought that he had glimpsed His familiar shape and had raced with his cart in that direction. Now all he saw was a profusion of fish and weeds on the bank of the canal and a boy who was walking away. Lelio laid down his cart and stared after him. What was it that he had seen?

Merchants sailing from the Adriatic, through the sea-gate of the Lido, would see rising into view before them a vast glittering expanse of domes, cupolas and towers, jewel-greens, purples and golds, with outlines that shimmered and shifted against the vapour that rose up from the Lagoon. Their astonishment would grow on drawing into the quay at San Marco and finding it not mirage but real.

To sit in the midst of it, as Marin did now, was something more splendid still. Venice, glorious, triumphant, unrivalled, the axis of the world. Noblemen and merchants of every race and colour pursued their business and trade. Africans in perfumed robes of musky crimson, Arabs in billowing jellabas, Russians in brocades and furs and cloaks of beaded velvet. Greeks, Slavs, Albanians and Turks. Buying, selling, the artful negotiation in between, the clasping of hands, the kissing of rings, the slow smile that signalled agreement.

At the base of the Campanile, in a row of wooden booths, sat the money-changers, discreetly counting their coins into piles before sliding them into boxes stacked by their feet.

The whole Piazza was crowded, its every space taken up with stalls and booths selling anything a person could ever want or imagine. A man in red breeches, ran to and fro on top of a platform of crates. 'Do you see this bottle here? This one here?' he shouted. 'One spoonful of this every day for a week will rid you of any ill, any ill ... the pox, lepra, bad humours in the blood. Anything that ails you ... the holding of water, melancholia of mind ...' Nobody paid him much attention.

A crowd was gathering in the corner nearest the Mercerie. So tightly packed together that Marin could not see what they watched. As he drew nearer, he heard the sound of metal on metal, small bells. He pushed his way through the people in front of him, and then he saw the girl. Straight away, he thought that he knew her. He remembered the face on the water.

She was dancing, whirling round, but with neither rhythm nor grace, rather the haphazard fluttering of something that was caught in the wind. Her steps, tangled and uneven, seemed hardly to touch the ground. There was something about her so fragile he was struck by the notion that, if she were to move too quickly in one direction or another, she might disappear like a quick gleam of light on the water.

Despite the chill of the day, she was almost naked. The thin slip of gauzy white suggesting a greater indecency than had she been wearing nothing at all. The bells he had heard were painted red and attached to the toes and the heels of her slippers. Mesmerised, Marin pushed his way forward to the front of the crowd. Her hair was the colour of marzipan cakes, and her eyes were half-shut as though to block out the watchers around her.

She was so beautiful that he could not believe she was real. It would have seemed more probable that she was not. And in some way, preferable too. He stepped back.

She began to sing, her voice high-pitched and tight, breaking occasionally as it reached for notes beyond its range. She could not have been more than nine or ten years old, yet the movement of her body and the motion of her hips suggested the knowledge and experience of somebody much older.

The crowd stared in silence – the men mostly with a desire they did not trouble to disguise, and the women with a look in their eyes that Marin could not understand: perhaps something approaching pain.

When her dance came to an end, a short, squat man stepped forward from the front of the crowd and moved his hand over the girl's shoulders, displacing her slip so that a little more flesh was revealed. 'Ladies and gentlemen,' he said, 'the dance of entrancement. I will wager that none of you have ever seen a prettier sight. Now if I may ask for your appreciation, please ...'

With his right hand he removed his hat and began to walk through the crowd, smiling graciously at the coins they offered. With his left hand, Marin noticed, he quietly and skilfully cut the purses of those who had not given freely.

The girl stood absolutely still while he did this, her arms folded across her chest, her eyes fixed on a distant point in the sky. And then she looked at him. Marin was sure she looked at him. She was waiting. He felt she was waiting but he did not dare go forward.

When the man had finished collecting the money, he went back to her and attempted to rouse her by shaking her. When she would not move, he swung her into his arms, and Marin heard him call her Constanza. As he said her name, Marin saw her turn her face to kiss him.

Marin watched them go, saw how she twisted round in the man's arms as if it were him, Marin, she looked for. He followed them. He wanted to see where they went. But by the time he had pushed his way through the people standing about the stalls and reached the alley, they were gone. He ran to its end and then to the end of the street leading from it. There was no sign of them.

They did not come back the next day or on the day after that. For months afterwards, Marin went back there and sat, waiting, hoping that they would return.

He imagined that Constanza danced in front of him and sometimes, usually quite late in the day, he thought he saw her shadow swaying on the ground. And when he left there, he felt that she followed him as the softness in the air that brushed against his cheek. He heard her whispering into his ear as he lay on the ground to sleep.

At the age of ten, it seemed to Marin that the world would offer little comfort and for the next two years he lived his life as far removed from it as he could. The only person to whom he spoke was Constanza. She danced above him on the clouds.

October 1556 led into the coldest winter that the people of Venice could remember. By the middle of December the canals had been frozen for a month, and children skated back and forth on the ice between the Ca' Foscari and the Ponte di Rialto. Deprived of their trade, some gondoliers had set up stalls on this frozen stretch from which they sold cabbage soup mixed with an alcohol they had brewed from mouldering rice, scavenged from cargo ice-bound on the Rio dell' Arsenale. Their soup burnt the throat and stung the eyes and dissolved the paint on the bowls that held it.

With no money for food, Marin hunted through waste-buckets and gutters for the frozen discards of others. His tunic and jerkin were torn and his breeches worn so thin that his flesh was visible beneath them. All that he possessed by way of a coat was a blanket he had stolen from a yard next to the Rio di San Moise. As he had wrapped it around him he had felt it twitching with a life of its own, and now some of what lived there had moved to take refuge in his hair and burrowed into the warmer, moister parts of his body, beneath his arms, between his legs.

His feet sometimes bled through the holes in his boots, and sometimes when he walked, after he had gone, where his blood had been pressed into the ground, the ice and snow melted to water, and the dead, frozen grass that lay underneath straightened up, became whole and stirred in the wind as it turned back from brown to green.

If he slept at night, it was wherever he happened to find himself when he was too tired to walk anymore. Huddled into the corner of a sheltered doorway or spread flat under sheets of tarred canvas in a shipyard or warehouse front.

In the mornings when he woke he could feel the force of the cold biting at his bones, and sometimes the numbness in his limbs remained there for days. To warm his blood he would stretch himself over any source of heat he could find – bakers' ovens, the kilns at the back of the yard by the Rio di San Moise, the stoves of men selling chestnuts – until those that presided over this heat became tired of his presence and chased him away.

Sometimes when he woke, stiff with chill, and stood to fight his path through a raging rain or snow, he saw, hunched in doorways or lying untidy on the street, the still, rigid shapes of those who had found their final rest. And very early, usually before the dawn, the Collector's cart arrived. Marin saw him sniffing and picking at the corpses, taking off their clothes. And sometimes those who had only slept too deeply, woke to find the Collector carefully removing their hats.

Often, Marin heard the cart and the Collector's skipping footsteps some distance behind his own, stopping whenever he stopped and retreating when he moved to turn back.

There were workers appointed by the Administration to clear the streets of all refuse, including the dead, but as they sat in the Piazza waiting idly for the Marangona to toll the start of their day, the Collector had already come and gone several hours before.

In every district of the city there were people living on the streets, some of whom Marin came to recognise. Occasionally, they walked alone, but usually in groups of two or three. Marin always kept his eyes cast down. He preferred not to add to his present situation the weight of any acquaintance. Constanza's company was all that he needed.

Winter passed and then the spring, summer and autumn, with Marin scarcely aware that they had. As winter came again, he saw the frost and ice around him, but barely felt any change in the temperature. He wondered if the layers of dirt and grease on his skin had worked to seal it, or whether he did not feel any more because his ability to do so was gone.

Marin spent his days and nights walking the city, making for himself ever more complicated routes. From the Zattere at Dorsoduro to where the Canale di San Pietro flowed into the Lagoon. From the Arsenale shipyards to the furthest bridge across the Canale di Cannaregio. Exhaustion resulted in a welcome absence of thought.

Often, the only light at night came from the candles guttering at the base of the street-side shrines to the saints, and although Marin had come to know the city well, he would occasionally lose his way in the darkness. It seemed that when they were concealed from view, the districts considered themselves free to alter their shape.

His attachments to the world had faded. Even that which tied him to himself. Were it not for his footprints, there were times when he would have considered himself extinguished entirely.

It seemed that hunger and solitude had sharpened his mind, revealing to him matters which had previously gone unnoticed. In particular, the sounds of things that he had always assumed were silent.

The sullen conversation of the winter clouds as they joined and parted, disputing over position. The persuasive murmur of the night as it courted before approaching to embrace the city. And now, as he tried to sleep, a new sound. That of somebody calling his name. The last person to have spoken his name was Clara.

Standing up and pulling his blanket around him, he began to walk towards it, calling back in response that he was there. But when he reached the next street, it seemed that the caller had moved. Marin followed in pursuit from street to street as the voice grew further away. And then it appeared to stop, waiting beyond the Rio dell' Albero.

Beginning to run in case it should move again, he wondered who it could be, for nobody knew his name. As much afraid as he was excited, he turned into the Calle del Traghetto where he saw the men, close to the Canale Grande.

Dressed in rags, they sat in a circle round a small fire. Marin could smell the meat they were cooking. Was it one of them who had spoken? Slowly Marin approached, having forgotten that he still called his reply.

The men heard his voice and turned – at first moving together, braced for defence, with the thought that others had come to steal. Then they began to laugh at what they saw, at the boy who came with his arm outstretched, calling to the empty air.

Shrinking back from their ugly noise, Marin fell silent. He did not understand what happened, had been so sure he had found the source of the voice. But when one of the men rose to his feet, pointing to the knife in his hand, Marin turned and ran, still whispering under his breath his assurance that he was there.

The men did not chase him but the sound of the voice was

now lost, obliterated by their jeers and laughter. At the bridge, Marin stopped to listen again but all he could hear was the eager rustle of the night, now given freedom to advance.

Resuming their meal, the men were surprised to see how far the level of the canal had risen, and yet more surprised when suddenly it swept forward so quickly that they could not prevent it from drowning their fire.

The next day, shortly after dawn, Marin caught sight of himself in a shop window mirror. He had stood for some minutes, staring, before he realised that it was also he who looked back. His hair was matted, his eyes were wild, and he looked altogether smaller as though what it was that gave him substance had been stealthily sucked out.

The shadow fell so suddenly. He turned round to see what had moved. Behind him stood the Collector. He had been waiting at the corner, standing still but breathing so rapidly that the air gave violent motion to the holes in his skin. Trembling, he held out his hand to Marin, as one would greet an acquaintance.

Marin backed away, shook his head, heard his own voice saying, 'No.' And as he turned and began to run, the Collector's cart scraped the ground, picked up pace and followed, quickening as it hurtled through the deserted streets behind him. It rattled over the stones, gradually closing its distance, then as with one final burst Marin reached the Piazza's noise and life, he was aware that the cart slowed and stopped.

Lelio watched him go. So finally there had been a meeting. But it had left him no more certain than he had been before as to the identity of Death's companion.

Marin continued to run, pushing into porters, tripping over boxes. He felt that his heart would either crack or jump from his chest, but he did not stop until he reached the Riva degli Schiavoni where he hurled himself into the Lagoon with a splash that scattered the fishermen's nets and their baskets

He drank in the cool, bitter tang of the water and the silvery scales and the waste from the fish. Swimming, floating, turning, plunging. Past, present, future meaningless, leaving his mind with nothing to fight or dwell upon except the joyous swell of the water as it played with him, sucking him in and pushing him out to air.

As he rose to the surface, laughing, something hooked around his ankle and began to pull him back. He tried to struggle free but found he could not. He shouted out for help. Hands reached down and grasped his. A fisherman pulled him up and onto his boat.

'My catch today is uglier than usual,' the fisherman said.

Marin laughed. He could not stop laughing. 'As ugly as the one who caught it!'

As he walked back through to the Piazza, he touched at his throat, trying to recall how his laughter had felt.

He sat down on the ground outside the Procuratie, leaning against a pillar as the sun dried his clothes.

On a box, by the stall closest to him, sat a man selling boots he had made out of sackcloth and soled with punctured wood. The man's beard was a shock of yellow prickle into which were lodged pieces of the meals he had eaten over recent weeks and months.

Marin's clothes began to dry, the sun warm and heavy on

his head. In and out from the building behind him scurried the Procurators of the Republic, clutching papers, scrolls and files filled with words they could read to remind themselves of the importance of the tasks that were theirs. Today, the enforcement of the sumptuary laws written to punish, if not prevent, unnecessary displays of wealth, sinful extravagance and any other immoral behaviour. Excessive use of household articles made from gold or the lighting of too many candles, the wearing of wigs, of immodest dress or skirts with trains so long that they trailed along the ground.

Among these Procurators came Sebastiano Finetti, the Administrator, his step quicker and firmer than theirs, fired as it was by the knowledge of the duty entrusted especially to him. It was to him to drag the city's moral clime dripping from the mud, to wipe it down and clean it off so that he could hold it, burnished, up to God. He took comfort from the grey wollen cloak that itched at his skin and fastened it more tightly so that the fabric would scratch at his neck and his wrists.

Marin closed his eyes and he heard Constanza laughing. Beside him the man with the boots was calling for custom.

'The foot like the face must be allowed to breathe, and my friends if you are to avoid the suffocation of the foot, you must dress it in sackcloth, not leather.'

Spring came early in 1558. The air grew softer, the days grew longer, and the light winds that sighed from the south were tinged with the fragrance of orange blossom.

One evening, Marin lay down to sleep in the porch of a church and woke to find that someone had left him two scudi. They had placed the coins right next to his face so that they would be the first thing he saw on awakening. They had given money as one would to a beggar.

He picked up the coins, testing their weight in his palm. He had always considered begging to be a shameful thing. Thoughtfully he polished the coins with his tunic and put one into his mouth. Then he began to laugh.

He stole a bowl from a market stall and held it out in front of him as he walked about the streets, more slowly now, to allow the time for the opening of a purse. He was most successful in his new trade. Even at nights while he slept, he displayed the bowl next to his face. He kept it polished, imperfectly, to suggest efforts to conform to the ways of the world, which had, sadly, due only to harshness of circumstance, failed.

As the Other had never answered when called, nor given one single outward sign of his existence, Marin had decided by this time that he was gone if ever he had been there at all. It was preferable, by far, to have for his companion the dancing figure of Constanza.

So when the people who gave paused and smiled with a lingering look, he told himself that it was because they found him beautiful. Although he did admit to himself that this beauty was clearly of some unusual type, needing their attention and consideration before they realised it was there.

He spent time looking into mirrors. The need to believe that his face played some part.

If he concentrated hard enough, he found he could will people to look at him, and so be ready for the change as it came, hitting soft against his skin. The world began to seem a marvellous place and he began to sense some blending of himself into the life of the city around him. It seemed too that it no longer moved at a rhythm so variant to his.

People were generous. So much so that, if he had wished it, he could have paid for a decent lodging of his own. But then he found somewhere, quite by chance, a home which cost him nothing.

It was a spice warehouse, next to the Fondaco dei Tedeschi. One night he had made his way in there to sleep. The storage area was clean and, because of the price of its content, placed two storeys up from the ground, protected from the flooding of the canal. A pile of torn, frayed sacking in a corner at the back made a very comfortable bed. And there was a hole under the floorboards where he was able to hide his money.

Sacks of nutmegs, cinnamon, ginger and cloves filled the air with a heavy, intoxicating sweetness that caught at his throat, their mingled scents lulling him to peaceful sleep.

There were two staircases that led to the storeroom, but the merchant and his workers only ever used one. They came in from the front, on the canal side, so Marin used the other, which was broken and rusting, leading up from an alley at the back.

Incoming loads were stacked separately in an area roped off to the right of the door, there to be counted and catalogued each day by the merchant himself. Every morning at eleven o'clock, he walked round, pointing at each bag and shouting out its contents to a small boy who followed, with a pen and paper, behind him. He did this every day, even if no new shipment had arrived, for no other reason than the pure joy that came at declaring what was his. And at the end of the listing he would then approve or deny the latest requests for stock.

Approved items were packed and moved to a holding area to the left of the entrance, while those lists denied were torn and scattered in pieces from the window.

At five o'clock each morning the workmen came. Some to collect the orders for shops and markets, and others to pack and despatch what was to go by sea to Spain, or further north inland, across the mountains to Switzerland, Germany, France or the Netherlands.

Those who loaded the goods had no reason to go to the back of the warehouse where Marin had his bed, and it was most likely that he could have remained there undiscovered, had he chosen to stay while they worked. But always he woke early, and had left by the time they arrived.

He liked to sit on the cusp of the Ponte di Rialto and to watch there, alone, as the dawn rose and broke, separating into fingers of silver pink light to pull back the cover of night. And as the last traces of darkness were taken, he looked out onto the city, bathing in palest rainbow hues, the edges of the buildings and the statues still in blur as they slowly remembered their form.

The proceeds from his begging accumulated. It seemed that the generosity of the citizens grew. But even greater than the pleasure of these coins dropped to his hands was that from the feeling which came when they gave. And when people chose not to give, it was not the lack of coins that made him want to draw back into himself.

He could feel the thoughts of those around him caressing his skin in waves or crawling over his body like ants. But the thing that made him shiver, in a way that left him breathless, was to be looked at with love.

A year passed.

Marin sat in the sun, outside the Procuratie. A group of officials hurried down the steps, so intent on their order to rid the streets of unlicensed beggars and vagrants that they noticed neither him nor his bowl at their feet.

One of them dropped a coin from his purse and Marin, gratefully, put it into his own. It seemed that the world now conspired to his benefit. He closed his eyes and began to doze.

A new sound blended with and then emerged from the usual background noise. The irregular, discordant beating of a drum. Marin opened his eyes.

From the far side of the Piazza a group of people approached. They were led by two children aged perhaps eleven or twelve, wearing pink tunics with white swaddling bands bound round their legs. Walking a few paces ahead of the others, they were banging a drum, strapped to hang between them, so that it fastened them together.

Behind them walked a woman, her skirts and bodice in pinks and lavender, gathered in flounces and pleats. Her sleeves were puffed, cut into sections and tied back with ribbons that trailed to the ground. Strapped to the soles of her shoes she wore pattens at least two hands high, which were covered in palest pink leather. The steps she took were tiny, hesitant, and without the support of the servant on whose shoulder she rested her hand, it seemed improbable that there would have been movement at all. The wind caught at her skirts, causing her to sway from side to side.

Marin stared at the man with whom she walked. Despite the years that had passed, he remembered his unusual height, recognised his distinctive features. It was the eunuch who had tried to escape from the freak show. What had been on display that day was now covered. Today, like the others, he wore pink, a curious garment, neither the tunic of a man, nor the dress of a woman.

Looped around his ankles was a fastening of what looked to Marin like ribbon, and he carried in his arms an ape. A small half-grown creature with a skirt of pink cloth tied round its middle, and another strip fixed round its rump.

Behind him and the woman came more children, in various shades of pink and dancing in formation. Marin could not tell whether they were girls or boys.

As the group proceeded through the Piazza, the woman turned to smile at the passers-by who paused to stare, but as she did, they averted their eyes and quickly hurried on.

They drew nearer and Marin could see that the heavy powder and rouge on her face were melting in greasy furrows. The dark pencil around her eyes ran in runnels down her cheeks. It seemed that she cried black tears.

She looked at him and he stared back, hard, wondering if she would give him money. She looked away, walked past, but at the end of the street he saw her look back. Marin watched as they came to a halt outside the dressmaker's shop, a short distance further on. They all went in, the boys with the drum turning sideways to enter through the door.

A few days later Marin saw them again. He watched as they went from stall to stall, and provisions were packed into baskets carried by two of the eldest children. It was the chief servant, the eunuch, still carrying the ape, who conducted all transactions. And even when the weight of his mistress's hand was not upon his shoulder, he always walked with his body slightly bent, his head and his eyes fixed downwards, as though seeking some small thing mistakenly dropped to the ground. So that even when addressing someone of a lesser stature than himself, his stance and the direction of his eyes suggested that whatever the height of the other, his own was always the lower.

Marin could see the woman looking in his direction and then through a gap in the crowd she found him. She waved her hands in instruction to her attendants and they all turned, straggling behind her through the Piazza towards where he was sitting.

They came to a standstill in front of him. The drumming stopped and the children at the back paused in their dancing and began whispering, fidgeting, craning their heads to see the cause of this disturbance to their usual routine.

The woman stared at Marin and then at the begging bowl by his side. She bent down, as far as her shoes would allow, to look at the coins he had collected. The servant looked too, his small black eyes shining, staring, but giving the impression of ceaseless movement, as if his thoughts skimmed in eddies on their surface.

'Agostino,' she said, ' give him money. Give him the purse.'

'All of it, Contessa?'

She pretended she had not heard him speak. 'And also give him that ring you are wearing.'

Agostino's expression spoke what his lips did not. He turned his back to her, took the purse from the bag he was holding and with a disdainful movement and a yawn, spat into it before flinging it and his ring towards Marin's feet.

'I would advise you to be careful, Agostino,' the Contessa said, without looking at him. 'Otherwise I will see to it that life deprives you of even more than you have lost already.'

Standing behind them, the drummers shrieked with laughter. As the procession turned away towards the Mercerie, Marin could hear the beating of the drum, uneven, breaking, shaking with the movements of their mirth.

For the next weeks, Marin sat in that same place and each day the Contessa came to give him money. She entered the Piazza with her attendants from the corner by the Campanile and left them waiting there while she walked to Marin alone.

Sometimes, as she came towards him through the rows of booths and stalls, he saw that she seemed weary, unwilling, as though forced into an appointment she did not want to keep. So he regarded it as a triumph on his part that she continued to come, that she could not help but do so, and that she continued to give as generously.

She came to sit. She stared. He felt the restless beating of her thoughts pulling at his skin.

He was curious about her and would have liked to talk, but she always brushed his questions aside or made as if she had not heard them.

Then, one afternoon, she said, 'Please do not speak. I do not come to hear you speak. But I think I pay you enough for your time?'

He told himself that he did not mind this, for he would not have been able to put her conversation into his purse. So if what they played was a game, he still, surely, was the winner.

But it became a game he no longer enjoyed. Contact with her began to tire him, to give him headaches, even though she did nothing but sit beside him on the bench and look. And her thoughts had become too heavy, like weights, pressing, easing through into the cracks they had made.

He began to hide from her, sometimes watching concealed from behind a stall as she turned her head, bird-like, to the left and to the right, as if trying to sense his presence.

And then he found that he did not want to see her at all. Not her money, nor her gifts, nor her eyes that looked into his and beyond them in a way that made him feel he had vanished.

Marin moved his daytime begging place northwards to the Campo San Giacomo.

In the corner nearest the canal, three brothers from the Levant ran an unlicensed stall selling household goods, perfumed soaps and candles. The youngest of them kept watch from the top of a box for the approach of any official; and at the signal from him, in an instant, the whole stall could be packed up and gone.

But inspections happened rarely, and for most of the time their trade was brisk. Thus, those who bought there carried off with them not only their goods but the conviction that there was money saved and therefore to spare. And in the flush of generosity born of unexpected gain, they often gave some of what they considered saved to Marin.

Across the square, under the porch of the Church of San Giacomo di Rialto, the bankers dealt in fortunes without so much as a scudo changing hands. Recording transactions in files and writing bills of exchange, debits, credits with a whisper and a smile. Overseas disaster or financial downfall nearer home brought a greater stream of custom arriving with anxious, trembling hands, but always greeted, their bills exchanged or torn to shreds with only ever a whisper and a smile.

Marin continued with his own banking, taking good care not to keep on display all that he had been given. He slid the coins cautiously into purses, concealed and sewn to the innermost seams of his tunic.

He was afraid of thieves on the street. The week before, a stall-holder here, too mean with his money to pay for a lamp-carrier or a gondolier, had walked home alone in the darkness and been set upon and cut with a knife so sharp that not only had it parted his throat, but taken half of his face.

Tied into small paper parcels and hidden under the floor by his bed, the money Marin had was plenty enough for him to have stopped the begging if he had chosen to. Counting it at night by candlelight, he saw that there was provision here for him to have lived as he wanted, in comfort, in a room with a bed, a home his by right not stealth.

But still something made him hesitate when he considered his move to that life from this. A fear that to step towards this happiness too quickly might cause it to evaporate or flee – a thought of his future as a bubble which, if too carelessly approached, might burst.

So he decided to wait until the winter before taking other lodgings. He imagined them somewhere near the Ponte di Rialto. He would rise or sleep at whatever time he pleased and, when the canal was frozen over, he would skate to fetch his bread in the mornings.

Marin had grown so practised in his begging that people very seldom refused him. Staring directly at those who came, he would open himself wide in his mind and concentrate, abandoning himself completely until he felt them falling in.

And the reactions that others had to him seemed to be growing stronger, ever more pleasurable. The feeling of their love raised his pulse. He needed it, he longed for it. It made him feel alive.

But when a day went by where his trade had been slow or his customers less than usually forthcoming, as he lay down at night to sleep he was aware that a part of him hungered.

In the corner of the Campo San Giacomo, an official nailed a notice to a board while another standing beside him spoke the words aloud for the benefit of those who could not read them. Some people stopped to listen briefly, then moved on, satisfied that the subject was no concern of theirs.

The official continued to read. 'And the regulations regarding beggars will henceforth be more strictly enforced. Those without license will find themselves consigned to the state galleys for a period of not less than two years.'

Marin listened for a minute or so before returning to sit where he had been before, setting his bowl back at his feet. Proclamations were often given. Hardly a week went by without a warning of a new restriction or an addition to the detail of some previous law – measures which were not always put into practice.

So it was much to his surprise that, later in the afternoon, he saw the rounding up of beggars begin. Dragged without ceremony from where they sat, their proceeds confiscated, their hands roughly tied before being marched towards the Piazza and the stall for registration at the waterfront.

Hastily concealing his bowl, Marin stood, patted his clothes to remove what dust he could and began to walk towards the Campo San Polo intending to take up a position there. But on reaching the square and finding a suitable place to sit, it was only minutes before news rippled in whisper through the stall-holders that the officials were on their way.

Over the next days, the arresting of beggars continued, the most fortunate of these only banished from the city, while their companions in trade stood in line on the Riva degli Schiavoni, in chains, heads shaven, this sorry spectacle a warning.

Marin walked the streets, not daring to stop, to rest too long in any one place or to display any other behaviour which might lead to the accusation of 'beggar'. He left his bowl at the warehouse and when people came near, he turned from them.

But even though he did not lack for food, having money enough to buy and fingers nimble enough to steal, he grew conscious of a gnawing emptiness that developed into a pain. He hungered for thoughts of love.

After a week, he could bear it no longer and although the vigilance of the officials continued, he began to beg again in the most discreet way he could, in a less busy place, at the end of the Calle di San Silvestro. Quiet solicitation for what people gave along with their money.

As the first person came – an elderly man – and Marin looked into his eyes, for a minute he found himself unable to speak, unable even to thank him, wanting only to keep perfectly still as he felt the tumble of the man's emotions spilling onto his skin.

Days went by, and Marin ceased to keep as close a watch. But on the fourth afternoon, his outstretched hand was unexpectedly grasped in another's and he looked up to see Sebastiano Finetti, the Administrator, taking a length of rope from his belt. Hauling Marin to his feet, Sebastiano pinched at his arms.

'A strong boy like you will be of use on our galleys and there you will have no choice but to obey the regulations and you will have cause to wish, I am sure, that you had learnt to do so earlier.'

He began to tie Marin's wrists and was about to add to these words of admonishment but suddenly forgot what his next words should be, for all at once he was overcome by something quite inexplicable. A sense of vast and immeasurable peace, a feeling to which he was not accustomed. And as the boy smiled at him, the feeling expanded, melting his anger to pity.

Sensing this lapse of concentration, Marin tried to slide free but Sebastiano tightened the knot in the rope, staring at him, blinking, trying to recall where he had seen him before. He was aware of a twitch on his forehead, small spasms above his right eye. He pulled Marin closer, touching his face, and Marin felt his thoughts, their anxious probing, gentle, almost fearful.

'Perhaps you are hungry,' Sebastiano said. 'Perhaps that is why you sit here.' Leading Marin by the rope, he began to walk back towards the Rialto, continuing to speak and providing his own answers to the questions he posed. 'When did you last eat? I am sure not for some time. Do you have a home? A warm place where you can sleep? It does not seem to me that you do. I could use my capacity to provide you with shelter. And food. Yes.'

Marin gave an experimental tug at the rope but Sebastiano was a large man and had wound the end of it around his hand. Now he wound it again, more tightly.

As they walked, Marin rubbed his wrists together, trying to loosen the knot.

'At the convent of San Barnabo Redentore,' Sebastiano continued, 'we have a new Shelter in the grounds. There is provision for boys of your age.' Seeing the change of expression on Marin's face, he asked, 'Is this a place that you know?' Perhaps he was one of those who occasionally came there for food. 'You know this place?' he repeated.

'My mother came from there,' Marin replied.

'Your mother?'

'Her name was Clara Sannazaro. She took me with her from there.'

'Impossible.'

'No, I tell you the truth.'

'Impossible, I say. Impossible.' He began to grow angry and impatient at Marin's persistent protests. 'No, I say. It cannot be so. I never forget a nun in my charge. Clara Sannazaro sold her child, exchanged her roundness for trinkets and pearls. This was before she came to the convent, and when she left, she was not of an age to bear more.' Seeing the boy's bewilderment and the signs of incipient tears, Sebastiano was sorry to have spoken so sharply. He remembered the business of the sister's child, a claim which he had never believed. He sighed. 'You must understand that Clara Sannazaro was not a woman much given to truth. But with us you will have a home and we will be your family.' Gently, he touched Marin's hair. The boy looked to be about fifteen, which would be the right age. But that he had anything to do with Clara Sannazaro came as a disappointment.

Marin ceased to fight with the rope and as Sebastiano walked faster, he now followed quietly behind. His legs were shaking and Sebastiano pulled at him harder, no longer looking back, mistaking Marin's stumbling for struggle.

Marin closed his eyes as they approached the convent. He felt the stones of the courtyard under his feet and when they stepped inside the entrance, he heard Sebastiano pick up and fumble with keys.

Opening his eyes, Marin saw San Barnabo's plaque in front of him. And while Sebastiano muttered in irritation, unable to find the correct key, Marin read the words, repeating them under his breath, frightened to let his attention wander elsewhere. And for the first time in his life, he prayed.

Two nuns approached in silence, making the sign of the cross as they passed. Distracted for a moment, Sebastiano glanced up and, seizing his chance, Marin sprang at him, kicking him with such a speed and fury that Sebasiano lost his balance and fell. Marin ran through the courtyard, free.

Walking back to the warehouse, he pondered Sebastiano's words. If not Clara's son then whose? Where had he come from? Or from nobody and nowhere, appearing for no reason like the growth of moss on a stone.

The recent notice regarding the punishments for begging remained nailed to its place, and the stall for the registration of labour remained open. But the man who sat there was idle, the officials responsible for the rounding up now unexpectedly charged with other duties.

Marin took up his previous position near the Rialto. From time to time he saw Sebastiano and then he took care to keep himself concealed. It seemed that all would continue as before, and so for a while it did.

It was only gradually that matters changed, that occasionally with some who came, he became aware of a dull pain, a crowding and tension in the back of his head. Other people's thoughts, too many of them, entering even when he did not invite them.

The headaches became more frequent, still occurring when he was alone. Particularly when he was tired and almost always when it rained.

There had been a time when Lelio had known, without a doubt, that Death was often near him. He had seen Death's playful wink from behind the eyes of the sick, and His nod from behind the heads of those who thought they were well but would soon be confined to their beds. And there was always the chance that, tarrying in His work for a moment, Death might delay just long enough for Lelio to touch Him.

Surely this would be all that was needed, a stroke of His hand, a sip of His breath, or even a brushing of the hem of His cloak. A contact that would cut the threads that tied him to this world and release him, finally, into the next.

August 1561 came to a close with rains. Grey skies and torrents. Marin sat under awnings or huddled in doorways as the canals spilled their banks, seeping up through the pavements so that they were awash with weeds and soil.

He walked slowly through the Rialto now, wondering in which street he should live. Perhaps somewhere behind the Fondamenta del Vin? Was it necessary to wait until winter? He could move, if he wished, today. And he thought about Clara, wondering what she had tried to hide and why. But he could not properly concentrate on any line of thought because the rhythmic pounding of the rain on the stones set off an echo that struck through his head where something was beating and drumming an answer.

Passing a tavern, he stopped in the doorway, for a moment, to shelter. From inside came sounds of loud raucous talk, laughter and song.

Cautiously, he pushed open the door. The room was filled with such a number of people, pressed together so tightly that the mass appeared as one.

He stepped back to leave, and somebody took hold of his arm.

'Why so fast young fellow? Why are you rushing to soak your bones outside? Stop and take a drink with us. Come now. It would be most ill-mannered of you to refuse.' The man who spoke was tall and red-faced, with a head of oily, close-cropped curls. He took Marin's hand, pressed his lips to it, and led him to a table. The men already seated there moved to make room, and one of them pushed across a cup filled with wine.

'A new friend to join our party,' the first man said. 'And the first rule for new friends is a drink.'

Marin drank because he did not know what else to do and was nervous of their reaction had he not. He took the first sip unwillingly, not prepared for its effect, so he was surprised to feel it warm and relax him, and to find that it immediately stilled the noises in his head. He drained the rest of the cup and the man poured him another.

Marin realised he was no longer nervous. And as unexpectedly agreeable as the wine's effect came that of the company of others. The men at his table were joking, laughing, and when they addressed him, Marin found he had words to reply – even though, as soon as he had expressed them, he could not remember what he had said.

The man with the curly hair put his arm around Marin, and one of the others pulled it away. Then these two began to shove and shout at each other, ending in an embrace and murmurings too quiet for Marin to hear. They left the table without farewell, and Marin saw that the others prepared to follow.

'Why do you leave now?' he asked.

'A man cannot drink without coins,' one of them replied.

At that moment, nothing mattered to Marin except that this afternoon should continue as it was, with the wine and the drinking and his friends. So he did not hesitate before pulling his purse out from under his tunic. He opened it and tipped it up, so that the coins rolled out across the table.

'I have money enough for us to drink.'

The man looked at the coins in astonishment. 'Such riches,' he said, 'for one so young.' He paused. 'And yet you did not choose to share this with us before.'

'You did not ask me, and I did not know yet that you were my friends.'

The man scooped the money from the table. He disappeared and returned some minutes later with a flagon in each hand. He set them on the table. 'I will be back with more,' he said.

Men who had not been sitting at the table before came forward and began to help themselves to the wine. At first Marin was offended. He had not meant to buy for them. But then he wondered if, after all, they were those he had met first because as his thoughts and his vision became more confused, all the faces around him were now coming to seem alike.

And as he tried to distinguish which of these had been his friends, he began to feel sick, very sick, and suddenly vomited, bursting the contents of his stomach over those closest to him, onto the table and the floor.

Arms hoisted him up, and he felt people strike at him as he was dragged away to the door. They threw him to the pavement, and he heard a lock slide closed behind him.

He lay there laughing, and still laughed as he staggered back to the warehouse through the darkened streets. Just stopping for a moment while he reassured himself that the footsteps he thought he had heard behind him were nothing but the echoes of his own.

He slept through the next dawn and the workmen's collection, and was woken only by the merchant shouting out his list. Marin lay quietly, wrapped up in the sacking in case today the merchant felt moved to count what lay at the back. But satisfied with the sound of his usual place, he and the boy soon left.

Marin stretched himself, aching, still weary, and tried to remember the day before. The air in the warehouse smelt different, bitter, but looking about him he could see no reason and nothing around him had changed.

He rolled over and checked that his money was still safe as he had left it. He thought that most probably what he smelt was his own fear and stupidity, and what remained of the wine and the sickness still coming on his breath.

How much had he spent in the tavern? How many had seen what he had? A sudden impulse came to gather everything up and move. But he was too tired to think it through and put the idea behind him.

His head was spinning as he walked down the stairway, but today, at least, there was respite from the rain.

The sun hurt his eyes so much that he was only outside for an hour or so, yet when he returned he knew that they had been there; and when he looked beneath the floorboard, every ducat, every scudo, every gift had gone.

But they had neatly folded the sacking he used for his bed.

Autumn arrived with a rush in October, trailing damp winds and rains which fell heavy and unbroken, day after day.

Temporary walkways were erected across the flooded streets, balanced each end on stacks of paving, slabs of stone, or any other material to hand. Some people paddled about their business on stilts, cut from lengths of wood. A cargo of fine oak, bought for renovations at the Incurabili Hospital, had disappeared, one night, from a warehouse and reappeared a day later, being sold on the south side of the Ponte di Rialto, sawn to shape, fixed with footholds and bound with rope into pairs.

There was hardly a person on the streets, and Marin did not bother to hold out his bowl or to smile to those who did pass. He did not have the will to start it all again.

On the fifth day of rain, just after dawn, he walked slowly into the Piazza. Mists rose up from the flood waters and spiralled down from the sky, and in the wavering haze of their meeting, he saw a man coming out of his tent. The man stretched both arms towards the heavens and then it seemed that from the middle of his chest he uncurled and stretched up a third. By the time Marin had reached the tent, the man was back inside.

The tent was yellow with fringes and above the purple flap of its door was a notice advertising perfumed oils.

Marin walked around it for some minutes, waiting to see if the man would come out, and when he did not, began to make his way towards the Mercerie, kicking and splashing at the water.

As he approached the Rio San Salvatore, he saw the funeral procession. Four men came out of the waterfront door of the large house on the corner. On their shoulders they carried a small black coffin. They made their way slowly across the sloping pavement to the funeral boat, jolting the coffin as they fought to keep their footing, slipping on the stones.

Behind them came a group of mourners, mostly women. They walked, clutching each other, arm in arm, as though only through their collective strength could the burden of their grief be borne, a load so raw and heavy that falling on single shoulders would have crushed them. Their faces were red and swollen from weeping.

Waiting by the boat was a priest who, as the cortege approached, opened a prayer book from which he began to read in a low, melodious voice. The rain became heavier, and his robe clung in dripping folds to his body. The hats and the cloaks of the mourners were sodden. The women formed a circle around the coffin, bunching tightly together, as words from the book prepared the occupant of the box for the trials of the journey ahead.

Four small boys, in cassocks far too big for them, stood behind the priest who led the litany, chanting at the end of each verse.

Marin drew nearer, his boots scraping noisily on the incline to the canal. One of the women at the back turned and saw him. She glared. He glared back. She turned away and then back to look at him again. She tugged at the elbow of the one standing next to her, and after a moment she had turned too. This one whispered to the one next to her, who also turned to look.

A moment later all the mourners had turned to face him. The priest read his sermon to their unheeding backs, and the children's chanting went unanswered.

The first woman called out, ' Torquato!' And she took a step towards Marin. He didn't move. 'Torquato,' she called, 'I see you.' Gathering up her skirts from her ankles, she broke into a clumsy trot, slipping and slithering on the incline in her desperate efforts to reach him.

When the others hoisted their skirts to follow her, Marin ran. They chased him through the Mercerie to the Rio de Baretteri and towards the Rio del Ponte dei Ferati.

'Torquato! Torquato!' The sound bounced from the buildings and through deserted streets, swallowed then delivered back by the mists, echoing from all sides in the driving rain and winds. They called him by the name of another, yet deep inside he was not surprised.

At the end of the bridge, Marin slipped, lost his footing and fell, hitting his head hard against the stone.

To the women approaching from the far side of the bridge, through the clouds of damp and spray, it seemed as though he had suddenly evaporated into the air.

One of them shrieked. 'Aaieeh! God has taken him. He came to say goodbye and now God has taken him home.'

After the others had turned away, Marin knew that one still stood at the base of the bridge, waiting. Then she too left and he heard her weeping grow fainter and fainter until it became lost among all the other noises in his head.

He closed his eyes for a moment, and when he opened them again he saw his surroundings grow bright, then blurred and very far away. He heard the women's voices, even though they were long since gone. Torquato.

Trying to rise, he found he could not. Time turned in on itself and stopped. On the edges of the darkness he saw Constanza dancing, moving swiftly from his view. Then the sound of the bells on her slippers faded gradually to silence.

Lelio sniffed at the boy and bent closer. At first he had thought he was dead. He lay half in, half out of the water, was being slowly dragged down by the current. Lelio pulled him up onto the bank and tried, without success, to prise open his eyes. Then he arranged the boy's limbs to make it seem they were confined by a coffin, and for a while he lay on the ground beside him.

Marin could not tell whether it was one day that passed or two, whether the intervals of darkness came from within or without.

Then the endless disjointed murmuring in his ears began to clear, and he heard a different noise, separate, distinct, from very close by. The beating of a drum. As it stopped, there was a scuffling and commotion and a foot kicked his ribs. Somebody shook him.

He heard the Contessa's voice. 'I will look after you and make you well again,' she said. Marin opened his eyes.

The children moved forward, jostling, whispering, and at the Contessa's order they hoisted him up and onto their shoulders. She shouted at them that they were to bear him gently, and the procession moved off towards the Piazza.

The children spoke softly to each other as they went. Marin heard one of them refer to him as their brother.

There had been no rain for a day but the streets were still flooded. The children waded through the market place, and with quick, sly movements, flung water at each other. Marin thought they would drop him.

Through half-opened eyes, he saw other people turn to stare and, to his right, swinging so close they touched his face, the folds of Agostino's cloak and the hand of the ape he carried.

At the quayside by the Pescaria, three gondolas were waiting in line. As the sun emerged from behind a cloud, drops of moisture glittered briefly, bright against dark polished wood.

'Into the first, and onto the settle,' he heard the Contessa call.

Struggling to keep control of his weight, small clumsy hands carried him on board, across the deck, into the cabin, and lowered him awkwardly onto the couch there. The Contessa made a great fuss around them, criticising the way they held him, poking and prodding at them, but she made no move to help.

When at last they laid him down, she waved her hands and sent them away. The gondola shuddered and moved from the shore, and she hesitated for a moment before sitting beside him to stare, passing her hands to and fro above his face.

The journey had been under way only for a minute or so when the rain began again. A barrage above their heads. A while later, the tapestry across the doorway to the cabin was pushed aside and Agostino entered. His hair was spread flat and soaked to his head, and trickles of reddish dye from his cloak ran over his hands, his robe, dripping around his feet. He held the ape in his arms. The Contessa took the animal from him and began to brush its fur dry with her sleeve.

'I told you,' she said to Agostino. 'I told you to stay outside.'

The pain in Marin's head grew worse. He closed his eyes.

Marin was woken by someone tugging at his clothes. His limbs felt soft and heavy, and when he tried to move them, he found that he could not. The Contessa had gone and the children crowded around him. As soon as they saw that his eyes were open, they pulled him from the settle, heaved him onto their shoulders again and, staggering under his weight, carried him out of the cabin and across the deck. He opened his mouth to tell them to leave him but was unable to utter a sound.

Two at his shoulders and two at his feet, they carried him down the boarding planks, onto land and through a garden, lush and green and patched with red. Their feet slid on the sodden grass. The rain still fell, streaming, steadily.

From somewhere out of sight, he heard the Contessa call, 'Take him to the blue room.'

They carried him through a series of narrow porches with arches shaped at the top to points and columns either side carved as serpents curled round the trunks of trees. Then through an enormous entrance hall, hung with embroidered fabrics that flapped in the draught from the doorway and past other children who, clutching tapers, were climbing ladders to light the rows of torches extending like branches from the walls.

A steep stairway led up from the far corner of the hall. By the time the children reached it, they were gasping for breath, their legs buckling beneath Marin's weight.

Following a few paces behind, the Contessa watched. She did not try to help them. She did not want to touch him yet.

Ascending the stairs, the children were too weak to hold him fast, and at each landing, as they swung him round and turned towards the next, he slipped sideways. The third time they let him slip so far that his head knocked against the wall, rendering him unconscious.

He dreamt that he was swimming and diving like a fish through the waters of the Lagoon, and woke to find the Contessa forcing one of her fingers into his mouth. It tasted of wine at first, sweet and strong, but left a strange bitterness on his tongue.

She smiled at him and took her finger away. 'I have special medicine to make you better. You must drink,' she said.

He lay propped on ribboned pillows in a large bed, surrounded by heavy drapes. She lay next to him, on top of the sheets and quilts. Her mouth and the skin around it was stained a reddish brown.

She held up the bottle, kissed it and laughed. 'I do believe that there is no ill in the world that this will not cure. Now that you are here, you must call me Flavia, and we are to be friends. And this will be your room. Tell me how you like your room.'

She swung her feet to the floor, stood, stumbling slightly, and pulled back the drapes around the bed.

The room was the finest Marin had ever seen. The walls were

hung with velvet panels, threaded through with beading and tiny knots of gold. The furniture was decorated with mosaics and carvings. Clusters of tall, spindle-shaped candles were burning in brass candelabra even though, he could see by the light from the window, it was the middle of the day. The linen sheets on his bed were inlaid with circles of lace.

As he opened his mouth to speak, the Contessa pushed another spoonful of the liquid between his lips. He spat it onto the sheets.

The pain in his head was growing worse, and he heard a beating becoming louder, as though something trapped inside there knocked impatiently for release. Unable to move, he closed his eyes.

'No,' she said. 'No.' She tapped the back of the spoon against his cheek. 'You must look at me. If you would drink, it would make you better.' He opened his eyes.

She took hold of his chin and turned his face towards her. She stared at him silently, her pupils moving rapidly as if she were trying to commit to memory the movement of the sky in a storm. He heard her whisper a name but was sure it was not his.

She looked into his eyes, and he tried to turn away, but she held him fast, tightening her grip. He pretended to faint, giving a sigh and letting his body fall limp.

He heard her sharp intake of breath, felt her trembling fingers on his face, trying to prise open his eyelids. He rolled his eyes up and back into their sockets so that when she succeeded, they stared back at her, unfocussed and blank. She began to pinch and prod at his cheeks and pummel at his chest. He stayed perfectly still. She cursed and leapt from the bed. He heard the bottle smash against the wall, her footsteps uneven, staggering across the room, the door opening and then slamming shut.

He could still feel the pressure of her hand on his face, long after she had gone. As though having touched him too hard, for too long, a part of her had stuck.

The Contessa came back at the first light of dawn next morning. She lay on the bed beside him, turned his face towards hers, put a bottle to his lips. The same liquid as before. Too weak to resist, he drank. He felt its effects running through his veins. Straight away, it soothed and stopped the pain in his head. He realised that he had been fighting something, and that now the fighting had stopped. He did not mind that she was there and that she looked at him. He did not mind anything any more. He looked up at her and smiled.

She leant over him, eyes fixed fiercely on his, tears and laughter coming at once. Her thoughts, a warm tide which took him up, caressing, touching softly every part of his skin, causing him to quiver with a pleasure so intense that at times it came near pain. Arching his body, he heard himself cry out.

But as the feeling grew stronger, suddenly he was afraid. The pressure of her thoughts began to suffocate as they washed over him in waves. He felt himself drenched by them, breathless, gasping frantically for air. His fingers twitched and grabbed at the frame of the bed, searching for something to hold to so that he would not be swept away. The Contessa stroked his brow. He heard her say the name 'Piero'.

Marin could hear conversation, disjointed phrases, unrelated, rambling, unfinished. But it was only one person who spoke. He heard a train of thought. Inside his own head, the thoughts of another. And while this voice grew louder and more distinct, the presence of his own thoughts grew weaker.

A haze filled the room, veiling its contents and the Contessa from view. He heard cannon fire, gunfire, saw streaks of grey smoke curling from barrels in clouds that caught in his throat. A bugle called in vain to men who would never rise again. He walked through red fields, lurching forward over grass crushed and torn and trodden to mud. Bodies, some tidy in heaps and the parts of others haphazardly strewn – pieces lurid on the ground for as far as his eyes could see. Then men in rags, singing, marching on narrow stony paths through fields of yellow flowers. And Marin knew that it was not another he watched, but himself. The feet that trod the paths were his.

It had seemed that all these things had happened in minutes, but it occurred to him now that it might have been for the whole of the day because, as he became aware of the Contessa drawing back, he saw that the sun had gone, the room was dim, and the candles were burnt to butts. He lay back, exhausted, trembling.

The Contessa sat on the edge of the bed with her back to him, swaying slowly from side to side, saying the name Piero. Then she jumped up, ran from the room and out onto the landing. He heard her weeping there, retching, and then the quick spatter of vomit on the tiles. Another door on the landing opened and closed.

He was soaked with sweat and the buttons on his nightshirt had broken from their fastenings. When he tried to pull it closed, it would not fit. It did not reach over his chest. His body had grown. Slowly, he reached to touch his skin, and felt coarse hair, hardened muscle, scars.

There was no light from the window but he could see shadows which jerked and danced across the room. Reflections, echoes of the thoughts of somebody else, the thoughts of Piero, now finding life through him.

Marin put his hands over his face and he wept, and then he laughed at his stupidity because, of course, the signs had always been there, only he had not cared to see. Today was nothing more than fulfilment of the promise that life had whispered before.

What people saw when they peered at him in that fixed and peculiar way had nothing to do with any beauty of his. It was the face of another they saw, somehow behind his own. He was the mirror in which they saw their thoughts, and in which this one appeared, the one they wanted, this other face that to them was preferable to his. And he knew that today it had been this one, the one preferred, who had talked inside his head.

He realised now that when he had, in the past, felt the need to hold fast to himself inside, it had been because the image of another was vying for its place. Was he really there at all? And if so, of what worth was something that could be so easily moved aside?

He wondered who it was that Clara had seen when she held him in her arms and whether perhaps, just occasionally, it had been his face, Marin's, she saw instead. And who it was that Vittorio had loved so much that the upset of their quarrel had been cause to take his own life?

Of course he had tried to shut from his mind the knowledge that the blame lay with him. But now to allow himself, finally, to think on it, brought a strange relief.

Yet still he was afraid. Turning onto his stomach, he pushed his face deep into the damp, rumpled pillows and, eventually, lulled to exhaustion by the medicine he had drunk, sank to restless, fitful sleep.

The battlefields and marching men returned in fragments, as specks of dust passing before his eyes, fainter, fainter and, by the morning, gone.

The next morning, Marin found his body returned to his own. The Contessa did not come to visit him. Instead she sent some of the youngest children, who brought him food, smoothed his sheets and plumped his pillows. They entered the room on tiptoe, and mimed each action before they performed it, so as not to cause him alarm. Small hands testing the temperature of his brow, three times waving through the air above it, before daring to touch his skin.

For most of the time he slept, aware, whenever he woke, of the rain drumming, ceaselessly, disconsolate, at the window.

And one day, when he opened his eyes, he realised that the rains had stopped. His head was clear. Climbing stiffly from the bed, he walked to the window and watched the slow, swirling withdrawal of the flood waters from the island and from what they had tried to reclaim as theirs.

The Lagoon was scattered with islands. Some large enough to have earned the right to be named as districts. Some, such as the Contessa's, just big enough to take a palazzo, maybe two, and their gardens. Some of this same size but with lesser intentions, displaying more modestly their humbler housing and perhaps a family vineyard or crops. Others, lonely places where the dead from the plagues had been buried, visited now by no man; and then those emerging only occasionally, momentarily, before slipping back beneath the thick-layered mists on the surface of the water, surrounded by treacherous sandbanks, marshes, in truth little more than mounds of mud, retreat only for birds, a few fishermen or wandering souls for whom the concept of home was unknown.

For another week, Marin did not see the Contessa. Instructions as to what he should do, what he should eat, what he should wear came scribbled on pieces of notepaper or relayed through one of the children.

He was so used to rising early that every day now he was awake before dawn. Except for the kitchen staff, the household here rose hours later than was usual, and what had been designated their daytime carried on far into the hours of the night. This rearrangement of their clock was at the Contessa's command, emphasising the separation of herself and hers from the life that was lived outside.

As Marin walked through the garden alone, on his first morning out of bed, he wondered whether it was he who moved or whether it was another within, waiting to appear whenever he should so please. And if it was the case that he, Marin, could house another and think his thoughts, then where or what was he? And he pondered on the nature of evil.

While the strangeness of the household pleased him, he told himself that he would leave in the spring. He would stow on a boat, swim to shore. She could not hold him against his will. But, for now, he would allow himself to be held.

He spent his time observing the others in the house. He concealed himself in corners, doorways, listening to their conversations, watching.

The Contessa's room was next to his, with the curtains on its windows always drawn. On the landing below was Agostino's room and the dormitories for her most favoured attendants.

These favourites, for the most part, were young, no more than ten years old. Indulged as if they were children of her own, they had, it appeared, no duties other than to accompany her on excursions and to scatter for her the silence of the house. The clamour from their games floated up and down through the stairwells.

In addition to these who walked with her were other servants, less favoured – the kitchen maids and those whose lot it was to sweep and clean the grounds, the gardens and the boats.

Agostino, it seemed, was in a category of his own. Marin watched him as he went about the house and gardens, hunched down to a shape too small for him, stooping as though to squeeze himself into a cage that only he could see. And whatever the outside event or insult, his eyes remained unchanged, unconcerned, as if he only watched what happened to another who was in no way connected to him.

But Marin saw that Agostino knew that the cage had gone, and it was only the others who did not. Agostino still took its shape only because he chose to. It was the others who were the fools.

He knew that Agostino watched him too, guessed that he had been recognised, and while this knowledge made him afraid, the urge to spy and follow was stronger.

Repelled, yet fascinated, Marin observed him. How might it feel to live untouched by the thoughts of others? And, having made this divide, would the result be loneliness or freedom?

He was aware that it would be wise to approach and attempt to make his peace but, lacking the courage to initiate their meeting, he hoped instead that something would occur to prevent it.

The rains began again, roaring and moaning from the sky. But, from his window, Marin saw that one of the gardeners, a boy about his own age, was still working, replanting the heart-shaped flower beds nearest the water's edge.

The boy worked carefully and methodically, not seeming to mind or even notice that the wind and the rain whipped and washed from their places what he had put there only minutes before. This, so that when he had worked his way round and back to the start, there was no sign of his having begun.

Marin pulled on his clothes, left his room and moved quietly to the stairway. The door to the Contessa's room was slightly ajar. At the bottom of her bed, Marin saw Agostino sleeping, stretched across her feet like a dog.

As he reached the foot of the stairs, he could hear the kitchen servants preparing the meals for the day. The clattering of plates and cutlery, the hum of their voices subdued and, now and then, a burst of smothered laughter.

Marin went into the garden and sat, settling to watch, on the path at the start of the steps to the water.

Jacopo replanted the roses. They were of a red so intense he could feel it pulse in his hands, a soft palpitation reminiscent of the pumping of blood. He liked to dip his fingers into those flowers in bloom.

He did not mind how many times he had to replant them. He enjoyed this work more than any of them would have known or understood. But he would never tell them so, because he knew that its purpose was not to give pleasure.

Only occasionally did anything other than the work in hand intrude upon his thoughts. The swifter, harsher passage of a bird, sudden changes in the light or, as now, the approach of the new boy.

He had heard the whisperings from the others. They said that the Contessa's strange excitement was caused by the effect of some spell this new arrival had cast. Perhaps what they said was true, and perhaps it was not. But there was something about Marin that made him uneasy. He carried with him a promise of upset, like the smell in the air that signalled a storm.

So he was not particularly pleased to see Marin that morning, and relieved that again he halted some distance away. Out of the corner of his eye, Jacopo saw him sit where the path stopped and folded to steps to the water. He tried to shut Marin's presence from his mind.

The next morning again, at the same time, Jacopo saw him come from the house and stop to sit as before, perfectly still, at the steps. It was the following day that Marin continued down to the flowerbeds and, without a word, began to furrow the earth, digging in circles with his hands, in an effort to do as Jacopo did.

'Does she know that you have come to help me?' Jacopo asked.

'She has not told me that I should not.'

Jacopo sat back on his heels and regarded Marin. 'Yes,' he said. 'The others say that you have put a spell on her.' Marin stared back at him impassively, until Jacopo found he had to look away. Then Marin began again, cupping his hands and plunging them back in the earth.

Laying a hand on his arm to stop him, Jacopo said, 'If you want to work with me, you must watch what I do.'

Marin changed the movement of his hands more exactly to follow Jacopo's.

Jacopo heard the sound of boats by the water and the crash of oars flung violently against the wood. He knew that they were watched. He moved a little further away from Marin.

Sometimes the Contessa watched Marin from her window. She noticed that, mostly, he hung back from the company of her attendants and her servants, and that soon they, as though by collective, unspoken agreement, began to keep their distance from him.

She had never believed in magic or witchcraft wrought by man. To her these notions were nothing more than labels for the convenience of Church and simpletons. Means to describe that which made them afraid or that which they could not understand. So what was this? The fact that when she looked into Marin's eyes, she saw Piero. For that was the truth of the matter.

Piero. Rather than run the risk of his leaving, it had seemed at the time preferable for her to leave first. She had gone without explanation. And now after ten years she saw him again, with no understanding of why.

But she could not see the boy too often. His effect was similar to that of the laudanum she kept in her drawer. Too much turned her head, made her sick, made her mad. She would just sip from him on occasion. And she would never let him go.

She watched him now as he worked with the gardener boy, and she wondered what they said.

She let the curtain fall, moved from the window and turned to face her mirror. For years she had approached it like an enemy, one to be treated with caution and care in order to exit the encounter unscathed. Then she had realised that, rather than aim towards some semblance of beauty, it was easier to pretend that she had forgotten its face. Yes, it was better to set one's sights low, and better still for it to appear that one did not have any at all.

In the semi-darkness, she dipped her fingers into the jars of cosmetics on her dressing table, smearing her eyes, her lips, her cheeks with careless layers of waxy colour.

Marin's meeting with Agostino came unexpectedly, on the stairs, where there was no possibility of either of them turning away. For a moment they regarded each other in silence, and Marin saw that Agostino waited for him to speak first.

'I have been wanting to say,' Marin said, 'that I am sorry. That I am truly sorry ... I did not mean to spoil your escape ... It was an accident.' But not having planned his words in advance, they sounded confused and strained, even to his own ears unlike any rendition of truth.

Agostino smiled, drawing his lips back to show his teeth, nodding as if satisfied to have heard what he expected. And when he raised his hand, the gesture was so sudden that Marin stepped backwards in fright, missed his footing and only prevented himself from falling by grabbing the rail on the wall.

Gathering his cloak around him, Agostino continued down the stairs, laughing as though the encounter had pleased him. And he was not fooled by what had been said. What were accidents other than actions for which people wished to disown their guilt?

However, he was not happy at the boy's arrival, this sudden disruption to circumstance, which previously had at least been composed of matters he understood. He sensed Marin's strangeness, the impression he gave of things held in check. There was something about the boy that was unusual, which made him want to peer closer, and on some days he felt he had come near to knowing it. But whatever it was remained half-formed, irresolute, therefore impotent like the power of a prayer only half meant. It seemed that the boy bound himself, probably without knowing that he did so.

Perhaps the Contessa would soon tire of Marin, and he would be despatched as quickly as he had come. She had taken a fancy to others before, and Agostino knew that in equal – or more likely greater – measure than her pleasure in them came that of demonstrating to him the fact that he could be replaced.

But he doubted that she would do this, and as he made his way out of the house he thought of her. Their intimacies begun at her signal, the duration and completion in silence. How astonished he had been the first time but now coming to see how the ties of hatred might prove as irresistible as those of love.

And then he thought of Ettore, whose face suddenly he saw everywhere, present without the need to recall. Would he learn that the ties of hatred could serve as suitable substitute?

One, two, three, four. Agostino turned backflips down the steps leading from the rear of the house to the gardens. The ends of the ribbons covering the chain around his ankles whipping through the air behind him. He knew what the others saw, and he did not care. Everything in its time.

He continued down the path towards the trees, the gravel hardly marking his scarred and calloused palms.

Such small displays of lunacy, he found, served to keep the others at a distance. Except the Contessa. But with her mind so taken up with the boy, he guessed that today she would not follow him.

Once into the trees, he began to walk through and beyond them to the place where the ground sloped in layers of weed and stones to the water. From this lower level, he could always hear the approach of any intruder before they caught sight of him. He closed his eyes, stretched his arms out above his head, then behind him, then in circles on either side. Nothing and nobody. Alone. He had come here and done this on the first day he arrived, and had he been a man who cried, had anything of that part of him been left, he might have soaked the grass with his tears.

Throughout the day and night, a keeper had been present to watch them. For ten years he had not spent even one minute alone. His every action open to comment and a possible cause for amusement. And the only one whose company he still wished for, he would never see again.

Now he considered each day that passed, each humiliation endured, as progress on his journey, taking him closer to the place where the hand that held the power would be his. So from here he could say that his survival had purpose, that having been spared he made use of it. It was necessary that he find some reason.

Opportunity for escape from the island must come. Until then he would wait. Among other things, he had learnt to bide his time.

He could not remember a time when he had not been listed as the property of another. Counted as chattel since infancy. Then clipped at the age of nine by his master to maintain the purity of his voice, he had been sold a week later to a neighbour in exchange for some coins and a half-sack of corn.

Agostino remembered the argument over his price, the coins unwillingly pushed across the table. He remembered the years that followed, the coins more or less, the outcome the same, until he had been sold to the freak show.

Although his time there was finished, every night he returned in his dreams. The rank stench of their cage. The howling of the wolfman told for so long he was a wolf that he had come to believe it was so. The only one who was caged alone, the straw where he slept heaped with half-chewed and decaying remains of the vermin he had been taught to accept as food.

The dwarf, reciting from the Bible, his voice falling and rising from whisper to shriek. Always the same verses. Genesis, Chapter One. 'In the beginning God created the heaven and the earth. And the earth was without form, and void; and darkness was upon the face of the deep. And the Spirit of God ...'

The keeper who lit small balls of straw, which he then tossed through the bars of the cage, laughing at the terrified scramble to smother them.

And Ettore. At nights he and Ettore remained close together, awake long after the curfew, while the others tossed and moaned in troubled sleep on the damp, fetid straw beneath them.

During the day when they were not travelling or exhibited he would usually remain silent in a corner while Ettore spoke or read his palm. Ettore liked to talk. Agostino remembered the sound of it. Tales of places far different from where they were now. And of a small place to the north of Umbria. Far enough from the rest of man to make it closer to God. Ettore used to joke that the reason he was able to read the hands of others was because he could practise on three, rather than two, of his own. This third, the size of a child's, extended from a small withered arm that grew from his chest.

But Agostino's mind had always been more on the feel of his hand in another's, and gratitude for the friendship it implied. So when Ettore had traced the lines on his palm, given a translation as to their meaning, Agostino had not listened. It had been preferable to close his ears, rather than to nourish expectation for events he thought could never come to pass.

He had never imagined at that time any hope for his future, never seen there a possibility of any great degree of change. Only perhaps another cage in exchange for this one and another after that. And so on and so on, until they opened it one morning and found that he was dead.

Then when change did come, Agostino had no more than the vaguest memory of what it was that had been promised.

Nobody knew how the fire had started. Possibly some carelessness with a lamp or candles too near the straw. It took hold within seconds, darting from the keepers' tent across the dried grass in the yard, to the wooden carts that took the show from town to town.

Agostino had watched as the flames came nearer their cage, blowing bright embers onto the straw at his feet. Around him, the others were screaming and banging at the bars with their fists. But the keepers ran past to the gates of the yard and out to the safety of the street. Then one came back, running zigzag across the ground, jumping over small heaps of burning straw.

He fumbled at, then released the lock to the cage, by now filled with blackened shapes writhing, alight, clinging to the bars, before falling twisted to the floor. Agostino could smell them. He turned and, for a moment, saw Ettore illuminated, flickering, then crumpling down from view. Trying to beat back the flames, Agostino plunged into them to reach him, but the keeper dragged him back, pulling him out and to the ground, hitting him over the head, and taking him senseless to the gate.

Out of the twenty who had been in the cage, eight had been saved but only three, including Agostino, were still of an appearance to be sold. The burns on his hands were patched and bound, and the day after the fire he was taken with the others to be sold at the slave market on the Riva degli Schiavoni. The Contessa had offered the highest price.

He remembered how afraid he had been at the circus. All the

time afraid. Afraid of where he was, yet afraid of being elsewhere. Afraid that there were things of which he should have been afraid, if only he had had the wit to know them. But on the night of the fire, filled to its capacity and further, the place where he had held his fear had burst, and since that time he had felt none because there was no longer a ground on which it could grow.

And as the Contessa prepared to take him away, the children skipping on either side of him, he did not heed their curiosity or their questions, or their fingers that plucked at his gown. Neither did he flinch as the keeper struck him one final blow. Already he had discovered that it was possible to feel things differently.

Thoughts about leaving came into Marin's mind. He did not act on them. They passed.

He and Agostino greeted each other with smiles and a respectful nod of the head and eased their days with the requisite words of politeness. Not from any dawning of friendship but knowledge that further confrontation would bring to an end the peaceable status that, at present, was of benefit to both.

It became habit that Marin and Jacopo worked together each morning in the garden while the rest of the household still slept. Only rarely did they speak. Scraps of conversation, started with no way of introduction and then left, sometimes mid-sentence, when that thread of thought was through.

Marin waited for the Contessa's summons. It did not come. Instead he saw that she avoided him. Sometimes he caught a glimpse of trailing skirts as she hurried away round a corner. At other times she rushed past him in the garden or in the house, as though she had not seen that he was there. And when she did stop, and they talked for a minute of small things, about which he saw she did not care, she would pretend that their meeting had been by accident. Marin knew that it was not. He could see by the look in her eye that she had needed to ready herself in advance.

Early one morning, just after dawn, he heard her pacing outside his room. He lay back on the pillows and waited. Through the half-open door he heard her shuddering breath, then her turning so quickly away that her shoes slipped on the tiles.

He climbed out of bed, went to the window and saw Jacopo picking grasses by the water. He pulled on his tunic, went down to the garden and, as he approached, saw Jacopo turn and narrow his eyes, uncertain, as if trying to see more clearly something partially obscured from view.

Jacopo stood up straight and waved. And who did he see, Marin wondered. Himself, or another, more pleasing, instead?

Suddenly at a loss as to what to do with his body, Jacopo returned to his work. He remembered that when Marin had arrived, he had decided that he did not like him and that at the time there had seemed very good reasons for this. Why could he not remember them now? Why was he only conscious of the strongest desire to hold him?

It was curious, the way in which Marin's features appeared to change so that each morning it seemed that his impressions the day before had been a mistake. Jacopo wondered if, blindfolded, he ran his fingers over Marin's face, he might have detected a different shape again.

When he reached Jacopo, Marin put his hand on his shoulder. 'Who do you see when you look at me?' he asked softly.

Jacopo continued to pick the grasses, gathering them into bundles and fastening them with twine. He did not reply.

Marin persisted. He had to know. 'I see by the way that you look at me that you see another face along with mine.'

'You remind me of the open fields and hills that were my home. I used to walk there with my father.'

'Do you like these thoughts?'

'Yes.'

'Would you like me otherwise?'

'Those are my thoughts. They are not you.'

Marin looked away.

An hour later, when Marin returned to his room, the Contessa lay waiting on his bed. She had the ape with her. She dandled it on her knee. She ruffled its fur, pulled at its paws and pushed into its mouth the bottle from which she had been drinking.

She curled her mouth into an unnatural smile. Marin saw the red-brown stains on the skin around it. He did not allow his eyes to meet hers. He stayed by the door and looked to the window. She raised the bottle to her lips.

She did not ask him to turn, because she did not want to hear him say no. She sighed. What to say? Where to start? What was it that would make him stay? Did she really want him there at all? The initial shock had turned her head. But did she truly want all that again? Had she not arranged her life precisely so that nothing of this kind would happen?

Love. Creeping into corners where it had no business and smothering every thought and motion of the mind even while one slept. Much better, surely, she had decided years ago, a semblance of sorts which could be kept to its place. She had chosen these people, Agostino, the children, the servants, because there was no possibility, on either her side or theirs, that the likelihood of love would arise.

But since the boy had arrived, she felt it all differently, and their presence only reminded her of what she had intended they replace.

She had learnt to marshall her feelings like soldiers trained to obedience. But now she felt them slipping, sliding from their ranks in answer to a call much stronger than her own.

All this time she had been longing for something once there, now gone, but still leaving the imprint of where it had stood.

Was it true that anything dead would, if left unburied, roam until it found proper rest? The thoughts in her head still wandering, desperate for salvation, quiescence, repose. She knew she thought too much. She envied those whose lives had been sufficiently sweet for nothing more than the bare rudiments of thought ever to have been required.

She saw now how Marin would not look at her. How he could not even bear to come near.

'Are you happy here?' she asked.

'Happy enough,' he replied.

'And your room, your clothes, the company you find, do they please you?'

'They please me well enough.'

'And you would not want to leave here?'

He paused. 'I think that Agostino does not like me.' Immediately he regretted having spoken of it. If the Contessa were to punish Agostino, it would not make this situation easier.

But she dismissed his words with a flick of her hand, as if she considered them unimportant. The expression on her face suggesting that they told her nothing new.

'It is not for him to choose what he does not like. Here, he will like what he must. This is your home now. You have no duties.

You will live here as my guest, my friend.' She paused. 'All I ask in return is that from time to time you sit and talk to me.'

Marin said nothing. Seeing her try, and fail, to smile, he thought back to what had happened before. The tingle on his skin was fear mixed with longing, a longing to feel it again. He wondered, was it like that, the sex act? Could it really be better than that?

The stall-holders at the Rialto had teased him when they saw how women were drawn to him, asking whether he was yet man enough to follow their interest through. They used to thrust their hips and roll their eyes, and tell him things so disgusting that he always blushed with shame. He had never told the stall-holders the truth, which was that the effect of those women's thoughts was enough. He had not been interested in anything further, had even suspected that anything more might impair the taste and sully it, like an excess of salt in a stew.

He told himself that if he lay or sat with the Contessa again, now knowing what to expect, and so more fully prepared, if it grew too much, he could simply gather himself and run.

He saw the anxious expression on her face, was pleased to know that he was its cause and made her wait some minutes longer before he nodded and said, 'I will stay.' It did not matter. He would go when he had had enough, when he chose to.

Only now did the Contessa relax and complete her smile. He would stay for as long as she wanted him to stay. Even if it was not by his own free will.

'May I go to the garden now?' he asked.

She smiled again. 'Of course.'

At the bottom of the stairs, Jacopo was waiting.

'They say she was a whore,' Jacopo said. 'Did you know?'

Marin continued out to the garden without slowing. He knew that Jacopo would follow. 'On the street?' he asked.

Jacopo quickened his pace. 'What does it matter where she did it?'

Marin shrugged.

They stopped on the path. Jacopo was silent for a moment, then he said, 'They say that one man signed to her everything he owned in exchange for her word that she would never leave him. In those days she called herself Maria. Other people called her "Maria No-Hands".'

He saw that Marin did not appear to be listening.

'She spent fifteen years in Rome when she would sell herself to do things that would turn your stomach if you knew. Did you know that she was famous for what she did? Maria No-Hands. She could squeeze her customers tight, tight, tight, without ever lifting a finger. She could make your instrument sing any tune she wanted, make it do things you never thought possible – all without using her hands. They say she has fingers down there, you know, inside.'

He had spoken so fast that he was breathless and his face was flushed. Now he was ashamed. The Contessa had done him no harm and she had given him a home. He had only wanted Marin to like her less, and perhaps him a little more.

Marin smiled. He was intrigued by what Jacopo had said and found the idea of the Contessa as whore, now victorious in her good fortune, pleasing.

From down by the water came the clatter of metal objects, of tools thrown onto the deck of a boat. Jacopo turned. 'I have work to do,' he said, and he ran. Away along the path, to the boathouse, out of sight.

Later in the day, Marin saw him again. This time with one of the gondoliers. The man's name was Ludovico. Marin had seen him with Jacopo before. Marin did not like him, and from the way that Ludovico looked at him, he knew that this feeling was returned.

Ludovico and Jacopo were polishing a gondola at the landing-stage. They each had a cloth that at intervals they dipped into a jar of wood-black. They were standing so close together that their bodies were in contact from shoulder to thigh. They were leaning, bending, rubbing, swaying as one.

All at once they stopped, throwing down their cloths, even though the task was only half-done, and ran across the stage towards the shed next to the boat-house.

Marin waited a few moments, then went down to see. Through a crack in the door he saw Jacopo's body, naked, pressed hard, pulled back, then slapping again against the mildewed wooden walls. Jacopo mewled like a cat.

The next day, after he and Jacopo had dug through the beds and piled up the weeds to be burnt, Marin suggested that they walk to the trees and look at some eggs he had found. He told Jacopo that they had the most unusual markings, like nothing he had seen before.

Marin laid his arm on Jacopo's, looked into his eyes, and he knew he would not refuse. He saw how Jacopo hesitated before he sighed, put down his tools, and followed, and he had also seen at the back of the boatshed, as it strained carelessly out to obtain better view, the shadow of a watcher.

There were no bird's eggs and anyway they would never have reached them, because as Marin had hoped, as they reached the trees, Jacopo stopped and touched him. Jacopo's lips felt rough against his, and as the morning sun caressed their heads, Marin saw through half-opened eyes that it was Ludovico who watched.

That night, Jacopo made a cross out of two pieces of rosewood, tied together with string, which from then onwards he wore always around his neck, concealed beneath his tunic. He never took it off. The smell in the air that signalled a storm had grown stronger.

The Contessa was fond of entertaining. She plied her guests with food and gifts and addressed each that came as 'true, dear friend,' because usually she did not know their names. The words that strung their conversations together were light in substance and form. She had seen that it was a mark of success in the world to have, as the most important matter on one's mind, the length of a train or the cut of a shoe.

After Marin had been at the house for six weeks she gave a party, a picnic, in his honour, so that she could demonstrate to him the wealth and society into which he had arrived.

On the appointed afternoon, she stood at her window and watched them come, their gondolas a thin, black trail on the water. Thunderclouds drifted, sagging in bunches, blackening the sky.

In the house, below her, she could hear the preparations underway. She had taught the children to sound eager in their tasks. Promotion or demotion through the ranks of her service were possible. It used to please her to see how this promise made them vie for her favour, and it used to please her still more to bestow one or the other for no good reason at all. It had pleased her once but it pleased her no more, and now she wished them all gone.

She walked down to the garden to meet her guests. They rushed from their boats to greet her. They ran across the flowerbeds, the women turning up clods of grass and blooms with their shoes. Then suddenly they were all around her with their murmured compliments, lies, apologies for gifts forgotten, not bought, and kisses they did not mean.

It was the same as always. She knew that. But today they were poison, not balm.

So what did one do with the truth when it surfaced? Push it back down to where it had been, or pull it out in welcome? Or the coward's answer, which was to turn away and to let it drift, untouched. She smiled warmly at her guests and held out her arms in greeting.

They followed her across the grass, towards the rugs and blankets laid out near the trees. Admiring, comparing, stroking, as they went, new clothes or the new colour or cut of somebody's hair.

There was always much talk of fashion. It was Agostino who chose the Contessa's clothes and, when somebody at a party spoke of this or that, the latest thing, he would clap his hands together and declare that one must straight away be bought for her. However unflattering she knew it would be.

And she knew that his desire to make her ridiculous came because what she had, and what of it she gave to him, were now what he must count himself lucky to receive.

Today she placed Marin to her right, where usually Agostino

173

was seated. She ordered Agostino to help the children serve the food.

She had dressed the ape in ribbons and a collar of golden beads, and as it skipped and crawled around the guests, they patted its head and pretended that they were pleased to see it.

Marin had not wanted to come to the picnic. He did not feel well. But the Contessa had insisted that he be there.

There had been constant rain over the past few days, and it had seemed to press its way into his head. He felt himself smothered by the weight of the damp.

It was only so that he could rise from his bed that, finally, he had taken the laudanum. She had pushed the bottle against his lips, and he had drunk it all. It had flattened his pain out to nothing. He could feel its effect swirling blessed surrender, a reminder that his torment was caused only by struggle and that ceasing to fight could, in an instant, bring relief.

The grass on which the guests sat was wet. Marin wondered why the Contessa had not arranged for them to sit in the house. He could see that some of them were already uncomfortable, fidgeting, and that the dampness had soaked through the rugs. He and the Contessa sat on bearskins, remaining perfectly comfortable and dry.

When the Contessa rang her hand bell, Agostino and the children came from the house, carrying bowls of rosewater and strips of linen with which they washed and dried the hands of the guests. Fifty guests, one hundred hands.

Agostino's expression, as he washed with care and then patiently patted dry, was of such complete content that those who had heard of changes in the household were convinced that, contrary to what had been said, these changes must have been to his benefit, not loss.

The Contessa hated it, that no matter what she said or did, he still smiled in that serene and peaceful way, the stillness within him seeming a cruel and purposeful reminder of the turmoil within her.

Once the washing of the hands was completed, Agostino and the children returned to the house, coming back a few minutes later bearing trays of golden goblets filled with foaming peaks of sherbet. And then back and out again, more slowly, with crystal pitchers of wine balanced carefully on their heads.

Agostino walked silently in front, his steps on the slippery grass kept short in order to accommodate his chains. He heard one of the guests ask the Contessa a question, so close to him and so loudly that there could have been no doubt that he would hear.

'Is it true,' the man asked, 'that these eunuchs are still equipped, in some way, to perform?'

The Contessa smiled and spoke loudly in return. 'Well, the answer to that depends on the manner of performance you mean. There is a type, the parading and acting, at which you can see he excels, but of course he used to be in a freak show, you know. Did you know? Until I gave him a home. But as for anything else, the more meaningful arts of congress that I think you have in mind – oh, no. Not possible, I am afraid. Not possible any more.'

Taking her glass, Agostino refilled it with wine. He straightened the man's napkin and smoothed it. Their conversation sufficient distance from where he carried himself, inviolate.

With a snap of her fingers the Contessa ordered Agostino to serve Marin's food. She smiled and nodded at the two Procurators, and they smiled and nodded at her. They would take back home with them flagons of her finest wine and a purse of ducats apiece. And in exchange she could serve as many courses as she wanted, displayed in or on whatever manner of gold she pleased, and no complaint of her breaching the sumptuary laws would ever find a hold.

Dish after dish was brought. Oysters, jellied sturgeon, roast guinea fowl served with herb and spice pastries, quails cooked in Sicilian wine, boiled pigs' brains, roast peacock stuffed with plums, roast swan nesting on a bed of gilded vine leaves.

Marin had no appetite. He picked at his food and threw the rest to the ape, who seized it up and scurried off to the trees to eat it.

The guests ate with their usual relish as if this food was the first on their plates for weeks, but now as the sun went down, adding to the discomfort of the damp on their flesh, came a sharp and bitter chill.

That her guests were cold made the Contessa glad. So much so that when children appeared on the edges of the grove, carrying flaming torches, she ordered them back to the house.

The last of the main courses was pigeon pie. Five separate pies were brought from the house, of such a size and on serving dishes so heavy that each required four children to carry it.

The Contessa stood and, as was custom, with a silver knife quickly sliced away the pastry crusts to release the birds. They fluttered out, bewildered, rising in drowsy, crooked flight up and over the trees. Marin watched one of them, lurching, stumbling sideways through the air, then suddenly collect itself and soar.

All this, as was custom, to the accompaniment, of the practised sighs and murmurs of awe and delight from the guests. But today their responses were muted. Cold and damp, they wondered at her behaviour. Had they fallen from grace? It really was too bad of her to treat her friends like this. But still they smiled like mandarins, and no word of complaint was uttered. Bearing in mind what they had received in the past and what they hoped for the future, pneumonia was really a very small price to pay.

Marin watched the children bringing trays of marzipan cakes and lemon biscuits, trudging in line from the house as heavy rain began to fall. Agostino walked behind them, carrying two more pitchers of wine. Looking around him at the guests, Marin saw that their faces were running with trickles of dye from their hair and cosmetics and that their clothes now clung crinkled to their skins. He huddled into his cloak.

The Contessa put her arms around him. 'Are you cold, my sweet?' she asked. He turned away from her. Always these terms of affection. She never used his name. He looked up at her. She held him tighter and kissed him. He was too tired to struggle. He watched the rain drops roll down from his hands, slowly, lingering. He felt them on his back, his neck, his sides.

He saw smoke rise in wisps from the grass and he heard the singing and the boots on stone. A reddish tinge to the air made it seem that the guests, now silently, sullenly, eating their cakes, were leaking a watery blood. Then from the smoke, he heard gunfire, felt it searing through his stomach. Everything around him turned to black, and he rolled sideways onto the grass.

One of the guests leapt up from his rug and ran to where Marin lay. He grabbed at Marin's head, plugged his fingers to his throat, and then he began to cry, wiping his eyes with the sleeve of his suit of cheap, tasselled silk which was now shrunk and ruined with damp. He turned to the Contessa, his face streaked with tears mixed with the black on his lashes. 'I am afraid the boy is dead,' he said.

A short distance away, the ape rolled on the grass. It was squalling, the edges of its mouth darkened and spotted with froth. Its paws reached up in contortions, twisted like the twigs on a tree.

Marin was carried to the house by the children. The guests hung back, wringing their hands. They did not want to come too close, fearing that, even now the boy was dead, further damage, therefore disfavour, might be occasioned by any ill-advised action or touch. And that if blame were to be apportioned, it might find its way to them.

But the sudden emptying of Marin's stomach, speckling the children's shoes, assured them that all was well and that a man's clothes were indeed a mark of his worth.

Marin drifted in and out of consciousness. On the first day of his confinement, Agostino was taken to the slave market on the Riva degli Schiavoni to be sold.

The Contessa purged the poison from Marin's system, pushing into him water-filled tubes to wash it away. She lay beside him on the bed, her hair unpinned and loose about her shoulders, and with her tongue stretching out and curling in, she licked from small glasses of laudanum.

The pain from Marin's stomach moved back to his head, and when the Contessa offered him laudanum to drink, he took it. And when she looked at him, and he felt the pleasure streaming along his limbs, he remembered that there was a need to protect himself but his mind was too muddled to recall what to do. For an instant he did not care, and then it was too late.

Piero came softly at first, then so loudly that his voice rose above the Contessa's when she spoke. Piero's thoughts, his speech, and a battlefield which overlaid the room like a gauze.

Tossing and turning in fever, delirious, Marin fell further into Piero's world, losing his hold on his own.

With tear-streaked faces the children nursed him, struggling with the weight of stone bowls, brimming with his waste and urine which dripped and slopped to puddles on the floor. Marin watched their satin boots walk unstained through the bodies of dead men.

Only when there could be no more denying that he had not long to live did the Contessa call in the doctors. They listened to Marin's incoherent mutterings and tasted the spittle that dribbled from his mouth. They held a lamp close to his flickering eyes and tested his throat with their fingers.

'Ah,' they said.

'We think he could live,' said one.

'But you understand, I am sure, my lady,' said the other, 'that the best medicines come at a price.'

Their prognosis was that the poison had gone but that its passing had left the boy with bad humours which they could see still lodged in his head.

The Contessa said that she would pay in triplicate for the medicine and for whatever they usually charged for their time.

The doctors conferred in whispers, shrugged and nodded solemnly, indicating that the favour done was theirs. They unfastened the rows of buckled straps on their bags, and then the treatment began.

They held Marin's mouth open and poured into it syrups of traganth and compound of powdered gold with hyssop. And when they burnt his head with cautery irons to dispel the humours they said were causing the fever, the room was filled with the smell of charring flesh and hair. They tied his arm with leather and, with the quickest flick of a knife, they cut it, so that with this stealth and speed they could catch the loosened humours unawares, pour them into a bowl and inspect them.

Marin did not know whether it was day or night, or how many had passed, when he realised the doctors were gone and that now he was alone with the Contessa again. Her fingers on him, cradling his head and stroking his face, holding him still so that he had no choice but to look at her. He tried to steady himself to fight it.

As the pleasure came, his hands clutched at the sheet, and his breathing grew faster. He felt his skin itch, had a sense that it stretched, and there was an aching in his muscles. He was aware that she kissed him. Then when he lay quiet, she went without a word, locking the door behind her.

His sheets were soaked with perspiration. He pushed them away and reached out for the jug of water on the table beside the bed. He reached too far, lost his balance and slid down onto the floor.

In front of him, in the long mirror on the wall, he saw the man's reflection. The man crouched too, as he did. He wore an embroidered nightshirt of the exact same design as Marin's. He had a face left pitted by the pox, a nose that came in lumps and ridges like a turnip, and a beard that was shaped to a point. He had brown scorch marks on his forehead. Marks such as a cautery iron would leave.

Marin raised a hand to protect himself and the man, in response, raised his too. Slowly, Marin lowered his arm and watched as the man did the same. Marin turned from the mirror and touched a hand to his face. The pitted skin, the nose in lumps and ridges, and the pointed beard were his.

His hands began to tremble. He pulled at this face, trying to rip away what he felt there. Slowly at first, then building to a frenzy, he dug deep with his nails trying to uncover his own features beneath. He felt his skin break and he cried with the pain. But when he stopped, exhausted, and turned back to the mirror, he saw the man looking back at him, his face scratched, torn, bloodied but underneath all this, unchanged.

Rolling himself into a ball, Marin rocked slowly back and forth on the floor, running his fingers over his face, the beard, the pockmarks. Without looking at the man in the mirror, Marin knew that he did this too.

'I am Marin,' he whispered. 'I am Marin.'

And he prayed that it was true.

When the doctors unlocked the door the next morning, Marin twisted round in his bed to face them. As one they shouted, reaching for their crucifixes as they dropped their bags for they saw that he had been possessed in the night: that there in the poor boy's nightshirt was a demon who stroked his beard, opened his bloodied face and laughed at them.

Marin heard the clatter and slipping of their panicking feet on the stairs. Moments later they ran back, warding off what they saw with a fervent repetition of prayer. Shielding their eyes with one hand, they seized their bags with the other, for these were filled with instruments and medicines too valuable to leave, even when faced with a devil.

Marin knew that he would die if he stayed there. Reduced to ash by cautery irons or, more likely, lost forever as another settled into his place. His own passing unmourned.

He climbed out of bed, crawled to the landing and clinging to the rail pulled himself, as fast as he could, down the stairs.

The sun was rising over the gardens as he limped towards the water. He heard shouts from the house and tried to hurry, but the effort was too much. He slumped to his knees with no strength to move any further. Suddenly, from behind, somebody seized him by the waist, lifted him and half carried, half pushed him into the shed by the boathouse. The door closed and he heard the key turn in the lock.

Footsteps came running, the door was rattled, and Marin heard one of the boatmen say, 'No, leave it. Ludovico has that key, and he is still asleep. The boy will not be there.'

Marin huddled down between the wall and a pile of splintered planks and waited. Throughout the day, he could hear the coming and going of boats. As darkness fell, he heard the boatmen slamming their vessels to the stage, tying them fast to the posts and walking back towards the house, cursing because they had not found him.

He squeezed further behind the planks and lay down on the floor. His body was itching. He reached to touch his face, his chest, and felt his skin moving under his fingers, altering its texture and shape, from Piero's body to his. His head was beginning to clear. He slept.

The sound of the key turning softly in the lock woke him. He rose stiffly to his feet, leaning on the wall for support, climbed over the wood and pushed open the door. The gardens shimmered in the light. There was nobody to be seen.

He stood for a moment, stretching his legs, hesitant in case somebody waited to trap him. Then he took a deep breath and ran, stumbling, flinging himself forward over the grass, onto the landing-stage and from it into the water.

As he rose to the surface and opened his mouth to gasp for air, somebody pressed him back, plunging him down so suddenly that his nose and mouth filled with water and, as he coughed more of it went into his lungs. He reached his hands up to try and force those that held him away, but they stayed firm where they were. Too weak to move them he felt himself pushed deeper.

Then he was hauled up by his hair, so quickly that when the air and sunlight struck him, his first instinct was to recoil. A hand struck him across the face.

'Don't you want to live?' It was Jacopo.

Marin could not believe what he saw. Lacking the strength to return the blow, he took hold of Jacopo's arm and bit it. Jacopo slapped Marin's face again, then crawled back out of his reach.

'You tried to kill me,' Marin accused.

'I saved your life. Perhaps I should not have taken the trouble. If he is watching now, he will probably kill me.'

'Who?'

'Ludovico. It was he who poisoned you, not Agostino. And don't swim in the direction you were going. There are nets in the water. They will catch you. She cannot bear to see you go.'

'And you? Are you happy to see me go?'

'I saw you. I saw you run from the house. I saw what you were, what you had become.'

Marin began to speak. Jacopo interrupted. 'Save your breath for your swimming. I do not want to hear your lies. Do you want me to say that I am filled with sorrow because you are leaving? No, I will not say it. Go. You must swim out towards the sea and then round in an arc to the city. Now go, or we will both be dead.'

'How will I know which way to go and when to turn?'

'You should ask the one who keeps you company to guide you.' Jacopo stood, ran from the landing-stage and out across the garden.

Lowering himself back into the water, Marin began to swim. The sunlight dimmed, and yellow-grey vapour gathered and thickened, hiding him from view. After some minutes, he realised that he had lost all sense of direction.

It occurred to him that if it was true that God and the Devil both took care of Their own, then one or the other would come to his aid.

The quayside at the Riva degli Schiavoni loomed so suddenly that Marin hesitated before swimming forward because he did not believe it was real. And he could see from the position of the sun in the sky that again it was morning. He had spent a whole day and a night in the water. He remembered thinking that he was drowned and dead, even though he had been aware of his body still swimming. But here he was. Alive. He was safe. Was it God or the Devil to whom thanks were due? Had something been demanded in return? He tried to remember more of the journey and whether he had given a promise.

He approached the quay, exhausted, his arms and legs so beyond his control that they knocked into fishing boats and caught in the nets which hung down in the water. He grabbed at the edge of the pavement, where he struggled, twice slipping back, before he could haul himself up and onto the stones. He lay down, shaking, coughing the water from his lungs.

Too weak to stand, he rolled his head to one side to look at the scene around him. He had imagined that it might seem different, this bustle and shouting with each person only concerned with and hurrying after business of their own, but it was all the same as it had been before. And as he did not appear to be a likely source of profit, nobody paid him any attention. He lay there until the chill of the stones drove him to stand. Still shaking, he tested one foot in front of the other.

He had no plan as to where he should go, so he decided to walk for a while in the hope that one would occur. Passing the slave market, he paused. Four boys, aged about eight or nine, tied together at the neck like animals, were being herded onto a cart. One of them turned back to look at two others left standing on the platform and waved. And beside these two, Marin saw Agostino fastened to a post. A merchant was pinching his arms and pushing back his lips to examine his teeth, but then he shook his head and selected the man behind Agostino instead. This one of far more docile appearance.

Agostino must have been brought there day after day since being delivered from the island for sale. Agostino's head was still bowed, but the look in his eye told clearly that this stance was a lie. It would be a brave man that took him away.

Marin wished that he had the money to set him free. What a fine thing that would be. Explanations accepted, forgiveness, blessings on both sides, and Agostino no longer a slave.

But as he thought these things, another merchant arrived, prodded Agostino and paid for him with coins drawn from a purse of red fur and leather.

His new owner had skin glistening blue-black like pitch and a string of ivory amulets hung around his neck. The tattered hem of his crimson robe trailed in the dust behind him. He wore no shoes and his long, flat feet, grey with dust, slapped like fish on the stones as he dragged Agostino away. He had tied Agostino's feet with a chain which drew blood from the first steps he took.

Shrinking back from view, Marin set slowly out towards the Fondaco dei Tedeschi, to the warehouse, and found that there too, nothing of what was had changed. He felt Constanza's breath on his ear as he lay down on the sacking and turned to the wall to sleep. His plan came to him. He would find her.

The next morning, the merchant arrived, still shouting out his worth.

All morning, Marin sat in the Piazza, watching the women and girls who passed. Would she be wearing her hair in coils, or braids, or pulled back with combs and jewels? And how would she have grown? How would he know her? Would he know her? Of course he would. Among all these lesser things, she would be perfection.

At noon he stole some bread for his lunch and, walking along the quayside, saw the children from the Contessa's household disembarking from a boat.

They came in single file, in silence, clutching identical parcels tied with cloth, walking in line as far as the Piazza where they separated, dispersing into the crowd. He did not see Jacopo among them.

An hour or so later he saw the Contessa, alone, coming from the Pescaria. She swayed as if drunken, her head nodding loosely like a puppet's. Weeping, she stopped passers-by, pulling at their clothes and asking them for help.

Marin watched. Had she stopped her crying long enough to

raise her head, she would have seen him only a very short distance away. But she moved on into the crowd and out of sight.

He sighed and rubbed at his feet which were numb and bleeding from walking a day without shoes. There was dust in the cuts on his face and, still wearing only his nightshirt, he was shivering from the cold. He walked back across the Piazza.

On the ground next to the money-changers' tables, he saw a fish, alive, flipping in frenzy up to the air in desperate efforts to breathe. The sight made him drop the bread he was carrying.

The weed on the fish's back was still wet as if it had come, that instant, from the water. Marin stood staring until for one last time it threw itself up, contorting itself, to breathe in what would kill it. Kneeling, he took it from the ground and cradled it in his hands.

That night he dreamt he was carried through the streets in a procession. He lay motionless across the people's arms while they gently bore him forward. When he woke he at first thought he had lain there in their hands, asleep, but then he realised that he had not been moving because he was dead.

Marin stole new clothes and shoes from a stall at the Rialto, deliberately choosing some that were bright. If Constanza were also looking for him, he wanted to be sure that she would find him.

But the only one he saw who searched was the Contessa. She passed close by as she cried, still never appearing to see him.

He began begging again, but in even the briefest encounters he felt himself slipping away. As if boundaries, having been pushed down too often, had lost any will to rise. He became afraid of looking too closely at people, and he did not want them to look at him for fear that something could catch him unawares and turn his mind so thoroughly that there would be no question of return.

On the island, that last time, he believed that he had tried to fight it. Was it possible that, all the while, another part of him had been quietly whispering 'yes'?

Over the next days and weeks, in and around the Piazza, on

pavements and on the tops of walls, on the highest rungs of the warehouse staircase and other such impossible places, Marin saw more fish, small things from the water, not yet dried, as if they had arrived only a moment before he had, there to display themselves to him.

And the dream of the procession would not leave him. It stayed firm and fixed, growing in detail.

One frozen February morning, about a month after he had returned from the island, Marin saw Agostino in the Piazza.

But he had to look twice to be sure it was him for Agostino no longer stooped, his head was held high, and he now looked about him with a calm and tranquil hatred. His face was covered in blood and bruises, and he wore the robes of the merchant who had bought him.

A commotion set up, rolling forward through the crowd as barefoot men in orange robes came running forward, cutlasses held out in front of them the more quickly to clear their way. Agostino began to run too.

A group of monks were walking in the formation of a cross from the far side of the Piazza towards the Palazzo Ducale. They wore white hooded cloaks, their eyes were cast down, and their lips moved in a rapid muttering of prayer.

Agostino ran towards them as the men with the cutlasses closed in. When he reached the monks, he pushed his way through an arm of their cross and disappeared.

The men with the cutlasses began to curse and shriek, thrusting out at the people nearby, accusing them of having hidden their prisoner. One pointed towards the monks, but the others pulled him back. They had seen that those who quarrelled with the Venetian Church often found that a meeting with its God or theirs came much sooner than expected. So they stood back, respectfully, to let the monks pass. It was only Marin who saw that from beneath the cloak of the monk at the end of the cross trailed a tattered crimson hem.

As he left the Piazza, he saw, piled into a doorway, close to where the monks had walked, the battered body of a man who still held tight to his rosary.

The smell of burning flesh filled the air. Blackbirds flew overhead and then away again, because there was nothing left of a quality that they would eat.

The stages where the slave market had been held were burnt to ashes, and tied to the posts at the site of the main one were the bodies of the men who had run it. They were naked, dismembered, their insides slashed, hanging out half-attached, and their private parts, which had been removed, protruded from their mouths.

Often Marin thought he saw Constanza. A sudden, particular lightness of presence or a fleetness of movement that he imagined might have been hers. But as the girl drew closer or he ran to look at her face, always he found that he had been mistaken.

One afternoon he was sure that he saw her. In a blue dress, tied with pieces of floating silk. He ran across the Piazza but, before he reached her, felt himself sliding over the ground on soft things that crushed to an oiliness, slippery, beneath his feet. He looked down. Fish. Their scales, their eyes, their blood, some still living, dozens of them. He could not breathe. He coughed water from his lungs.

All around him, covering the stone, he saw more fish and weed, still wet and glistening. Everybody else in the Piazza – the stall-holders, the pedlars, the merchants – carried on about their business as normal. They made as if they did not notice the plants that clung to their ankles or the fish trod to pieces by their shoes.

If the sun rose the next morning, nobody in the city saw it. The skies remained obscured by rolling red-grey cloud, the colour of ancient blood, which gradually pressed down, descending so far as to shroud the towers and the spires of the buildings. Its movement a slow pulsation like breath.

People came out from their houses, lighting torches as they huddled into groups and whispered.

The dust began to fall at mid-morning. Some people returned to their homes to shelter. Others stayed to watch. So that they could say afterwards that they had done so, or with the thought that if this were the end of the world, a final mark of God's displeasure, they could say at the Gate that they had been the first to come forward and admit the sins that were theirs.

Small cindered specks blew down in eddies, spinning ever more quickly before exploding to scatter. Soon the buildings and the streets were covered, and the water in the canals flowed black.

In the late afternoon, the rain came to wash it away, and a glow of silver light could be seen through the cloud. The water fell in drops that grew in size and speed until they became a continuous flood, a wall, solid, unbroken, sweeping out with the wind and then sucking back into itself.

The frames of the stalls in the Piazza were flung into the air, into splinters. Roofs and the upper storeys of buildings cracked and shattered and slid to the streets and canals. Ships at the quayside were torn from their moorings and smashed against the stones.

Some crouched on the ground and cried up prayers for mercy and forgiveness. Others ran with vague thoughts of escape through the streets, waving their arms above their heads or rushing in circles, weeping, because they knew what they did was futile.

Lelio felt the water pour through him. He watched the wind seize up, toss round and throw down those who had lain in his cart.

Then from one instant to the next, the rain grew less, and the air grew calm. Hesitantly, people came out from where they had sheltered. They ceased to pray.

Some way in front of Lelio, two men rose to their feet. He could only see their backs. In the gathering light, it seemed that the body of one dissolved and reformed with the brightness, its outline shifting and changing, shaped by the last drops of rain. Lelio could see right through him to the streets of the city beyond. He recalled having watched such a thing before and tried to remember where.

The men both turned and moved but, in the flooding of the light that followed, Lelio could not see their faces.

They mounted horses. Rode in opposite directions. One rode bareback while the other had a horse with jewels in its saddle and long scarlet fringings which whipped out flat from its bridle as he rode.

Years later, people said to each other that this was the day on which the dying had started and they should have known that a darkness approached.

God had sent them warning, just as He had two hundred years before when fireballs had flown through the sky and the bells of San Marco had tolled, untouched – sounding for the souls of the dead from the plague who were yet unaware that the knell was in welcome to them.

Alvise dressed in front of the mirror as had been habit when his vision was good, but sometimes, recently, it had become so misty that he had to press himself close to the glass. His sight varied from day to day and often during the hours therein, from what was close to clarity to the near blackness of his approaching hell.

But however little he could see of himself, he still made great efforts to present a perfection to others. He had his barber keep his hair in a fashionable crop and his beard rounded neatly to his chin; and from the bows on his shoes to his striped, padded hose, every item of his clothing was there only as result of the lengthiest deliberations. Sometimes, the emotion at what he saw so moved him that he would kiss the toe of his boot or the frill of his jerkin, but most often his own reflection.

He was invited to the most exclusive salons and dinners where he knew that he was admired for his charm, his dancing and his wit. The higher in society he climbed, the more he enjoyed the view.

The story he told was that he had been raised in the Indies and it was a maharaja who had taught him to dance. The marks on his calves where a whore had knifed him after he had refused to pay, he said were from the claws of a tiger.

He knew that people envied him and that there were many who gladly would have exchanged their lives for what they perceived to be his. But the truth was somewhat different to that which he chose to present.

He had never travelled further than the shores of the Lido, and his father had been a thief. Of the successful sort, however, and the family had never lacked for comfort. But now that the money his father had left him had gone, Alvise could not even remember how he had spent it, other than vague recollections of whores – those whom he had had no choice but to pay – the most expensive tailor who made him clothes he wore only once and, in general, those things incumbent on a man of his standing. Pleasures that he saw as invitation to happiness, to serve as accessories once it arrived.

Having a horror of poverty, he lived by the premise that to surround himself with sufficient proof to the contrary would discourage its filthy approach.

But now he was dying. Fallen to the French pox. A whore's parting gift, something for which he hoped he had not paid. He had seen the effects of this pox on others, and knew that what waited was disfigurement, rotten bones and blindness, so that the madness to follow would come as a blessed relief.

How ironic it was – for the joke was not lost on him – that having always insisted he be surrounded by beauty, he now kept company with a crawling ugliness of his own.

Sometimes the small eruptions on his face leaked through the powder he patted there to hide them. On those days he wore a black velvet mask, set with rubies at the temple. Most becoming. The rise to fashion of the seeping pustule was something he had yet to see. Perhaps a matter which deserved discussion.

Of course he had tried every treatment: charms tied onto his body, supposed to chase off the demons who nourished infection; liquids taken from mummified corpses dug from their tombs in Arabia; the desiccated dung of frogs; arsenic in tinctures to his tongue and on poultices to his piece; laudanum and ambergris; and a healing powder shipped from the East which had left blue stains all over his clothes. But congress with a virgin had been by far the most enjoyable.

Alvise whistled softly under his breath as he rode across the Ponte di Rialto. It was a good day, a fine day. His pustules remained matt under his powder, and when he had dressed in front of the mirror he had seen, clearly, his reflection smiling back. He had spent the morning undressing and dressing, several times, to celebrate the fact that he could see himself do so.

He leant down to smooth out the scarlet fringing on his horse's bridle, only looking from the way in front of him for a moment, when seemingly from nowhere there appeared a bundle of rags and dirt coiling around the animal's hooves.

The horse shied up. Alvise tried to hold it still and watched in astonishment as the rags drew together, drifting over the ground, and stood to form a man.

Alvise rubbed his eyes and squinted. He recognised him. He had never seen him so closely before, this one they called the Collector who followed so soon on the heels of death that some whispered that he brought it himself. Not an acquaintance that Alvise cared to make.

Lelio laughed and laughed again, uncertain as to what he should do next. He was aware that the gaping holes on his face meant that a smile, however kindly intended, would not necessarily be well received.

He had remembered where he had seen those things, the changing, before. At the San Barnabo Redentore Shelter. He did not know what he hoped the man might tell him. Only that what he had seen on the day of the storm and remembered of the child in its cradle seemed reasonable indication that this man was not as others were. Therefore one could assume that, as he was different, he would know different things, be privy to the preserve of the wise.

If the properties of the Elixir were all that were claimed, God would not have entrusted its creation to any ordinary man. It would not be available to any fool with money enough to buy the ingredients and a spare afternoon during which he could mix them.

Surely, this must be the man he sought. But if this was the infant grown, he appeared older than Lelio had imagined he would be, and any similarity to previous acquaintance was gone. However, he recognised the expensive decoration on the saddle and the bridle of his horse. The other man he had seen had ridden bareback. And no man who knew enough to shift his shape would have forgotten to saddle his horse.

Lelio looked at the one now in front of him. After so long, a chance for deliverance. But what could he offer him in return?

Lelio saw that the man looked back at him in the way that most people did. As though he were a figment from their darkest dream. A spillage from the inferno. And he saw that the man's hands moved on his horse's reins, ready to turn it round.

Jumping up, Lelio swirled in the air so fast that shreds of him came separate. Then he beckoned in the most casual way, with what he considered a friendliness, a camaraderie, the manner in which one wise man would greet another.

He whirled in pieces from the ground to demonstrate that he knew secret things too. Beckoning again, he walked to the end of the bridge, hearing the hooves of the horse as it followed and the voice of the man as he tried to hold it still. At the Riva del Ferro, Lelio stopped. The horse stopped just behind him.

Alvise could see that it was a man in front of him but with a smell that was beyond disgusting and looking unlike anything he had ever seen. He was more a pile of refuse that spoke. But what man, of refuse or otherwise, was able to do things like this?

Lelio moved so that he faced away from the light. 'Let me introduce myself. My name is Lelio. I see by your expression that you know me as something else. But I did have a name before that.'

'That was a fine trick you showed me just now,' Alvise said. 'Anyone else might have thought it was real.'

'It was. I can break and come together as often as I please, no matter how many times. No matter in what way the pieces fall or how small the parts of me are split. I do not die.'

'You hold sway over death?'

'I said I do not die.' And Lelio saw that the man was sick. The emptiness around his eyes, a card of introduction he had seen many times before. Why would such a man let himself grow sick? Was it that his power was only partial, like his? He did not want to doubt that he had found his answer.

'And what is it that you wish with me?' Alvise asked.

'There are things which are not generally known. I think you know something of such matters yourself? As I do. Because, clearly, neither of us is as others are.'

Lelio saw, immediately, that the man was not pleased by this drawing of a similarity between them and laughed, trying to make good his mistake. 'Please, do not be offended, Signor. I do not presume to suggest that my knowledge is even one hundredth the extent of yours.'

But the man had tightened the reins of his horse and turned it round. He began to ride away.

Lelio called after him. 'I would only like to say, Signor, that if you have sickness, then what I have will save you.'

The only sign that the man had heard was the slight hunching of his back. Lelio watched him go. The meeting had not gone as he had planned. He had been too familiar. He had not shown the proper respect.

As Alvise rode over the bridge, he was aware of a temptation to stay. It was reasonable to suppose that the man had heard of his knowledge – for his discourse in the salons was frequently lauded – but, all the same, he found talk of such strangeness disturbing.

Three weeks after meeting Lelio, Alvise was returning home from his tailor when the darkness fell as suddenly as if a cloth had been cast over his head.

He was aware that he had, instinctively, raised up his hands, waved them in front of his face. Aware too, immediately afterwards, of how ridiculous to any onlooker this would have seemed. He had been taken totally by surprise. Its descent before had always been gradual.

He stopped for a moment, fixed a smile to his lips, before continuing on in the same direction, trying to keep a straight line. But when he reached what he thought would be the corner of the street and turned, he walked into an obstacle which hit at his chest. He turned a little to one side, moved forward and met it again. He pushed. It gave way. With a crash.

Around him he heard people shouting. He stepped back onto something that rolled back beneath his foot. He fell. He tried to stand but could not for the darkness had crept into his limbs. He heard voices of people coming closer to see what had happened. He wondered if any of his acquaintance watched. In his head, he saw what they would see, how he lay there, stupid, helpless.

'He is drunk,' a man said. 'I saw how he walked just now, and now look, he cannot stand. Can you stand, drunkard? Can you even stand?'

'And where is the money for the stock you have ruined?' It was the candle-maker's voice.

Alvise felt the slime of mud against his cheek. He began to laugh. No, the joke was not lost on him. Someone touched his shoulder.

'It is I, master, come.' Mehmet's voice. His servant.

Mehmet pulled him to his feet and Alvise stood, leaning on him, while Mehmet paid the candle-maker his money.

Alvise saw nothing of their route home. What he did notice, however, was that Mehmet had said nothing about finding him this way. This lack of surprise suggesting he had seen it before. Alvise had always thought that his periods of darkness were secret. He imagined what it was that Mehmet might have seen. Things which he had never intended be witnessed.

For the next few days, the sliding to black and back continued without warning. Kindly reminder, Alvise supposed, of pleasures yet to come

He did not leave his rooms. Sitting at the desk in his study, he thought. Of all the things he had tried. Of all the things that had failed.

From the next room, he could hear Mehmet singing in his usual flat, peculiar way. Almost everything that Mehmet did had now become an irritation.

Over two weeks went by before Alvise felt his sight had settled enough for him to venture outside.

It was an early summer's day. Fresh, green uncurling of leaves and pale orange blossoms trembling before the air plucked them free and lowered them onto the ground. The pooling of sun on the water.

Did he only notice his surroundings now because, as each season came and went, there was a possibility he might not see it again? Should he try to remember their details or impose the blackness on his memory too and forget that he had ever had vision?

Some men were picking fish from the bank of the canal, scooping them up in their hands, rejoicing that for the past week there had been no need to set out their nets and catch them. Alvise looked at their rags and put his hand over his purse as he passed.

He thought of Lelio. Was it any more likely that he would find his cure from the dung of a frog than from the lips of a man of refuse? And if Death was waiting anyway, would it matter if he walked to meet Him?

Alvise stopped and began to walk back in the direction he had come. The men on the bank still gathered their fish, their voices raised in argument. Having filled their buckets to the brim, they now fought over those few that were left.

Next to the gateway of the San Spirito Hospital, Alvise sat down on a bench and waited.

In a small courtyard to his right was the outhouse where the corpses of the recently deceased were put until they were taken away for burial. Outside it, a woman was weeping.

She was begging a man to unlock the door so that she could go in and rescue her son. She insisted that they must be mistaken, that it was not possible for him to have drowned because he never went near the water.

Other men came out of the hospital. They told her to go. They picked her up and carried her into the street. They closed the gate to the courtyard.

Alvise sat on the bench for the whole of the day. As the sun went down, he got up and began to walk home. Approaching the Ponte di Rialto, he heard the rattle of a cart behind him.

Lelio called out. 'Signor! I beg your pardon, Signor!'

Alvise turned round.

Lelio would have prostrated himself and kissed the man's feet, had he not thought that to leave patches of his skin on the bows of those shoes would have produced an effect opposite to that which he wanted. This time he would be more careful, with his words and in his actions.

'I ask that you forgive me, Signor,' Lelio said, 'for the roughness in my manners on the last occasion we met. It was some time since I had had the opportunity for conversation. I ask that you forgive me, Signor.'

Alvise inclined his head slightly, pleased that he had not been forced to speak first.

'If you will forgive me, Signor, I believe that there are things that we could speak of.'

'Perhaps.'

'If you would come with me now, we could talk ... I could show you ...'

'I already have an engagement for this evening. I will meet with you tomorrow.' He would not come too easily. He would not put his desperation on display.

Arrangements were made for the following day, and Lelio bowed as low as he dared. Respectful. They parted.

As Alvise reached the end of the bridge, the woman he had seen earlier at the San Spirito Hospital hurried past him. In her arms she carried the body of a child. Its flesh was puffed and bloated in the manner that would indicate a drowning.

Alvise walked through the marketplace and along the small road that led to I Nastri.

His eyesight had been good when he left his rooms but now the blackness returned in patches that slowly joined together, making it seem he looked out through the shrinking holes in a shutter. He stopped and was about to turn back when he heard the cart behind him. Suddenly. He had not been aware of its coming.

'Good day to you, Signor,' Lelio said. 'If you will forgive that I say it, I am hoping in the most respectful way that our meeting today will benefit us both.'

He did not mention the man's sickness, its scent so sweet and so close that in other circumstances he would not have resisted the temptation to leap out and embrace it. The man walked as though he could not see and he kept his face turned away. But this last reaction, of course, was one to which he, Lelio, was accustomed.

'Please, Signor. Please, follow,' he said, walking slightly ahead so that the man might believe his stumbling went unnoticed.

When they reached the mud stretch, Lelio pointed to a piece of sacking that he had placed ready on some boards on the ground. 'If it would please you to sit, Signor?' he asked.

Alvise was about to refuse but, unsure that he could keep his balance for too long, he sat.

'May I speak?' Lelio asked. 'May I speak freely?'

Alvise gestured to show that he could.

'I saw you that day of the storm,' Lelio said. 'You did things ...'

Alvise knew he had done nothing. He had only sat and watched. He realised that Lelio had mistaken him for somebody else. 'Yes, I did things,' he said.

'If you would tell me ...' Lelio began.

Alvise interrupted. 'But I have seen that you are a man who does things too. And when we met on that first occasion, you said that you do not die ... that you have something that is a cure for sickness. I have a vague recollection of that.'

'You would rather I spoke first?' Lelio asked.

'I defer to you, Signor. I would.'

Lelio started his story. The stealing of the broth. The preservation of his youth, the excitements with the horses' hooves and the time after that when he had watched himself rot. 'But,' he finished, 'I have papers which come from the same place as the broth which I believe could have the answer.'

'And this is ...?'

'A cure, Signor. A making whole and the lasting of this for ever. The restoration of any body and the healing of any sickness. For any man. If he were sick, you understand. The answer is something called the Elixir of Life. Are you familiar with the art of alchemy, Signor? If you will forgive me for asking.'

'No.' Alvise had decided this not the most favourable time to air his views that such fancy was sweet syrup to feed what passed for brains in the gullible. Something to be believed only by those deranged and unsound of mind.

'If this answer you seek,' he continued, 'is in the papers you have, why do you not have it already?' He gestured at Lelio's body. 'It does not appear that you do.'

Lelio nodded acknowledgement that the man was correct. 'You are, of course, observant, Signor. I do not have it because I have never learnt to read. I do not pretend to be a wise man. Not as I see you are, Signor.'

'And what is it that you wish from me?'

'A part of your wisdom, Signor. If you could read those papers, Signor, we could work together, if you will forgive my suggesting such a thing, and uncover the secret they contain.'

'Where are the papers?'

Lelio handed him a scroll which Alvise opened. The lettering was too blurred for him to read. The paper felt greasy between his fingers. He was aware of Lelio by his side, hopping from foot to foot, wringing his hands, impatient.

'What do you think, Signor?' Lelio asked.

Alvise adjusted the position of the papers, held them towards what he thought was the light. 'I think they are most interesting,' he said.

Lelio stopped his hopping. Now he had no doubt that the man was blind.

'But I must take them with me,' Alvise said. 'To examine them more closely, to see if they contain anything of truth or worth. I must tell you this. I only work alone. If you are in agreement, we will speak of my findings at our next meeting. I will meet with you here, in a week at the same time.'

'Of course, Signor. Of course. And may I thank you ...'

Already Alvise was walking away. Lelio watched him go. Weaving, unsteady in the mud, past the blackened tree-stump, floundering, his hands out to either side of him as though he were wading through water.

Should he have kept his papers back? Insisted they stay with him? He had feared that the man might grow angry at his lack of trust and go, leaving him with his papers unread and useless.

Thinking back to the day when he had stolen them, Lelio wondered now if he had taken them all. There had seemed to be so many and, at the time, it was only the clasps that bound them that had been of any interest. But even if some small parts were missing, a man such as the one he had found would still, surely, be able to produce what was needed?

A wise man would have handled their meeting differently, would have learnt more. But at least he was wise enough to know that.

Alvise clasped the scroll to his chest. It took him until nightfall to reach his rooms. He would not ask the way.

Alvise slept. For a day. When he woke he took the papers to his desk to read.

All reason and sense would say that the man was a liar who had composed an interesting tale to account for his frightful appearance. But this would not explain what he had done on the bridge. So what was that – the breaking apart and coming together again? Reason and sense would say trickery. Clever and cunning trickery.

Alvise held the papers close to his face. They were written in a dialect with which he was not familiar so he had to read them through several times before he had, he thought, some understanding of what they said.

Which was that if the student faithfully followed all the instructions given there, he would have the secret of turning base metals into gold then, after this, the Elixir of Life, the Element of Absolute Change, which would cure all illness, return a body to its rightful state and prolong its life to many times that of its natural span.

Alvise put the papers down. A project for fools, no doubt. Yes. Something to be believed only by those deranged and unsound of mind. So did the fact that he considered testing it, even if only as form of diversion, mean that he already travelled that way himself? Yet so far nothing of reason and sense had found him a cure.

He read through the papers again.

Alvise met with Lelio the next week, in the same place, at the appointed time. The hungriness in Lelio's eyes unnerved him; and the way that Lelio reached out continually to touch him, sniffing, aroused in Alvise the strongest desire to run.

Lelio saw that the man was no longer blind. This surely more proof that he was something out of the ordinary. 'You think the work is possible?' he asked.

'Yes. I think it is possible.'

'You followed what it said and you thought so?'

'Yes.'

'Then?'

'I will carry out the work.'

'And I ...'

'I have said to you that I work alone. I will share with you the results.'

Lelio frowned and shifted from foot to foot. 'You will have expenses?'

'I expect that I will.'

'I would like to pay a share. Will you meet me here again so that I can give it?'

'The Ponte di Rialto,' Alvise said. 'On the Ponte di Rialto, tomorrow at noon.' A crowded place in daylight. He would never come back to this place again. A place left behind from when all was hell, or present in advance for when all would be so again.

He heard Lelio calling after him as he left. 'Signor, I would be most interested to know ...'

The next day, Lelio brought with him not coins but jewellery, rings of varying sizes, necklaces caked with earth.

There was a trader on the Campo San Zulian who sold the appurtenances for the effecting of spells, manifestations and witchcrafts from a room behind his bookshop. There was a constant demand. Alvise had wondered why. But not too often or for too long. The untidy workings of the minds of others were not a mystery which he cared to probe.

It was here that Alvise ordered what the papers said was required. The mercury, the sulphur, some varieties of salt, the powders. Lead. A furnace, a stand, a pan for his vessel, a crucible, condensers, retorts, scales, filters, funnels, copper tubes, bellows for the fire. When the articles were delivered the next day, wrapped in paper and sacking, Alvise nailed cloth over the windows of his study and told Mehmet that he was not to be disturbed.

The sulphur and the mercury which were needed to start the process of the putrefaction had to be stirred every hour, day and night, for one week. Only then did he add the mercurial water into which he had dissolved his golden ducats as an invitation to the changing and leave the mixture on a lesser heat to ferment for forty days more.

He did not sleep. He did not put out his chamber pot to be emptied. He took in the trays of food that Mehmet brought and then left them by the door, untouched. At times his sight became weak, flickering and guttering with the lamps, but it never left him so completely that he had to stop his work.

For seven more days he increased the fire until, bending close, he saw the first small streakings of white which the text had described. They were spreading, developing a deep yellow hue, then changing to blues and greens which quickened to flash across the surface of the mass like the feathers of a peacock's tail. All exactly as the papers had said, he realised, noticing that his hands were trembling.

Jumping up, he danced about the room. Backwards, forwards, backwards, forwards, between the bookcase and the door. Had God existed, he probably would have thanked Him. But when he returned to his crucible, breathless, Alvise saw that something was wrong.

The whole mass should have changed to white before taking on its final colour of deep red. Instead, the mixture now exuded a thin green oil which was rising to cover its surface. Frantically, Alvise seized the bellows. He had forgotten to regulate the heat.

He stirred the oil back and mixed what he had prepared in the crucible together with the molten lead. The result was a lumpen grey mass.

He had failed.

Alvise spent the day walking from one side to the other of the Ponte di Rialto. As the sun went down, he heard the wheels of the cart.

'Did you do it? Is it done?' Lelio's excitement was such that he could not keep still. Small particles came loose from him as he jumped, drifting out on the evening breeze and descending as dust to the ground.

'No.'

Lelio stopped.

'Not yet. It is a most complicated thing. Even given these instructions and ingredients, there is much else to be understood. Much that most men, I can assure you, could not even begin to grasp.'

'I meant no disrespect. It is only that I have waited so long for one such as you ...' Was this delay a sign that something of importance was missing? That not all of the papers were there?

'Your waiting is almost done. When the moon has come back to the auspicious house, I will begin the work again.'

'Of course, Signor. Of course. And Signor, I would be most interested to know, if it would not offend you to speak of it ...'

Lelio watched him go. Solid against the evening air. Quite different from the baby at the shelter for foundlings and what he had seen on the day of the storm.

Alvise spread the parchments on his desk. Did they contain anything of value? In the past he would not have hesitated to keep all that he found for himself.

But with his sickness had come the new weakness of uncertainty. Surely only that could be responsible for the laughable fear he now entertained that Lelio and his creeping decay would always be able to find him.

Alvise began the whole process again. All fifty-four days. This time he was certain that he had followed the instructions exactly, yet still his lead did not change. In fury, he swept the retorts from the table.

The next morning, as he picked up the broken glass from the floor, one piece cut his finger. As he sucked on it to draw the blood, it occurred to him what it was that was missing. What the papers referred to as the 'living red', which was to be added at the finish, had to be blood – not more of the mixture itself.

He left his rooms, went to the Ponte di Rialto and waited. And again, at the end of the day, he heard the cart.

Lelio appeared to have lost some of his former respect. And struck by the fear that he would request the return of his papers, Alvise had left hurriedly before the words could be said.

Sighing, Lelio turned to more neatly arrange the limbs of those newly come to his cart. He wondered at their scent of brine, the saltiness of their skin, and how it could be that beneath dry clothes he had found that their flesh was wet.

Approaching the Campo San Zaccaria some hours before the dawn, he heard voices, saw lamps. Four figures gathering firewood into a pile. Leaving his cart and moving quietly closer to watch, he realised that the officials for health and sanitation had come to work much earlier than usual and that what they carried to an untidy heap were the bloated bodies of infants.

From beyond the church, Lelio heard the footsteps of Death dancing pit-a-pat over the stones.

Alvise went through the processes again, this time putting in at the end of it a measured amount of his blood. Yet still nothing.

He took the papers in his hand, tore the cloth from the window, then stopped. Just once more. He would try just once more. Perhaps he had not put in enough of the blood.

He began again. This time he did not keep his appointment with Lelio and, over the following nights, he became aware of noises outside the house, but was unable to determine whether they were the rattling of the wind or the cart.

When the time came for the blood to be added he paused at the point of making the cut, recalling how painful the last drawing off had been. Putting down the knife, he called out to Mehmet.

Leading Mehmet to the table, Alvise explained to him that what happened now was a new and additional part of his duties. He dipped the knife down so that it stroked Mehmet's arm, but once the stream had started, it kept on and would not stop. Even when the blood filled the beaker and flowed out over the brim, Mehmet did not attempt to pull his arm away.

Alvise stirred the blood into the pan together with the substance he had made and the lead. Nothing changed. He watched, waiting. Mehmet watched too, blood still leaking from his arm, leaving small, dark spots on the carpet. But the lead remained unchanged.

Alvise kicked at the stand of the furnace. He tipped the crucible up close to his face to examine it. Crusted to one side were two tiny nuggets of gold.

Sitting Mehmet into a chair, Alvise gave him a cloth for his arm, fetched his cloak and raced out to the apothecary. He came back with an ointment that the man had said would stop any bleeding. Mehmet must not die.

That night, as he lay in bed, Alvise thought through the day. Could it be that one blood was different to another?

More blood. Clearly, the answer was more blood. More blood to bring more gold. And perhaps after that the return of his health and life?

Alvise began the work again. He still did not meet with Lelio. He ignored the night-time rattlings. He would not go out, not yet.

Every room was thick with the smell of Mehmet's ointment, even those which he had not entered. The wound had bled for another week. It appeared that Mehmet had the bleeding disease.

When the day came to add the blood, Alvise took his biggest beaker and lined two more up beside it. Again, he dipped the knife to Mehmet's arm and again he gently stroked.

Stirring the blood into the mixture, he added the requisite quantity of lead. They watched. They waited. Nothing changed. Alvise tipped the crucible to one side. Not even the smallest crusting.

Anger flared inside him – at the experiment, at Mehmet, but

above all at himself. What he had thought he had seen before had obviously been false, more trickery from his eyes. To have believed in such a thing, even for a moment, made him as stupid as those who gave their lives over to superstitions or to God.

He hurled the crucible at the wall, and darkness came all at once, completely. But he continued to search around his work table with his fingers for more things that he could pick up and throw. He heard Mehmet run from the room and his own voice echoing back from the ceiling in rage.

When he woke he could see gold amongst the shattered glass. Tiny rocks of it where the mixture from the crucible had landed. He picked one up. Slightly warm to the touch, it smelt of Mehmet's ointment.

He knew that this was impossible and yet he held the evidence in his hand. Or had he only crossed the quiet line beyond which this was real?

Alvise sat at his desk, drinking wine. The means with which he moulded the world and himself to the best of all possibility. With the gold had come something equally as precious – a return of his former assurance.

For the past days, the rattling outside had grown louder. It had entered his sleep, forming his dreams at night. Now it seemed that it grew louder still.

Alvise threw down his glass. He snatched up some of the rocks of gold he had piled onto the table and he ran out to the street. It was empty. He began to run towards the Ponte di Rialto, his footsteps echoing off the stones in the deserted squares.

With the darkness had come a mist so heavy that he felt a constriction in his breathing. He stopped, trying to draw in the air, and continued at a walk.

When he reached the bridge, he called out Lelio's name. Everything had become clear in his mind. The man was nothing but a devious old beggar who ate too little. An inventive trickster with, it must be admitted, an unusual talent for disguise. One who must have come by those papers in a way quite different to that which he claimed. Alvise smiled. Yes, he was back to himself, back to seeing things as they were. He threw the gold down onto the bridge.

'Here is your gold!' he shouted. 'Your share of the bargain. You shall have the remainder when I am done. If you are not in agreement with that, tell me now. I know you hear me. Tell me now if you are not in agreement.' There was no reply. 'And if you are not in agreement, what will you do? What can you do? If you hear me, answer.'

Crouching in the shadows, Lelio heard. And, some way to the side of him, he also heard Death laughing. When he looked down at his skin he saw that it dripped water.

Alvise walked from the bridge. He had drunk too much wine. Every building he could see, swayed fluid as if he gazed down on their reflection.

His feet were slipping on the stones. He realised that he hurried.

Seated on the bed, Alvise grasped Mehmet's foot and cut deep. From downstairs, he could hear the noise of the tavern. The discordant hubbub of the poor. He had moved Mehmet to this place because he could no longer tolerate the smell of the ointment or the spottings of blood on his carpets.

He patted Mehmet's foot as the blood spurted out, and put his arm across Mehmet's shoulder. 'When I am well again, you shall sit at my right when we dine, and the guests of the house will know that it was you who saved my life.' He did not look at Mehmet as he said this, and had Mehmet made any reply, Alvise would not have heard it.

He still held the beaker to Mehmet's foot but he was thinking of other things. How was it that now, that after so many more attempts there had been no further gold, and his trying for the Elixir had resulted only in noxious fumes?

As he was no longer begging, Marin now avoided the Piazza. There was no reason for him to stay there. A rich place or a poor place. It did not matter where he sat, but he preferred that it be somewhere where he no longer saw the Contessa.

Sometimes he thought he saw Constanza, and then, as always, his first reaction was to look away, to hesitate before he dared follow or examine a face. Delaying that moment when, again and again, he would find that it was not her. He imagined that she too searched and waited. And surely, as she was meant to be his, his fate – for how could it be otherwise – she would be the one who looked into his eyes and saw nobody else but him.

He would see her and be seen in return. And it was on the day that this last thought in particular had come to him that his delay in examining the faces that passed grew yet longer. So long that on occasion, by the time he raised his eyes, the one he had seen had gone.

Marin now spent most of his days in a small market square in

Cannaregio, to the north of the Jewish Ghetto, bearing in mind that his search continued. But taking pleasure in this period, this prelude, when all that was dreamt was possible and any fears, therefore, discounted.

He liked to sit leaning against the well in the centre, with his cap pulled down over his eyes and his sleeves and his hose rolled back so that he could feel the sun's play on his skin.

Most of the stall-holders there were gamblers. In the evenings, they cast their stakes in a tavern at the Rialto and during the day they sat under the beech trees behind their stalls.

Arriving at the market with dawn, they would unload their wares into chaotic piles from barrows, then hurry to their places at the trees to argue over what had been lost or won the night before and to flick and throw their luck again. They stayed until lack of light told them that it was evening.

It was in July 1562 that Marin first saw the boy, walking through the square on his way towards the apothecary. He wore a hat so large that Marin could not see his face and, even though the day was warm, a long woollen cloak, beneath which his feet were just visible, covered in red and brown bandages and caked with mud from the streets. And he left behind him a smell of such acrid intensity that Marin was surprised to see that it left no stain on the air.

The boy went into the apothecary, and some while later emerged holding a parcel to his chest. He walked past Marin again, round the corner and towards the canal.

As Mehmet approached the canal, he shifted the weight of the bottles – medicine for Alvise and ointment for himself. He pulled his cloak more closely to him and paused for a moment on the bank. He liked to look at the water. Flowing, vast, endless. He was a small shining, floating in its midst. Today the cuts hurt him but maybe tomorrow they would not. Unless there were more, and really that did not matter either. There was very little that really mattered, very little that was real. But if he closed his eyes, he could feel the water washing through him, and when he made himself small in his head, he liked to dance upon its waves. He could skip through the tips of the foam on its surface, so fast and so light that his feet left no trace.

After that first time, Marin saw the boy quite often. Always going into the apothecary. On some days, his bandages were red and wet and on others they were brown like rust, covering older wounds. Why he came and what he bought there remained mysteries.

Marin and the apothecary knew each other by sight. The apothecary did not tell the stall-holders that he had seen Marin steal food from their stalls; and Marin, in return, did not tell the apothecary's customers that what they bought as ancient healing powder from the East was simply dust from the canal bank behind the shop, swept up and bagged each morning, before being sprinkled with the powdered paint which gave it the deep blue colour.

Eyeing Marin warily as he entered, the apothecary moved to stand before his most expensive stock. Whenever he saw Marin, the thought always came to him that he should attend his Church more often than he did.

'Good day to you, Signor Apothecary,' Marin said. 'The boy who came in here just now. Do you know him?'

The apothecary began to polish the weights of his scales.

'Is he sick?' Marin persisted. 'Is it medicine for himself that he buys?'

'My customers' business is private. Their business is in confidence, as is yours. You would not like it to be known that you are a thief.'

'And I could say ...'

'You could say nothing. Because it would be my words against yours. And who would believe a filthy little thief. Now go before I report you.'

After Marin had gone, the apothecary sniffed the gold the boy had used to pay for the medicines. Piles of tiny sharp-edged rocks that smelt of the ointment he used on his skin.

It seemed fitting that he would rescue Constanza. That was something Marin knew. He would take her from whatever unhappiness she inhabited and set her free.

In the evenings, he now usually went to the Rialto where he liked to watch the street-girls. They and their trade still cause for fascination. He watched how they smiled at passers-by, the soft invitation to fleshly engagement. He had wondered if he might find Constanza there.

One day, as the light was beginning to fade, he watched three of them play a skipping game using small stones as markers. One in particular caught his attention. Her tiny breasts were bared, pushed up above the lace of her dress, the tight, modest buddings of flowers. She wore her hair coiled to her head, fastened with a band into which were fixed fragments of broken glass, copying the style in which noblemen's wives wore their diamonds.

Marin drew closer and closer. Could she be Constanza? She looked round. She smiled. He realised she had probably seen him some while before. She was not Constanza.

Signalling to her friends, she walked towards him. There were no words of introduction. She led him by the hand to an alley behind them and then she kissed his lips.

He felt her hand between his legs, unfastening his breeches as she pulled up her skirts and, reaching one leg up around his waist, climbed onto him. He wondered if she would ask for money and if it would be worth it if she did.

She steadied herself against the wall, guided his hips into a twisting rhythm. The band from her hair slipped and fell to the ground. Her skin was soft, moist and slightly sticky; her face not so different to Constanza's.

Marin's arms began to ache from her weight. Then it was over in a rush. It was done. She smiled at him, sleepily. He smiled back. He had forgotten that he should not look too closely. He had wanted to see what she thought.

Now he felt the beginnings of the confusion in his head. He tried to shake it away and looked down. On the ground by his feet, for an instant, the last of the sunlight struck the glass on the band the girl had worn on her head. A quick, unexpected brilliance. For a moment he stared, hypnotised, his mind moving away from hers. And at the same time, like a tide, he felt the pressure of her thoughts recede.

And that was when he discovered how to stay balanced on the edge of himself, on that blissful precipice with the pleasure of another's thoughts playing on his body, yet still able to hold himself as himself. All he had needed was an anchor to prevent the slipping away.

When he had recovered his breath, he pulled his purse from under his jerkin, fumbled with coins, unsure how much he should offer, but was stopped by the girl's hand on his.

'That was not for money,' she whispered into his ear.

'Thank you,' he said. He could not find anything else to say, so he fastened his breeches and left her.

He went quickly, half running towards the canal, to be alone. He sat on a ledge overlooking the water. On the rooftop opposite, in the dusk, he saw two birds fluttering in intimate struggle, and he wondered if it felt better for them.

On his way to Cannaregio one morning, passing through the Campo di Rialto, Marin saw a crowd pressing around a stall. Unlike the others there, the stall-holder did not boast of what he sold, and thus the people were drawn to discover for themselves what could be of such value that to proclaim its worth was unnecessary. They shoved at each other to get closer.

Pushing his way through them, Marin saw a man selling knives. Of all types and design – some small, for use in the kitchen, and others of a size nearer swords. He considered stealing one of the smallest and, asking the seller if he could hold it to test the blade and the handle, pointed out the one he desired.

The man handed it to him and, pretending to inspect the blade, Marin wiped it with the hem of his tunic. He had been about to turn swiftly into the crowd when suddenly another knife came spinning to knock the first from his hand.

Jumping back in alarm as the seller raised his head and laughed, Marin saw before him Agostino. Agostino free. Of a different weight, much larger and wearing a hat which, previously, had half hidden his face.

It seemed too late for any gesture of friendship and, giving a tentative smile, Marin was not surprised when none came in return. He picked up both knives from the ground and took out his purse, offering coins for the first. But Agostino shook his head.

'I am glad ...' Marin began. ' I saw ...' But he saw too that Agostino did not listen, having turned his attention back to the selling of knives and the requests of a man who wished to purchase a dozen.

Agostino watched him go – the boy grown into a youth but having in the process shed none of his strangeness. Twice responsible for his return to slavery, which surely was cause enough for hatred. But it seemed that hatred would not always come as easily as he wished. Trying to concentrate on the customer's questions, he pushed from his mind sudden thoughts of Ettore.

At the end of the day when Marin passed through the square, he saw two men quarrelling at the place where the stall had been.

One was demanding that the other repay him for a knife he had bought there. He complained that the blade was bent, that it would not cut and that in addition the handle was broken. And having discovered that the vendor was unlicensed, when it was the duty of the Administration to ensure that such things were monitored, it was to him, the official, that he came now for his money. He shouted. 'I want repayment from *you*.'

The official cowered and looked about him to see if his colleague was near. Seeing no sign of assistance, he dipped his fingers into his purse and gave the man his money.

The man to whom he gave the money was Agostino. In different clothing, with his hair brushed back, and now he wore a beard.

Marin began to beg again. But it was not as easy as he had first supposed, to keep that concentration on something else in place. So now when he felt himself slipping, he would recite in his head complicated calculations of mathematics, or the birth and death dates of all the Doges from the beginning. It was only after a month or so that he found he could leave the calculations and the reciting, that it had become almost reflex, this automatic withholding of part of his attention, as anchor, elsewhere.

When people looked, he could now look back. He raised his eyes to theirs, in casual inducement. He could tell, as they approached, which would probably ignore him or else regard him for a moment with mild curiosity, like a favourite toy long since outgrown, before going on their way. They were the ones who had an air about them of being complete, while the others betrayed, by a barely perceptible restlessness, their yearning for a piece that was missing.

Marin considered moving from the warehouse in case the thieves had seen he was back but he realised that even if he left there, they might still see him and follow to any other sleeping or hiding place he had. So he stayed where he was and hid his money in another place under the boards.

One morning he woke later than usual to see porters at the front of the storage area, putting together an order of spices.

They carried the bags down to a girl who then walked in front of them along the quay. Her face set sullen with no sign of the promise he looked for, and he saw as she passed with the porters that her movements were as devoid of grace as theirs.

Perhaps he would cease to search.

On the day that the girl came to collect the spices, Marin decided not to go to the marketplace. He walked.

He walked until the light began to fade when he found himself across the canal from the Ghetto, opposite a wall of tall, narrow houses, their uneven storeys stacked like dice and all windows facing the water bricked. The only lights to be seen were those held by the guards at the gateway.

As the sun went down, it seemed that the buildings moved to reach up after it, grasping at the last of its warmth.

It was almost the hour of curfew, and from every direction the people came hurrying, with their yellow hats or some piece of yellow cloth pinned to their clothes. They climbed into the boats which waited to take them across the canal. There were never enough boats for their numbers. They always had to stand, crushed, holding each other so that those on the outside would not fall out.

Marin began to walk back in the direction of the Rialto. Crossing the bridge, he saw the boy with the bandages coming towards him and, as he passed, Marin could hear him singing to himself, softly under his breath. Something flat, of no particular tune, a murmur in time to his steps. Marin followed.

As they came near to the Fondamenta della Misericordia, Mehmet slowed, stumbled and then fell. Marin ran to him.

'Are you hurt? Can I help you?'

Mehmet lay on the ground, dazed. Marin pulled him to his feet and supported him with his arm. 'You can lean on me,' he said. 'We can walk together.'

Mehmet gave no indication as to whether he wished this or not, but when Marin began to walk, he moved with him, leaning heavily on Marin's arm, but otherwise not acknowledging his presence. When he pointed to a side-street leading back from the water, Marin pulled him towards it.

A few houses in from its entrance was a tavern, and Mehmet stopped in front of its half-open door. For the first time, Marin saw his face clearly. Heavy features not held in any expression. The innocence of a child.

Sounds of laughter and the stamping of feet came from inside. Somebody was playing a fiddle. 'I live here,' Mehmet said, and he fainted.

Marin dragged him in through the door. The place was full. People jumped and swayed to the music. Marin waved to attract the attention of a woman close by, then realised that it was a man in skirts who sniffed in their direction, wiped his hands on his stained bodice and jerked his thumb behind him. 'Upstairs,' he said. 'To the right.'

Taking Mehmet under the arm, Marin pulled him past the dancers, up the stairs and into the room at the top on the right, which was separated from the landing by a curtain. Mehmet stirred but he did not answer when Marin spoke. Marin laid him down on a mattress in the corner and lit the lamp beside it.

Unfastening Mehmet's cloak, he found it was wet and, when he stretched the dark fabric up close to the lamp, he saw that it was soaked with blood.

He pulled the garment away from Mehmet's body and saw that he was bleeding heavily through a bandage on the lower part of his arm, and that in other places on this arm and on the other one too, there were smaller wounds leaking through the cloths that bound them.

'What happened to you?' Marin asked.

'They are old, most of them. My blood does not stay. That is why they still bleed. They need more ointment.'

'Ointment?'

'On the table.'

Next to the wall was a table and on it a bottle and several strips of cloth. Marin took the stopper from the bottle. The familiar, pungent odour filled the room.

Marin wiped and re-bound the deepest cuts. 'My name is Marin,' he said. 'And yours?'

'Mehmet.'

'What happened, Mehmet? Who did this?'

Mehmet closed his eyes. His breathing became more regular. Marin thought that he was sleeping. He wondered whether he should leave. When he stood, however, Mehmet opened his eyes and struggled to pull himself up so Marin sat down again. They stayed for a while in silence.

'I have some dice on my belt,' Marin said. 'Would you like to play?'

'I don't know how.'

'I will show you.'

Over the next weeks, in the evenings, Marin came often to Mehmet's lodgings. They played dice. Their conversations, for the most part, in silence.

Mehmet grew stronger, and the blue-grey tone disappeared from his skin. It was some time during the eighth week that he began to look worse again – that when they played, he now also kept his arms hidden under his cloak. He smelt more strongly of the ointment. When Marin asked him what was happening, he would not reply.

One evening, Marin suddenly leant forward, tugging sharply at Mehmet's cloak, trying to uncover his arms. Mehmet resisted. They fought. Marin left.

That night Marin tried to imagine Constanza with him. He sensed her approach but she stopped before he could see her.

Returning to the tavern the next morning, he found Mehmet's room stripped bare. The air there still smelt of his ointment. In the yard outside, the landlord was burning the mattress on which Mehmet had slept. No, he replied, he had no idea where Mehmet had gone.

Marin thought of Mehmet often, especially on days that were damp, when clouds of vapour rose from the canals to hang, drifting, on the air.

Marin looked for him but did not find him. He looked in the places where he had seen him before, and he searched the reflections on the water.

A year passed, twice during which Marin thought he had seen Agostino again, yet in two identities so completely different that he had had to watch for a while and even then he had not been sure.

The first time was in early March 1563, when he had come across some men building a hospital close to the Scuola di San Giovanni Evangelista. The foreman had looked like Agostino. Marin watched him pointing at plans and shouting at the workmen as they hurried with piles of bricks. Rubble they had cleared was piled at the edge of the site. Among this, Marin saw a broken shrine to San Barnabo Redentore which had remained unused for so long that somebody had tried to cover his face with another's.

The second time was almost three months later, towards the end of May. Marin thought that it was Agostino he had seen, walking through the Piazza in the flowing blue robes of a bishop. People had bowed to him as he passed.

Agostino strode straight and rapidly, his mind clearly concerned only with what lay ahead. And when some of those who bowed came too near and tried to touch, he pushed them out of his way.

For a short distance Marin had followed him, imagining how it might feel never to find it necessary to reach for the favour of others.

Walking back through the alleys to the west of the Arsenale shipyard, Alvise thrashed at the air with his cane. He had chosen one that was decorative, studded with gems and mother of pearl, to show that it was only to accessorise his clothes and not to aid his walking.

The canal had overflowed, sticking clods of waste to the fronts of his shoes; and now, as he came to a dip in the ground, there was no alternative but to wade forward through a brown tide which rose to his knees. Feeling it soak through the silk of his hose, the desperation he felt was such that he took out his bottle of cologne and held it to his nostrils.

Curse Mehmet for insisting that he be moved to a place like this. And so suddenly. And with no explanation. And still there was no more gold.

'And I believe it is for us to cast this Devil out.'

The crowd in the Piazza roared their agreement that it was. Sebastiano Finetti, the Administrator, made the sign of the cross on his chest in a silent entreaty to God. To give him the strength to do what he knew to be right and to take the sickness in his stomach away.

The woman sat strapped to a stool on a platform high enough for those at the back of the crowd to see her. Behind this was a large pile of logs covered with brushwood and surrounded by stones.

In an open box by the woman's feet lay the knives and long metal pliers which would encourage the truth from the Devil within her, for it was well known that always His first answers were lies. When the two hooded men began to pick up the instruments, one by one, measuring their length and testing their sharpness, the woman simply stared straight ahead, the tears on her cheeks long since dried.

The Inquisition official sitting next to Sebastiano on the

platform smiled and pared a thin slice from the joint of pork in his lap. He offered it to Sebastiano and cutting a much larger slice for himself, folded it into his mouth before signalling to the men in the hoods that it was time for them to begin.

The men approached him for their questions, then returned to the woman whom they hit on the breasts to wake the Devil in case He slept. And it was to her breasts that they spoke, each in turn.

They told the Devil that the woman's neighbours had seen Him copulating with her and then running with her through the public gardens in San Polo, having fused his body with hers and taking the form of a dog.

Marin was close enough to hear the woman answer quietly that this was not so.

One of the men hit her again on the chest, tore away her bodice to reveal her naked flesh and began to cut at her with his knife, red slashes from her throat to her waist, through which the Devil could more easily be heard. She screamed out for mercy, but this only enraged him further and he began to tear her more quickly.

'It is not your voice but the Devil's that we have come to hear. Tell Him to speak more loudly. Now He tries to hide from the face of God. If we do not hear Him, we will cut again until there is nowhere left in you for Him to hide. Now answer us, Devil. After the copulation, you persuaded this whore to cast away the form that God had given her. You led her to damnation. What did you do next?'

Sebastiano looked at the woman's breasts. He knew that the reason the Devil did not speak from the woman was that, unseen by the others, He had come to him and now edged for room on his chair.

The woman began to speak, her blood spreading on the boards of the platform, dripping through to the ground below. Again, the man raised his knife. She fell silent, and when she began to speak again, this time it was in a low croak, which cracked and stopped at every few words.

Pushing another slice of meat into his mouth, the Inquisitor nodded his satisfaction at the sound of the Devil's voice. He signalled that the questions resume.

'And is it not true,' one of the men continued, 'that you conspire with this whore to bring a pestilence to our city, a return of your plague? Causing our citizens to suffocate, to choke to death in their beds. Think, Devil, before you give us your reply. If you tell us the truth, God's justice will be merciful. If you lie and deny these things, you and your whore will burn.' He paused. 'Is it true, then, that you bring your pestilence to scatter on our streets?'

Quietly, she answered, 'Yes.'

The men looked back at the Inquisitor. He gave his signal. They raised their knives.

The woman did not see them put the torch to the bonfire behind her, because they had already cut out her eyes.

Marin edged his way back out of the crowd and sat down to think outside the church in the Campo San Zulian.

How would a person know whether they were damned or not? If the Devil lived inside you, would He announce His presence or just make Himself quietly at home?

From across the square two women approached, arguing, pulling at something held between them. Marin realised, as they drew nearer, that it was a long plait of hair which each was trying to wrest from the other. They were fighting over the hair of the woman who had sat on the platform.

He stood up, went into the church and knelt in front of the bench furthest from the altar. A service was ending. The congregation waited in line for the priest to pass his hands over them in blessing.

Marin took his place at the end of their queue. A man pushed his way in front of him. Their eyes met. The man fell to his knees, bowed his head, made the sign of the cross and reached out to touch Marin's foot. There were tears in his eyes.

Marin ran out of the church and knelt at the side of the canal. He asked God if he was damned. But as far as he could tell, God gave no reply. Perhaps He did not consider him worthy of His attention. Perhaps He was not even there. Or perhaps it was that his salvation swung in the balance, the deciding weight either way dependent on how he behaved. Whether he used what he was to bring happiness to others or benefit only for himself.

A child playing with a hoop rolled it towards Marin's feet. She smiled up at him, and he felt her thoughts tickling like feathers over his skin.

For the whole afternoon, Marin sat waiting for the Contessa in the Piazza, imagining what would happen when he spoke to her. She would cry, he thought. She would reach to hold him. And then he would take her by the hand and kiss her. But it was two more days before he saw her walking slowly from the Pescaria, her head bent, still calling but now not bothering to look as she did so.

Running from where he sat, he took her gently by the shoulder and smiled. 'Here I am,' he said. 'I have come back.'

To his astonishment, she pushed him to one side, continuing on her way. He ran after her. 'It is me, Marin. Don't you see me?' He took hold of her again. He led her kindly by the hand to the bench outside the Chiesa Ducale and kissed her softly on her brow.

She looked. He seemed different again. How strange. But to speak of his departure, giving him reason to leave once more? No.

Marin kissed her a second time. He suggested that, if it pleased her, their next meeting could be somewhere more private.

So it was arranged that their meetings take place in a tavern behind the Campo di Rialto. Rooms to let by the hour, for the enjoyment of activities unobtainable at home.

They arranged to meet there every week on the Sunday. He did not listen when she talked, aware that it was Piero whom she saw. He kept his mind fixed on the stain on the wall behind her. There was never contact between their bodies but did she see, he wondered, that he shuddered at the touch of her thoughts?

Sunday. The day dedicated to the salvation of the soul. He met with the Contessa for the same reason that others went to church.

Afterwards, she used to lie back on the pillows and whisper not his name but another's. Only then did he turn and put his arms around her, hoping that God saw this.

Their meetings continued. Winter moved into spring, and spring into summer. Time passed. And if not exactly in happiness, neither could he truthfully complain to God that there had been pain.

People had grown so used to finding fish and strands of weed on the streets in the mornings that some persuaded themselves it had always been this way. They spoke of God's bounty and benefice as they put the fish into their baskets.

Marin watched some men now, on the bank of the Rio di Palazzo, picking their day's catch from the ground. Every so often, he observed how they moved their shoulders slightly, feeling what they thought was a breeze on their backs.

Marin felt it too. But to him it felt like water.

The evening was cold, and Marin pulled his blanket more tightly around his shoulders. Always, still, this feeling he had had as a child that, if he walked long enough, or only in the right way, all the answers to his questions would come.

There was a place he had gone to on a few occasions before, each time unaware that he sought it out until he had arrived.

It was a tavern to the west of the Arsenale shipyard. An old wooden house, sunken on one side so that it stood in the mud at a slant, surrounded on all sides by water and approached by a bridge of splintered planks, bound together with rope.

Marin had never crossed the bridge. He had only stood before it and waited. Today, he smelt Mehmet's ointment before the tavern was in sight. He hurried on, across the bridge, and entered. He climbed the stairs in the corner of the room.

The door to the third room on the landing was open. A lamp set onto the floor was burning brightly but cast no shadows in its light. All the furniture had been pushed into a pile in one corner, except the bed where Mehmet lay, singing softly to the wall.

Mehmet fell silent. 'I thought you were dead,' Marin said. 'You knew I did. You let me think it.'

He walked closer, and Mehmet turned to face him. His face was ashen, his eyes glazed, and his left arm, which hung down from the bed, was dripping blood onto the floor. Marin knelt to fasten the bandage.

'Who does this to you, Mehmet? Why do you allow it? *Do* you allow it?'

Mehmet turned back to face the wall.

'If he had not taken me in as his servant, I would not have had a life to give. Now I do this, and I help him. Maybe I save his life.'

'What do you mean? Who is he?'

'He is my master and he is sick.'

'Who is your master? Look at me.'

Mehmet did not turn around.

'Come with me now. I will take you away from here.'

'No.'

'You would prefer it if I left you here? Left you to die for him?' Marin stood up, held out his hand. 'Come.'

'No.'

Marin walked to the door and paused. 'Do you have a God, Mehmet?'

'Yes.'

'Does He hear you? Do you hear Him? Do you really believe He is there? If you asked Him questions and He answered, would you listen? Would you believe what He explained?'

Mehmet did not reply but curled against the wall. Marin went to him, took the ointment, and began to re-bandage his arm.

He wanted to know the experience of others, whether their

conversations with God were more easily understood than his. And how it was that they could be certain that the words had come from Him and were not merely the mind's sly repetition of their fears.

Marin stole an apple and sat down on the stones outside the Fabbriche Vecchie. Placing his cap on the ground, he smiled at those who came near.

He had only been there a short while when he saw a woman approaching him. She was expensively dressed in a green satin dress sewn with cords and jewels. She walked straight towards him, smiling, her arms stretched out in greeting. He had no idea who she was.

Bending down, she took his hand. 'Good day to you, Signor,' she said. 'And how goes it with you today?'

Before Marin could reply, a man appeared beside her and began to shout and gesture. So wildly that people passing stopped to stare, believing they were watching a street show.

'A beggar? Another beggar now?' He shook her by the shoulder. She pushed him away. He shouted more loudly. 'The dirtiest, the lowest that the city has to offer. Even a thief works harder for his living. Look at him, this one. Not even the wit to rise up to the rank of thief. Destined to sit, for the rest of his miserable life, sucking on the pity of others.'

Marin saw that although the woman's face was turned in his direction, she was not really looking at him. Her attention was more on the man who stood shouting beside her. She was smiling, and when the man drew pause for breath, she took his arm and pulled him onwards across the square. Their servant girl followed, carrying two baskets of fruit.

Less than an hour later, the servant girl came running back. She handed Marin a note. It read, 'I would like to apologise for my husband's rudeness and beg the opportunity to do this in person. Please come, as my guest, at eleven o'clock tomorrow morning. With my kindest wishes. Tullia Paschini.' On the back of the paper was written her address.

The girl stood back, curling a strand of hair around her finger. When Marin did not look up or answer, she supposed he could not read and snatched the paper from him.

'I will tell you what it says.' She began to read, but when Marin looked up she stopped. He smiled. She could see he was waiting and thought she must have missed something he had said.

'What does she mean by this?' he asked.

'If you come, you will find out. Shall I tell her you will come?'

'Yes.'

She handed the note back to him reluctantly. She wanted a reason to stay.

The next day, Marin visited Tullia Paschini in a palazzo set back from the Canale Grande. The front of it had been painted in pinks, blues and gold. Flowers, leaves, hosts of flying figures.

He was not sure whether he should enter through the front gate or use the tradesmen's entrance at the side. He looked at the note in his hand and decided that it entitled him to use the front. He walked towards the gate, changed his mind and went round to the side instead.

The servant who opened the door looked at him in a way that suggested he considered even this entrance far above Marin's worth. He waved Marin through to the kitchens where he was left in the company of the maids and the cooks, without explanation, for almost an hour. The servant returned. 'The Signora Paschini will see you now,' he said.

Marin followed him upstairs and through corridors to a room at the top of the house, where Tullia sat waiting on a low pink silk settle, surrounded by cushions and rugs.

The walls of the room were panelled and hung at intervals with long strips of bright embroidery which were all joined at the top by a chain. In the far corner was a table laden with fruit and crystal decanters of wine.

Tullia stood to greet Marin, pulled him to her, kissed him on the mouth, then put her hand up to her own and laughed as if in surprise at what she had done.

She began to undress him. There was no word of the apology she had written of in her note or any explanation for what she did now. But Marin did not try to prevent her from taking off his clothes. It had occurred to him that enjoyment might only come with practice.

Tullia undressed herself. Bodice, skirts, petticoats, which she threw to the back of the settle. She pushed him back onto the cushions and as she moved astride him the settle rocked violently beneath. Her cries came echoing back from the panels.

After that first day, there followed many more, and sometimes Marin went there five times in one week. He was not certain what it was that she felt for him, nor why she continued to invite him. Was he really so skilled a lover? She offered him money. He took it, delighted at this upturn in his fortune.

Their physical love-making he continued to regard as the necessary and regular effort required to achieve an objective and, in the meantime, he sank with a sigh into the ecstasy that came from her thoughts.

One afternoon as they lay back on the cushions, Tullia said, 'I have been invited to the home of Giorgio Bobali next week, his palazzo in Santa Maria Formosa. His salon. Would you accompany me?'

'And your husband?'

'He will not be there. He does not like those people. He will not find out.'

'I have never been to a place like that before.'

'Do not be anxious about it, my darling. All you need do is be yourself.'

She stroked his head. His hair was too long, and it was stiff with dirt and greasy. She kissed it. Her favourite companions for intimacy were those she picked from the street. Oh, the allure of the dirty vagabond: their coarseness, the grime from their skin as it rubbed onto hers, things she could not resist.

She watched him dress. It was interesting that on closer acquaintance she found him more attractive. When she had first seen him sitting on the street, she had thought him rather ugly. Now something in the way he looked at her made her feel girlish again and happy, in a way she had not felt for years. Happiness of the delirious kind that came with being in love. But to be in love with the dirty little beggar? She realised how ridiculous that was.

Marin thought about the invitation all the way back to the Rialto. He had heard talk of such places and occasionally, as they passed, the conversations of the people who went there. He had seen their fashionable clothes, their elegant manners and the great lack of interest they always displayed in everything around them – the words of their companions and even their own, all met with yawns of boredom.

He squatted next to the doorway of a shop on the Campo di Rialto and looked out across the square. A few months ago, a new beggar had arrived there, and whenever somebody came near, he would roll his twisted body out from his corner and into their path so that they had either to stop or attempt to step over him. And if lack of agility forced them to stop, he would wave the sores on his arms at their faces until they gave him money.

Fastened around his neck with a length of fraying rope, he wore a notice advising the world that his name was Orazio, that he had no sin and that he was a child of God.

Marin watched him now, writhing in front of a merchant. But the truth of it was that Orazio was not a cripple. Marin had seen him dancing in a tavern near the Arsenale. Not a place that would be visited by those on whose purses he preyed. Marin remembered what Tullia's husband had said. Was it another truth that he, Marin, was really no better than Orazio?

And if he was to make a new life for himself, could the salon be its beginning?

Somebody had drawn a picture of Gian Pietro Carafa, Pope Paul IV, and nailed it to a post in the Piazza. Somebody else had thrown an egg at it. Another had added a note to the effect that the Pope having cancelled his visit was a sure sign he had deserted them. Officials were quickly ripping these papers down.

Marin was on his way to a tailor's shop on the Mercerie. He had with him a full purse of the money he had saved.

Inside the shop were displayed bales of cloth with samples of the garments that could be made from them, artfully hung alongside. Marin was aware of the tailor watching him. He turned to the man. 'I have money,' he said. 'And I am here because I want to look like a gentleman.'

The tailor surveyed Marin slowly from head to toe. He took a deep breath. 'You have dirt in your hair, young master. You have dirt on every piece of skin I can see. Unless you wish me to cover you entirely in cloth, may I suggest that you pay a visit to the bath-house?'

Marin was silent. How would a gentleman have responded to

that remark? But before any satisfactory answer came, the tailor was on his knees in front of him, measuring the length of his legs. A gentleman would have had his reply at once.

Marin was measured, and his clothes were chosen. Braided hose with ribbons and a garter below his knee, a tight jerkin with a skirt that flared and a doublet made of silk.

That afternoon, Marin folded the sacking he had used for his bed at the warehouse and pushed it into a corner.

He went to the bath-house where they soaped and steamed him and scrubbed his skin with bristles. And for one scudo extra, they rubbed onto him a tonic water which they said would strengthen his blood. Then he went to the barber who took two hours to clip his hair until it lay smooth and short, back from his forehead, with a small curl in front of each ear.

He then paid a month's rent in advance for lodgings at the top of a small house in the Calle dei Fuseri.

The next day he went back to the tailor, changed into his new clothes and told the man to burn his old ones.

Marin had imagined that when he walked back through the streets to his rooms, people would look at him differently.

All Marin could see on Tullia's face when she came to the door was anger. She hardly spoke as they walked to her gondola. She ordered her boatman to hurry. She told Marin that he was late. He knew that he was not. He wondered what was to come. Tullia made no remark as he stroked his breeches and ran his fingers over his perfumed hair. She pressed herself away from him into the corner of the cabin.

A servant opened the door of the palazzo of Giorgio Bobali and they were ushered up the stairs to a room full of people all talking, all laughing, their expressions varying degrees of amused ennui.

A large man in purple breeches came quickly across the room towards Tullia and Marin. He glanced at Marin, looked away, then pulled Tullia a little to one side. Marin heard him ask her, 'So where is your little beggar friend?'

Marin understood. As he moved away from Tullia and into the crowd of guests, he heard her calling his name. He walked around the room at a loss as to what he should do, and was just about to leave when next door a small orchestra began to play. A few couples separated themselves from the rest and moved in there to dance.

Marin stood under the archway dividing the rooms and watched. He had never danced before.

One man in particular stood out. He danced with such assurance and grace that, instead of him arranging his steps to the music, it appeared that the music should and did arrange itself around him. People stood back to make more room for him and his partner.

Marin had noticed him earlier and seen how, when he spoke, people clung to his every word, even forgetting their displays of boredom. And these words were discussed after he had uttered them in case there was still wisdom or wit they had missed, further treasure they could still squeeze out. The man wore expensive clothes, silks and frills, and the most delicate shoes of the softest leather with buckles and ribboned bows.

Alvise circled the dance floor. Tonight he knew he moved as he had done before the sickness came. It gave him joy when others stopped to watch him. And he liked it better when, as now, his sight was clear enough for him to see them look. To imagine himself through their eyes was even better still.

He slid his hand along the waist of the girl with whom he danced and, for a second, he touched her breast. He wondered how she was beneath her skirts.

Once the music had finished, he came back into the main room, passing Marin who was caught up, pushed along with the people who followed behind him. A group formed around Alvise in the centre of the room, waiting for him to speak.

Stroking his beard, Alvise began. His oration composed of

the conceptions of philosophers and scholars – Ovid, Dante, Boccaccio – which he featly combined and adapted before giving them out as his own. He was proud of his learning and lost no opportunity to remind those around him of what genius they had in their midst. Its brilliance served to blind those who might otherwise have looked too closely.

'My mother always said that it was immoral to be clever. What do you think of that, Signor? Do you like your women clever? Or do you agree that too much activity in the upper half, makes them wanton in the lower?'

Marin turned to see who spoke to him. It was the girl who had danced with the man now giving the address. She waved a fan of blue feathers in front of her face so that he could only see her eyes.

All the replies that came into his head seemed foolish, so he just looked at her and smiled. And when he felt what she thought, it was clear that no amusing reply would be necessary. As the tremor on his skin began, he let her speak, keeping in his mind an awareness of the flames of the candles on the table behind her.

Alvise watched them. Until only minutes ago, her eyes had been on him. Who was this youth? Not anybody he had seen before. She seemed completely enrapt, and yet he was not saying a word.

There were some degrees of beauty which required no assistance from speech and had the boy been possessed of looks of that kind, perhaps then he could have understood. But the boy was plain. His features had nothing about them to recommend or praise. So why did she look at him as though there were no one else in the room?

Alvise drew his talk to a close, ignoring the pleas to continue.

He walked across the room and pushed himself between Marin and the girl. He bowed and introduced himself. 'Signor Landucci at your service.'

'Signor Gaspari,' Marin replied.

Alvise smiled. 'I have not seen you here before. Our friend Giorgio likes to collect people he finds interesting. He has a taste for the bizarre. I presume you are a recent acquisition? Do you hide beneath your fine hose any unusual measurement, predilection or talent?'

'I have never met Giorgio.'

'He is the man in the purple breeches talking to the servant with the tray.' Marin turned and saw the man who had rushed to speak to Tullia and himself when they arrived.

'I came with a friend of his. Tullia Paschini.'

Alvise threw back his head and laughed. 'Ah! The Signora Paschini. And tell me, does she still like to entertain her guests in her pannelled room? I see by the expression on your face that she does. The Signora Paschini is a very generous woman, my friend. She likes to share with her friends and even her servants, the pleasures that come her way. I must tell you that the creaking I am sure you heard was not from the age or condition of the panelling, but from the excitement of those behind it.'

'They do not tell her husband?'

'I'll wager he was watching too.'

Alvise laughed again. 'Do not look so shocked, my friend. You were not the first, and I am sure that you will not be the last.'

Two women in men's attire approached. They wore identical shirts, jerkins and hose. One of them asked, 'Are the two Signors to keep their own company for the whole evening, or can we tempt them to dance with us?' She took Marin's hand and placed it on her breast.

'I have to leave now,' he said. 'I have an appointment elsewhere.'

Alvise smiled. 'By the way, if you are fond of dancing, I like to practise some mornings at home. If you have nothing better to do with your time, perhaps you would care to keep me company.'

As Marin left the room, the girl with the blue feathered fan lowered it from her face. He reminded her of a dog that had been beaten too often but would still rise to bite if it could. She was sorry to see him go.

When Marin met with the Contessa that Sunday, she did not comment on the cut of his hair or his clothes. Whatever it was that she looked at had obviously remained unchanged.

Sebastiano hesitated for a moment at the door of the church of San Zaccaria, then decided not to enter. As God would, in any case, have been aware of his thoughts, it seemed an unnecessary and provocative thing to spread them for view at the altar.

So he continued on his way north towards the Rialto where he was to bid farewell to the senior envoy from Rome, to make pretence that he was sorry he was leaving. Which, upon reflection, he supposed he was. For if there had to be presence from Rome, papal interference in Venetian laws and lives, then it was preferable that any visitor who reported back should be as easily fooled as this one.

Would the next also believe that there had been no increase in the numbers of those dying, that records to the contrary were due only to errors in the accounting?

The envoy was standing at the landing stage outside his lodgings, with the man who had come recently to oversee the running of his household.

The steward had features which suggested Eastern blood,

perhaps some heritage from Kazakhstan. Watching the two together now, Sebastiano could see that if asked to judge which was servant and which master, most would have said that it was the envoy who served. For there was nothing about the other that invited the description of servant.

The envoy's head was slightly bowed as if it were the more natural thing, despite their present circumstance, that he should defer to his steward.

The newly enacted laws intended to regulate the activities of Bravi were having little effect. There was no less brawling and fighting between the rival factions and no more evidence of restraint in their brutal settling of vendettas or the ferocity with which they gave their protection. The bloodshed continued, and they roamed and behaved as they had done before, defiant. Resplendent in the various liveries of their employers and the swagger that boasted they were well aware that a glorious and violent death might lie only minutes away.

The fight began at dawn at the west end of the Zattere. Marin watched the two sides approach, drawing slowly closer together from opposite ends of the Front – some holding their swords aloft, others swinging spiked metal balls on chains. Clearly, their meeting was planned.

Stopping a short distance apart, they waited for the signal for advance, the horses nervously pawing the ground and the men cursing at the delay. Then one of the captains shouted his challenge and, as the other gave his assent, the two sides surged forward with a roar, and the first blood sprayed onto the quay.

Men called out, exultant, as their weapons broke bone and flesh, and horses screamed in panic as their legs were cut and their hooves tangled in the bodies of those slain.

In their midst, Agostino whirled his sword, pulling his horse in a circle. None of his opponents dared to come near. Even his own side drew back.

As the sun rose higher, the fighting slowed and both sides, those few that were left, turned and moved back to their own. Enough had fallen.

Agostino rode ahead of the others, back towards the Rialto. This was a life that pleased him. His companions were thieves, murderers, vagabonds, renegades from the military service. The edges of society joined together in an untidy knotting of its fringes.

Their newest recruit said he was a poultry-seller and that he had lived in the city all his life, but he was careless enough in his movements for Agostino more than once to have seen, beneath his shirt, the soldier's tattoos on his arms. One so fresh that it was still lined with blood. It was that carelessness and the way in which he often laughed at himself that reminded Agostino of Ettore.

The man had a face left scarred by the pox and a nose that looked like a turnip. The others called him Piero.

Agostino rode faster and purposefully into the paths of those he encountered for the satisfaction of seeing them jump from his way. They saw what he was and knew that he would have welcomed a quarrel.

In recent months, the number of Bravi on the streets of Venice had increased. Their presence, a constant source of intimidation and menace as, disregarding the laws of the Administration, they brought, instead, their own. Selling their services to the owners of illegal gambling clubs or the richest courtesans who chose to flaunt the proceeds of their trade. To any who, because of their wealth, and often the way in which it had been gained, considered themselves at risk.

They provided armed escort through the streets and the strongest deterrent to trespass at home: a protection more personalised and vigorous than that from the sleepy night-time patrol of the peaceable Signori di Notte.

Marin had not seen Agostino at the scene of the fighting, for he had been distracted by the sight of the Collector running with his cart along the waterfront, shouting, 'Wait!' at someone ahead.

Alvise taught Marin how to dance and he taught him how to dress. He taught him how to stroll through the streets as though the ground existed to support his feet alone. He taught him what to say and how and when to say it. He oversaw Marin's purchase of a horse which he insisted should be one similar in looks to his own, and he had his tailor make a new coat and breeches so that they could ride in identical clothes.

When Marin protested at this continued extravagance, pointing out that his funds were limited, Alvise dismissed his words with a wave of his hand. 'I will pay. It is my pleasure to pay. Our enjoyments shall not be curtailed by coins.'

He revealed to Marin all the things that a gentleman should know, with one or two exceptions, for it was necessary that he remain the superior. That Marin was so eager to learn, and that it was to him that he looked to learn it, was most gratifying. He was, Alvise saw, a most unusual person. His demeanour, a curious mixture of defiance, fear and guilt, as if having committed some wrong he was unsure as to whether he was sorry or whether the punishment merited would reach him.

And there was something else. Was it only shyness? That way he did not meet your eye, gazing out from under his lashes towards a point somewhere else in the room and looking at the person to whom he spoke only with the occasional rapid sideways sweep.

They began to spend almost every evening together, returning to their lodgings late at night or early in the morning, their footsteps and their bawdy songs of love and lament echoing through the streets.

Alvise was usually drunk, very drunk, by this time. He liked to drink wine and laudanum. They distanced the thought of his illness, enabling him to be more easily that which he wished to present as himself.

But Marin had not drunk of either since leaving the island. Both wine and laudanum would, he knew, have soothed the recurring headaches but they would also have lessened the control he needed to hold his attention in place. For he had by now become a master in the art of the elliptical eye movement, of that shooting, evasive glance which required an absolute acuity of thought.

So Marin always refused when the tray was offered. Even though Alvise often tried to persuade him otherwise.

On those evenings when they returned with company, Alvise always insisted that they still stay together with their women. In the curtained cabin of a gondola, rocking the passage of the boat, or side by side on the bed or on the settle at Alvise's lodgings.

On these occasions, Marin was quietly dutiful in what he knew was expected. What he had wanted did not necessitate the removal of clothes, and his pleasure had usually come some time before, unencumbered by physical distractions.

On the evenings that Alvise did not feel well enough to leave his rooms, they stayed indoors. Alvise drank and they talked. Alvise said that his sickness was a rare wasting disease, one most prevalent among intellectuals.

To Marin, such a thing sounded quite as elegant as the circles in which they moved. An ailment which a gentleman could display alongside his clothes as indication of his character.

Marin was pleased to have Alvise for a friend. He was fifteen years his senior and much experienced, it was clear, in the ways of the world. When they walked together, arm in arm, he noticed people turn in admiration at the handsome spectacle they made.

Alvise was pleased to have Marin in his company, but one of the things he had learnt in life was that friendship came at a price that only the foolish could afford.

He could not understand how Marin drew to himself, almost without fail, any woman he chose. He had neither the looks nor the charm to make their surrender explicable.

Late one night, returning from a party, Marin practised the steps of a new dance that Alvise had taught him. As they crossed the Ponte di Cannaregio, he lost his footing on the wet surface.

Alvise caught him before he fell and, just for one moment, seeing Marin's face turned up towards his in the moonlight, he had experienced the almost irresistible urge to hold him closer, to take him fully into his arms and kiss him.

Instantly, he recoiled, letting Marin overbalance into the water. And only when it was clear that Marin would not need his help, did he reach down his hand to offer it.

As they bade each other goodnight, Alvise hoped that neither his desire nor his disgust had been evident.

Walking back that night, towards the Calle dei Fuseri, Marin paused by the Rio di San Salvador to look down at the canal. Surrendering to an urge to lower himself again, he lay down on the bank, crawling forward until the water touched his face and then his chest. He stayed there motionless for some minutes before pulling himself back to sit.

His hand still bled from his fall. Wiping it on the grass, he touched something soft, the dead body of a rat. He picked it up by its tail, swung it, held it for a moment in his palm before he felt its body warm, saw it shiver and curl to life, then jump to scurry away. It occurred to him that he should have been surprised.

He stood and walked along the bank, searching for something else. He hunted in the weeds. A little further on, he found a cat, half-buried. He could tell by its smell that it had been there some days. Tearing open the gash on his hand, he pressed blood to the animal's mouth, flicking at its throat to make it breathe. When a shudder ran through its body, he fondled its ears and calmed it with strokes of his fingers.

He looked up at the sky which remained quiet.

Marin found himself avoiding reflection upon what had happened. Much as a man might do with something of which he is ashamed.

That he had found Constanza was beyond doubt. Yes, her face was changed, but only in a way similar to that which he had imagined it might be.

Marin had seen her on the Mercerie, wearing a dress of scarlet ruffles. Her face was bare, untouched by powder or paint, and as she walked her servant moved like a quick shadow behind her. People muttered, loudly enough for Marin to hear them saying 'courtesan'.

She did not walk in the manner that most women did, but so swiftly that he had to hurry to keep up with her.

For the next weeks, he followed her at a distance. Prolonging this time before they met when anything he dreamt could be real. Usually, he followed closely, but sometimes further back, so that he could gaze instead on the image that he still held in his head. Every afternoon he followed her.

On the one occasion when Alvise asked him how he spent his days, Marin replied that he slept in preparation for their evenings. Slept the hours he followed Constanza or sat at Mehmet's bedside.

Alvise said that he slept also. Slept those hours he was draining Mehmet's blood.

Although Alvise had not seen Lelio for some months, there were days when the rattling in his ears was constant, as if Lelio raced about with his cart, out of sight, behind him in his study or hidden by a building or passers-by on the street. He would rather the sounds had been Lelio than the full onset of his madness.

Marin had twice come late for their meeting and the Contessa had wondered why. Now she followed him and the girl, watching as the girl's usual routes gradually became his. Seeing how he wanted to approach her but dared not, how he called to her without speaking, she knew that the girl would soon come in answer even if she did not know the reason. Sometimes, the Contessa saw her half-turn in his direction.

The girl did not wear oil on her hair, nor did she use cosmetics or powders. Probably the only woman in Venice who left her face bare. Was it that he found this nakedness, the idea of it, alluring?

And she saw what she was, this girl. Knew how she had come by her clothes and her jewels, and why she rode her horse with such finesse and practised ease. She went through the streets with a pride which the Contessa had never considered possible.

Marin waited for his Constanza in the Campo San Salvatore, knowing that within minutes she would pass through there. But in the middle of the square, a disruption had started.

Officials from the Administration had cleared a route to prepare for the procession of the Flagellants only to see that the band of refugee soldiers, with whom they had argued earlier, were now emerging from the crowd, coming to sit where they had been before. Drunken, singing battle songs, insisting on their right to access, they linked arms and refused to be moved.

The officials tried to drag them away but the pushing and scuffle continued, still blocking the route, as the first of the procession entered the square at a run. Declaring their penance in song, they came rapidly forward. Each held a stick with three tails of leather, studded with thin metal spikes, and with these they scourged themselves, joyously tearing open their backs and their arms in rhythm to their chanting. As new beads of blood appeared, they urged each other to strike harder, faster, to show the sincerity of their intent.

Withdrawing hastily to the safety of the crowd, the officials raised their eyebrows and shook their heads to make it clear that they had done all that could be expected. As soon as they were gone, the soldiers rose unsteadily to their feet. The spectators lining the edges of the square shouted their encouragement.

The Contessa saw the girl that Marin watched. She wanted to throw her from her horse, push her face into the mud on the ground. She could not bear the sight of her aloof composure and, as her anger built, she found herself pushing her way through the crowd and walking slowly towards her. She approached until she was near enough to see that even in the jewellery she wore, the girl remained defiant. As the Contessa had suspected, the necklace was of pearls. And it was the sight of these, so casually worn, that had finally robbed her of reason.

'It is forbidden by law for whores to wear pearls,' the Contessa shouted. She seized hold of one of the girl's legs, tugged at it and reached up, trying to grip the beads. Retaliation was sharp and immediate. The girl struck the Contessa across the top of her head and pulled her away by her hair.

With a cry of rage, the Contessa hit out again at the girl and her horse. The animal reared up in fright and plunged forward into the centre of the square as the fighting between the Flagellants and the soldiers began.

Marin saw his Constanza come suddenly out from the crowd to disappear an instant later into the mayhem which now grew as spectators surged forward. Stepping in with their swords and their sticks, this an unexpected bonus to their morning's entertainment.

In panic, Marin urged his own horse forward and rode in to where he thought she should be.

He tried to clear a space around him and shouted at the men to stop. The noise and the pleasure at combat were such that his voice, if heard, was not heeded. Men from both sides struck at him.

The battle had spread throughout the square and Marin had not found her. He thought she must be dead, lying cut and trampled beneath them. Then he saw her and realised that she was waiting for him. She was laughing.

He made his way around the fighting, approached her. 'I wanted to save you.'

'And have you now come to claim your reward?'

'Helisenne?' he asked, riding beside her towards the Rialto. 'You have never changed your name?'

'No.'

She saw that his disappointment weighed so heavily that for some minutes he was bereft of speech. How ill at ease he was, the ceaseless movement of his horse's reins suggesting that now he could not wait to be away. She would rather he stayed.

'I think it only fair that you receive some reward for your trouble, Signor Gaspari,' she said. 'Wine? Cakes? Almonds? Gold dust in rosewater to settle your heart after your exertions?'

Marin did not answer. He was trying to remember and compare. Her face, her grace, in comparison to what he had searched for.

Helisenne stopped her horse outside a house in the Calle dei Cinque. 'I live here,' she said, handing her reins to a servant.

Before he was able to insist that he was neither hungry nor thirsty, Marin found himself following her through the shadows of the entrance hall and up the stairs. The living room smelt of musk and rose. Lengths of yellow silk flapped in the breeze from the window.

Helisenne sat down, half-reclined, on a couch draped with animal skins, the greys of ash and charcoal. Her fingers lightly stroked the fur, moving back and forth across it.

She saw Marin look around the room and asked, 'Did you think I would live in a box in an alley, Signor, with a cloth over my head to hide my shame?'

'No! No I did not. I ...'

'I would rather hear nothing than a lie, Signor.' She laughed. He shook his head, laughing too, unsure as to whether she teased him.

Marin watched her give orders to the servant who had brought in a decanter of rosewater and a tray laden with cakes. He looked for signs that her happiness was pretence. There were none. From the first moment he had seen her, it should have been clear that rescue would not be required.

Helisenne crumbled a cake with her fingers. She could not understand why he had come. Why the display in the square? Why go to that trouble and yet now make no advance towards her?

Smiling, she poured rosewater into the goblets on the tray and handed one to him. 'There is nothing that you are forgetting, Signor?'

It was some moments before Marin replied, 'There are things I would if I could.'

'Such as your purpose this afternoon?'

'Which is not the one I suspect you believe.'

'So then ...?'

'Does to speak of something make it easier to forget?'

'There are some things that are impossible to forget, whatever one does.'

What was it, she wondered, that haunted him? That when he thought of it, caused him to tighten his muscles as though it gave him pain?

Knowing she watched him, Marin tried to still the quiver in his hands.

They ate the cakes and they drank the scented water. They sat quietly and talked of ordinary things – the price of cloth, the weather – as though this was the way in which they had always spent their afternoons.

But at times Marin could not hear what she said because of the rushing in his ears. And he was unable to tell whether the pulsing he felt was from her thoughts or from his.

Helisenne was puzzled by the curious movement of his eyes, the rapid sweeping glances which fixed on her only momentarily, before settling on those things apparently of primary interest – the ceiling or the hangings on the wall behind her.

They talked through the afternoon, the evening and into the night. Marin did not want to stay longer.

'I will come tomorrow,' he said.

'Yes.'

'At noon. If that would be a convenient hour for you?'

'Yes. At noon.' And as he looked at her briefly, she saw that what he hid was fear. But not of her. What she saw was his fear of himself.

Turning away, he asked, 'I remind you of somebody else?'

'No. Quite the reverse.'

'Till noon tomorrow, then,' he said.

'Yes.'

When he left, he kissed her eyes so firmly that she could not open them.

Love came like a robber in the night, to make off with a person's senses – so fleet of foot and wily that it was useless to chase for their return. Helisenne knew that Marin would not come that day. It was very seldom that robbers came back.

Finally, one who was different. To whom or what could she compare him? Nothing in her experience. Yet it seemed that he would pass through her life as quickly as a breeze, and equally as impossible to grasp.

At noon, she walked around her living room and straightened all the hangings. Hand-painted silks from Constantinople. Beneath them, spread out on the floor, precious Siberian furs, and on the table, in pots for her guests, honey from red bees in Russia.

The truth was that she was happy. She had a beautiful home, fine clothes and servants. She earnt five times a banker's salary and well knew that the disapproval or outrage expressed by others was often thin and poor covering for envy.

And what indeed was the truth of anybody's life? Nothing

more than a rough piling together of all they had chosen to accept as real.

For Marin, Helisenne had become the tapestry onto which all other thoughts were printed. But he had seen by the light in her eyes that she had found what she sought. So how long would it have been before, at breakfast or dinner one day, with a careless word, she revealed who it was?

And what manner of man would harm what he loved? He knew he should keep away.

A week after meeting Helisenne, Marin was invited by Alvise to a dinner at the house of a merchant.

'He shouts all the time, and one could enjoy better conversations with a tree,' Alvise said.

'But you still want to go?'

Alvise laughed. 'Of course. He is so rich it would not matter to me if he slit the throats of infants in their cots. My dear Marin, how little of life you know. And how secretive you are about the past that has formed this foolishness in your head.'

When Marin said nothing, Alvise laughed again. He could wait. It would come. He was in good spirits that day for he had seen clearly, in the mirror as he dressed, the sight he would present to others.

Next to the gates of the merchant's house, a group of men stood in the shadows. Their swords were drawn, glinting in the light from the lamps. An air of nonchalant menace implied that they would rather see trouble than not.

'Bravi,' Alvise whispered. 'Our friend has bought himself some Bravi to protect the wealth he has gained from his pirates. More things he can add to what he reminds us is his.'

Agostino drew back as Marin came close to him, his hand on his sword, recalling that once he had wanted to kill him. Whatever life had dealt him had not been soothing to his complexion, and his elaborate costume did nothing to disguise his pallor. There was still an awkwardness in the way he moved as though his clothes were either too small or too large, to be shrugged off as soon as he could. Or was it that the source of his unease lay deeper? Marin's own skin his ill-fitting coat? Pinching at his arms, constricting his chest, it being this that gave the discomfort. Revealing Marin perhaps to be no more suited to this world than he was. Agostino let his hand slide from his sword.

Behind Marin and his companion came Domenico Tarabotti, the man who said he was from Naples, who always introduced himself as a trading merchant but also always with a smile to indicate that those with intelligence would see that he was something more. And if he saw that an acquaintance did not immediately grasp the point, he would hint so heavily that now the whole of Venice knew that a papal spy had arrived from Rome.

Agostino's displeasure at his arrival had lasted only until he saw that Domenico was as much a fool as the envoy before him.

Inside the house, the rooms were hung with ribbons to celebrate the birthday of the host.

'One more thing he owns,' Alvise whispered. 'One more year. And here he is, our host, Pepin, come to greet us. Now listen. He will shout our names too.'

Marin looked across the room at the man who came towards

them. It was the merchant from the warehouse in which he used to sleep.

Pepin lightly touched the arms or backs of the other guests as he approached, moving his lips as he did so. If only for this evening, he could count them all in as his.

He touched Alvise and Marin on the arm when he reached them. 'I see you are admiring my hangings. My sailors brought them back in my ships. Welcome to my house. My servants will take good care of you. My food, my wine are here for you to enjoy. And have you met my wife, Constanza?' he asked, pointing to where she sat.

The woman sitting by the window turned, and Marin immediately recognised her face. She was the one he had seen, two years before, ordering spices at the warehouse. He remembered how, afterwards, his restlessness had persuaded him to change his routine. It was most likely, he now realised, that she had also come there in order to meet with her husband.

He waited for her to stand, for reassurance that it had been only the clothes she had worn or the particular light on that day that had made her movements seem dull.

As she moved towards her husband now, greeting guests along the way, a slight unsteadiness to her steps made it seem that she walked in her sleep. Marin dug in his mind for memories, trying to bend those he found to fit, for she did not resemble in any way the picture he had carried in his head.

Beside him, a woman began to talk about the price of oranges. Their cost, he agreed, was scandalous.

Pepin accompanied Constanza around the room, introducing her to the guests she had not yet met. Her attempts at coquetry were inelegant, gauche, suggesting an unskilled imitation of the behaviour of others. Having dreamt of this moment for so long, Marin's instinct now was only to draw back in denial of that which he saw. She came closer, and a tremor went through his hands, causing wine to spill from his glass.

'Signor Gaspari, you have not met my wife.' Pepin said.

Marin bowed, unable to speak. He supposed she must think him rude. He glanced at her, looked away, then felt compelled to make sure …

'Signora Pasquati, did you dance as a child?' he asked.

She paused before giving her reply as if it required debate. 'Yes, I danced.'

It seemed as if she waited for him to say more but, putting both arms around her, as if to protect from incipient theft, Pepin pulled her away to display her to another.

A servant appeared and rang the bell for dinner.

All the places at the table were marked. Marin was seated three places away from Constanza's right and across the table from Alvise. The woman who had spoken about oranges changed her card so that she was now seated next to him, then separated and petted her skirts to position as though they lived and must be settled and rested before she was.

Dinner was served. Had Constanza spoken, Marin would have been close enough to hear what she said. But even when Pepin addressed her, she only moved her lips into the shape of a smile. Always the same reaction and one to which he must have become used, for he betrayed no sign of surprise. It occurred to Marin that maybe he preferred it like this – that she, like his other treasures, was silent.

Marin was not conscious of what food passed his lips as he

watched her from the corner of his eye. Love? Surely he should have been aware of its presence? He put a hand to his chest, testing for sensation and movement. But his heart, having leapt at the sound of her name, had since slowed, moribund, stilled.

He heard Alvise talking of his time in India, of the tiger that had savaged his leg.

The evening progressed. The guests drank, and noise in the room increased.

Two men stood up on their chairs and shouted at the ceiling that they were noble by blood and by birth, that all life was theirs and that now they were going to claim it. They did so by loudly passing wind and lighting the gas with candles.

Others took the food left in the serving dishes on the table and threw it around the room.

Constanza yawned. They did this every time. Even in their displays of rebellion, nothing ever changed.

She noticed that one man to her right did not join the revelry. Perhaps it was that which drew her attention. But as one feeling was so much like another, such a problem to sift them apart, she could not really be sure.

If it had not been Pepin that she had chosen, would that have made the difference? She waited for something to wake her. Yet Pepin's jealousy had taught her one thing, which was to look about without seeming to do so. She had only looked at Marin once. Now she looked again, aware that she stared too long, forgot her normal caution.

She knew that it was because he saw this that Pepin stood and came to kiss her on the lips. She did not mind. She did not feel it. It did not matter that others still came to kiss the hands or the lips of her corpse.

As her eyes met those of the man to her right, and lingered, she became aware of vague thoughts, perhaps memories which she supposed could have been hers. Things that had been hidden, forbidden, secrets: a distant thrill that stirred, rising to shake itself, moving to taste the air.

When at last the evening was over, and they walked to their gondola, Alvise linked his arm through Marin's and said, 'You were very quiet this evening, my friend.'

'I had some pain in my head.'

'And was the cause of this pain anything to do with the wife of our host?'

'No.'

'There are very few things that escape my notice, and I saw that your downcast eyes were wandering in her direction.'

'Do you think her beautiful?'

'She is too thin, all pale and drooping, like an asparagus that was kept from the sun. And most likely she has the same bitter taste. I advise you to be careful. Our friend Pepin does not tolerate any handling of his goods.'

Once the last guests had gone, the captain of the Bravi ordered the night's camp prepared. Agostino was one of the few he addressed by name, for it was the captain's policy to treat those bravest as favourite.

The one they called Piero remained where he was, standing next to the gate. The captain shouted at him that he should do as he was ordered. Piero did not move. The captain shouted again.

Piero said something to some others close by. The captain heard them laugh. It was not the first time that Piero had failed to follow his orders. Nor, he suspected, was this the first time that Piero had made him a cause for the men's amusement.

If ever a man tried to seize his command, it would be somebody like Piero.

After their camp had been set, the captain saw Piero walking alone, out through the gate towards the canal. Setting down his blanket, the captain followed him along the bank. The night was quiet, and the darkness relieved only by an intermittent, watery glow of moonlight. Looking around, the captain assured himself that they were alone.

He had not set out with murder in mind but, as he drew closer to Piero's back, this was the desire that consumed him.

As he grasped his sword, he was suddenly aware of the darkness shifting beside him. But before he could turn, Agostino had slit his throat so that it gaped smiling from ear to ear.

Before Piero had time to utter his gratitude, Agostino had mounted his horse and ridden away. He did not want to hear Piero's words. He had simply saved one where he had not saved the other. There was nothing more to be said.

To fight in battle was Piero's first love. This had become his source of ecstasy and despair. And his new position as Bravi captain did not fail to give sweet supply of both.

His Flavia had gone so suddenly, without ever giving reason why. But not too long afterwards he had discovered that a wound or a blow, whether given or received, touched just as well, as deeply as any lover's kiss.

He had not expected to see Flavia again and, when he had, at first hardly recognised her. There was not much in her appearance of the girl he had known.

But as he saw her more often, sitting on a bench in the Piazza, and as the days went by, each with its riding past her, he came to the conclusion that he must have been mistaken because in reality she was not so much changed.

The Contessa wondered if he had seen her sitting there and, if he had, whether he thought her ruined. But in truth she had hardly recognised him, for the Piero she loved now was as tall as she had always wished him, with a beard shaped to a point in the way she had often suggested would suit.

Alvise had noticed the change in Marin's mood and decided that the only logical reason was that he had fallen in love with Pepin Pasquati's wife. This infatuation leading perhaps to a cosiness in which there would only be room for two. Leaving him, Alvise, alone, robbed of his strange new pupil and also his gratifying deference.

They had dined together at Alvise's rooms, and they sat now, one either side of the fire-place. For over half an hour Marin had torn pieces from a roll of bread and thrown them into the flames. Alvise noticed that, from time to time, he looked at the flagon of wine from which he, Alvise, was drinking.

Why did Marin never drink? And what would happen if he did? Some revealing of the mystery or an amusing lapse of that irritating self-control? Amusement had been far too short in supply of late.

'You are quiet *again* this evening,' Alvise said.

'I have a headache,' Marin replied. He did not turn away from the fire. He thought of the things he had believed to be true. How many more among them were false? Was it that nothing of his life had been fated or planned? The abilities he had nothing more than a random bestowal of fortune? Gifts he had regarded with fear?

'Take a drink with me. A small one. It might ease your pain. It might also ease your spirits.'

Marin looked up. 'You know I never drink wine.'

'Come now. A drink with your friend Alvise.' Tipping the water from Marin's glass onto the carpet, he filled it with wine.

To his astonishment, Marin accepted it, running his fingers around its rim before placing it on the table. Yet, as Alvise sighed, Marin picked it up again, raised it to his lips and drank deeply. 'To future freedom,' he said.

Domenico Tarabotti was not happy in his work, for it pained him to live in this way, as something so much less than he was. He knew that if people were aware of his true importance, they would treat him with more respect. They would surely bow instead of nod, they would make way at his approach, and when he spoke they would listen.

As things were, he arrived at dinners and functions eagerly with, pinned to his handkerchief, a note on which he had written reminders of all the amusing things he could say. But always he was interrupted and, as the evening went on, he became more downcast because there was never opportunity to say them.

The only one who treated him with anything close to the respect he knew to be his due was Sebastiano Finetti, the Administrator.

Now, as he walked along the Calle Larga, he pulled his hat down over his ears, huddling against the chill. He could not bear the Venetian damp. He longed for a posting to the high, dry hills of Siena or to the endless sunshine of Naples.

He sniffed. Perhaps he had caught influenza. Perhaps on the

grounds of ill health he could plead for transfer elsewhere. A more hospitable clime instead.

But he knew that they would never allow it, and that he would be forced to stay, whatever his health, until he had fulfilled his duties. Two matters, the investigation of which, he considered, an absolute waste of his time.

The first was regarding the rumours of sedition, an uprising from the Venetian church, a plot to kill Gian Pietro Carafa, their pope.

Of course there were rumours of uprisings and assassinations. The murderous stealth and treachery of the Venetians were legend. To Domenico, it would have been far more alarming had there not been.

Then there was this second matter, this ridiculous business of the Messiah whom it was rumoured would now be coming of age. But as all attempts to find him had failed, there was now apprehension and anxiety that, having remained so far in hiding, he would suddenly appear in the midst of the people as Saviour and usurp the throne of their pope.

Domenico sniffed. As if any Messiah, given his choice from the world, would elect to make his home in this damp, and select for his company the deceitful, duplicitous Venetians.

Domenico wiped his nose on his sleeve. He dared not use his handkerchief for fear he would smudge his notes. It began to rain.

Even if a Messiah had been born there, had initially arrived by mistake, Domenico did not suppose for a moment that he would find him. If he, Domenico, were a Messiah, he would have moved, by now, to Naples.

'Today, you must tell me who does this.'

Mehmet gave no response.

Replacing the stopper in the bottle of ointment, Marin rolled it between his hands.

'How is it that you accept this? Why will you not come with me? Why? You could have your freedom.'

'You do not understand.'

'What do I not understand?'

'I was born a slave. I am still a slave. And what a slave has will always belong to his master. It is my fate, and it is not possible to run from fate because fate will always run faster and win. Marin, you do not understand that we are not free.' Having raised himself to speak, he now lay back, exhausted.

Leaping to his feet, Marin flung the bottle at the floor, pulled Mehmet from the bed and shook him. 'Who says this? Tell me who. Who can tell us we are not free?'

Mehmet tried to scramble away from the splinters of glass that had opened the soles of his feet.

Suddenly quiet, Marin quickly lifted him, pressing him close before laying him back onto the bed. Weeping, he bound the cuts he had caused. When he was done he shut his eyes and felt Mehmet's hand on his cheek.

Mehmet smiled. Already the pain had gone, and he saw himself again as a small shining on the water. He had seen its tides in Marin's eyes. He felt Marin's arms around him, heard the whisper in his ear, 'You need not be afraid. I could always save you.'

He barely had the strength to murmur his reply. 'That would not be my fate.' He could see that the waters from outside had spread again and come into the room. Each day they rose, sometimes a gentle stream, sometimes torrents through the walls, yet always his bed remained quite still, and the current left dry what it touched.

Marin left the room and walked down the stairs, pushing his way through the drinkers and their songs of merriment. He punched the face of a man who did not move quickly enough. At least he, Marin, would not be bound.

Marin continued to meet with Mehmet. They played dice. They talked – usually without the impediment of words – of everything other than why they sat there.

A lvise had read the papers many times over, experimenting with different amounts of Mehmet's blood and at different phases of the moon. If the impossible had happened once, why did it not do so now?

Some days before, walking from the Rialto with Marin, he had heard the rattling wheels of a cart just a few paces behind them on the stones. But Marin had insisted that he heard nothing and turned to show him that there was nobody there.

Watching him gradually sicken as he made his way about the streets, Lelio knew that Alvise had not succeeded with the Elixir. And whether there had been more success with gold was not a matter of interest.

Obviously he had been mistaken as to his identity. And if Alvise had been a test planted in his way to measure the growth of his wisdom, clearly he had failed in that too.

Meanwhile, at night, he found the streets littered with signs of Death's activity. Yes, lately there had been much else to occupy his mind. His cart was overflowing. More than he could ever have wanted. So many with the same look about them, the swelling of the body, the puffiness of the skin, and often when he shook them, the trickling of water that came from their mouths.

And these were not from a general spread of the people, but mostly the very young and the old. Those too young to have left their cots, and those whose legs were too elderly or infirm to have lifted them out of their beds. Yet they all appeared to have drowned.

The number of those who died in this way was increasing, but no announcements had been made, and no warnings had been given. The Administration did not speak of it.

At nights he had seen the black boats, laden with corpses, gliding north from the Arsenale.

The Administration issued a proclamation which was read out by an official in the Piazza. It stated that the rumours of a plague were false, put about by enemies of Venice who envied her status and beauty. That any small increase in mortality was due only to the unseasonal damp, and that further spreading of the previous lie would be viewed as treasonous and punished.

The official pinned the notice to a board outside the Procuratie. A short distance away he saw, engrossed in conversation, a group of German merchants whom he recognised. They and their trade were regular visitors. They would no longer come if they thought there was plague. Neither they nor the others. Evidence so far had been buried on a small island north of Murano.

Smoothing the notice out, the official underlined the signature of Sebastiano Finetti. He looked out across the Piazza, knowing that this was possibly the last time he would see it, for that afternoon he was moving his family to the safety of Florence.

It pleased Alvise to see Marin foolish. How, unused to intoxicating liquors, he slurred his words or forgot them, or his coordination became confused. Accordingly, Alvise did all he could to encourage this new habit.

But no matter how foolish Alvise saw he was, he remained an object of fascination for others. They flocked to him, seemed to drink from him with their eyes as if he were intoxication for them. Why?

Was Marin truly an extraordinary person, or did he only behave as though he were? If there was anything which Alvise would dislike more than the first, it was certainly the latter.

For Marin now occupied the position of grace, previously reserved for him.

In the past, it had always been Alvise who wanted to be at
every party, every dinner, every salon, and Marin who, often
reluctantly, had allowed himself to be led. Now it was Marin who
insisted that they accept every invitation and in addition attend
events to which they had not been asked.

But Alvise saw that it was not the pleasure of his company or
the promise of that of their acquaintance that drove Marin into
this frenzy. It must be that his mind was still on Pepin Pasquati's
wife.

He could not understand why Marin had not gone with
Constanza already. It seemed that he could have any woman he
chose, so why did he hesitate now? Or was he hiding the fact that
already they were together? It was most likely that this was the
case. Well, even if it could not be prevented, roughening its path
might at least provide some amusement.

He watched Marin talking, laughing, kissing, making love with
the desperation of a man who knows that it is only his constant
movement that keeps him from drowning.

Pulling love to him from whatever source he could find, Marin's days and nights were a blur of sighs, of tangled limbs, lifted skirts and petticoats and bodies pressed onto his. To raise objection because he himself was purely incidental as they reached out for what lay behind would have been foolish. Sometimes the thoughts skittering across his skin became too many in number to register. The imprint of the world upon him.

In the brief moments when he was sober, he noticed how his relationship with Alvise was changing. And when Marin now questioned some hostile remark or move, Alvise only smiled to indicate that whatever it was, was imagined or merely a joke.

Marin could see that Alvise's sickness was growing steadily worse. His appearance had become dirty and careless, and his skin, now grey in tone, was creased and marked like damp paper, and pustules showed outside his mask. Often he walked into doors and walls, fell over pieces of furniture, and when he ate he left food on his face and his clothes. But whenever Marin expressed concern or offered his arm as support, Alvise would refuse, and nor would he speak about what happened.

Clearly, Alvise was dying, and Marin could have shown him that he need have no fear of death. But he had decided that he would not do so until Alvise came to him and showed that he considered him an equal. For he could see Alvise's jealousy at the success he had at love, at how the women found him impossible to resist, but also he saw the look on Alvise's face which suggested that he thought him still no more than a child whose achievements were only by chance.

So sometimes now, when Alvise corrected his speech or behaviour a little too loudly in public, Marin would choose a woman and take her into the garden, some empty room or a cupboard, just as a reminder that he could have this. Regardless of how he looked or spoke.

In time, Marin began to go out for his entertainment alone, and usually on returning, when he looked into his mirror at home, he noticed that something about his appearance had altered. A new birthmark, a difference in the thickness or colour of his hair, or his clothes suddenly an awkward fit, their size for a body other than his.

He noticed, but now he no longer cared. He continued to drink and considered it a sign of success that often he did not know whether it was day or night.

As the question of salvation was no longer of consequence, he ceased to meet with the Contessa.

From where he stood, waiting outside the warehouse, Alvise could hear the merchant shouting. It was most likely, he thought, that Pepin still shouted when he was completely alone, when there was nobody else to hear, just from the sheer enjoyment of doing so.

On seeing Pepin descend the storeroom steps, Alvise raised his hands to indicate pleasure and surprise as if this were a chance encounter. He bowed, greeted Pepin and placed his arm around the merchant's shoulder.

'How well you look, Pepin,' he said. 'My admiration for you is boundless. I must say that in the circumstances I would not have been so patient. Nor would any other man I know.' Alvise turned his face to one side and looked at the ground. 'Especially as there are so many that know of it. Your wife is a very beautiful woman.' He sighed. 'But I always thought that she was the type to remain true.' He caught Pepin's eye. 'I believe there must be something of the saint in you, Pepin. Yes, I believe that is what it is.' He paused. 'Oh, dear God, forgive me. You did not know. I see by your face that you were the only one who did not. Forgive me. I only wanted to offer condolence, but now I see that instead of lessening your pain, I have been its harbinger. Forgive me. If I had known or even suspected for a moment that you were not fully aware … He was my friend …' Gripping Pepin's hand, he squeezed it tightly to communicate the extent of his sympathy. 'Forgive me, Pepin Pasquati. I wish you good day.'

There were too many bodies for the funeral boats to transport each night, and too many bereaved families in too many districts for the deceit to continue any longer.

And the symptoms remained the same – the coughing, the bubbling from the lungs – while those who stood around the bed, burning herbs and counting beads, could only watch, powerless, as their loved ones choked to death.

New sanitation officials were employed to clear the increasing amounts of weeds and fish that were found on the streets each morning. Bonfires of saltpetre, brimstone and amber were built in the squares to dispel the excess damp in the air. A ceremony was held at which Sebastiano Finetti lit the first.

The search for a cure continued, as did the frequent and frenzied claims that one had been found. These from physicians, apothecaries, women who brewed herbs and bones in their kitchens and many others who had been quick to spot an opportunity for lucrative enterprise. And while all of them failed, there was no denying that they had done so the richer.

Having found nothing with which to assuage their fear, some people discovered that over time this feeling had changed to one for which it was easier to find an outlet. But having no real idea at whom to direct this anger, it seemed prudent to blame those who had been blamed for so much in the past. Within a month, there were five reported attacks on Jews as they returned to the Ghetto at curfew.

As the death rate quickened, others looked to the Church. They cleared the porches of card games and put back the pews in the places which had been used for the selling of second-hand furniture. Volunteers were despatchd to scrub clean the shrines on the streets.

Congregations of worship grew, and preachers who had gone to find other work now returned to their previous calling.

Each saint in turn was petitioned, and careful vigil was kept for a decline in the number of deaths or for any sign that their pleas had been heard.

Nobody could remember, afterwards, who it was that had first mentioned San Barnabo Redentore. Neither could they remember his feast day nor how long it had been since this was observed.

But when those who liked to make note of such things looked back through their calenders and checked, it was discovered that the feast day of San Barnabo had been on the day of the storm.

It was suggested that their negligence had angered him to such a degree that he had delivered this plague as punishment. And those who liked to pronounce on such things said that this was probably true.

When books were searched for his life and his history, it was learnt that many years before, in a plague of that time, it had been he who had saved the city. He had offered up his life to God, and it had been accepted in exchange for those of the stricken people.

Trepidation at having incurred such wrath was tempered by now knowing the means to redress it. So, in April 1566, the citizens of Venice began to pray to San Barnabo for his forgiveness and return. They swore their loyalty and their love.

Next to the window in the Austrian Earl's dining room, a man sat on a stool with a drawing board on his knees. So expert was he in his sketching of flattering portraits that sometimes all resemblance to their subject was lost. For few would pay for something which showed them only as they were.

He was presently engaged on a picture of the man who now spoke with the Earl's wife. The artist paused, undecided as to whether he should make the nose longer or shorter but knowing that, in any case, it had to be changed. However, as he pencilled in and rubbed out various possibilites, he found the picture suddenly ripped from his hand, with a look from its subject that discouraged any request for payment.

Agostino crumpled the paper and threw it into the fire. Having procured his invitation by claiming that he was a visiting prince, he had come in preparation for his next role, alert for the careless word or anecdote that might later be of worth. So far, however, the evening had proved unproductive.

Looking about him, he noticed Marin's erstwhile companion.

He had always considered their pairing a strange one and the advantages to each were matters which could only be guessed at.

The man was drunk, and his clumsy attempts to retie the ruff round his neck were resulting only in further entanglement. Imagining it a noose, Agostino stepped forward, smiled and offered to help fasten it more tightly, only to realise on doing so that nothing of worth would come from this action for the man was too drunk to speak. Leaving him to grimace alone in front of the mirror, Agostino prepared to leave.

Alvise rubbed at the glass with the palm of his hand, trying to focus on his fading reflection. If the plague took him first, at least he would appear at his funeral a more attractive corpse.

As the Earl ordered the floor cleared for games, servants scuttled forward to move chairs to the edges of the room and began to hand out blindfolds. Signalling to a servant to bring his cloak, Agostino's attention was unexpectedly arrested by the sight of four women pressed so closely around Marin that they all but pushed him into the flames of the fireplace.

He had seen before how people were drawn to Marin, so much so that they seemed unwilling to let him slip from their presence. How might it feel to be so adored that one's every movement was dogged? To step to the side only to have one's pursuers follow suit, gathering again like flies?

Now, as Marin bowed and tried to make his way to the door, Agostino watched the women follow him with something akin to greed, as though the pot had been snatched before they had eaten their fill.

Behind them came the artist, anxiously waving a sheet of paper, chasing approval and payment for his work, but by the time he had squeezed past the guests, now forming themselves into lines, Marin had left the room.

Agostino moved to follow, catching sight, as he went, of the picture the artist held in his hand. The face was that of a stranger.

Descending the stairs, Agostino could hear the laughter of the guests, indistinguishable from the whickering of donkeys.

Marin and Alvise had not seen each other for weeks, and when they met at a soiree at the Ca' Grasso, it was by chance. They greeted each other briefly, then they moved apart.

Alvise lay down on a couch, already so drunk that his glass dropped from his fingers, spilling wine onto his neck and his clothes.

He could barely see. Only the vague shapes of the room and the people who moved around him. He could hear Marin's voice and a woman's, their laughter.

Marin pulled the woman closer and looked into her eyes. He felt his body changing. It made him smile, this slipping into the form of another. He felt the itching of his skin as it stretched or shrunk to cover the altering of the muscles and bones beneath it.

Alvise closed his eyes. Soon this blackness would be permanent. Mehmet was dying. After that, who would give him blood? How would he know the type that was needed?

It was a curious thing that even when his sight was bad, when everything else was clouded, Marin's face was still clear, always seen with the same intensity. Curious too, to remember how when they first met he had thought Marin unremarkable.

When Alvise opened his eyes, it was to the red of Marin's hose in front of him. He could not take his eyes from him, and he was disgusted by his thoughts. He wanted to leap up, to seize him, to peel him like an orange, skin from flesh, and suck him dry.

As he stood up, unsteadily, the darkness closed in completely. Whirling round in frustration, he heard the sound of a vase shattering on the tiles of the floor and felt somebody's arm reach out to grab at him. Lashing out to knock it away, he heard Marin's voice and the crashing of plates and glasses on the table.

Stunned for a moment, Marin lay among the broken crockery, drops of his blood dripping onto the food. Then swinging his legs to the ground, he punched Alvise in return.

They were both propelled to the door by their host and, as they came onto the landing stage, they heard from inside the house cries of astonishment and screaming from the guests.

In the dining room, the pigeons that had lain as decoration around the pie were rustling their feathers, shaking sugar and gold dust from their wings as they rose to fly, tangling their feet in the hair of the guests and pecking at their faces.

Alvise pointed towards the noise from the window and laughed. He motioned for Marin to come closer as though he wanted to whisper. He felt at his belt for his knife, pulled it free and thrust it at Marin's neck, tugging at him, holding him close and trying to fix his lips to the wound as Marin fought to push him away. Alvise fell backwards onto the wood.

'Are you mad?' he heard Marin ask. He imagined the expression on Marin's face and laughed. He sat up, reached out, put his arms around Marin's legs.

Marin kicked at him. Alvise did not let go. He held firmly. He still laughed, pulling his face into a woeful approximation of the look he guessed Marin would have.

With one final kick, Marin freed himself. Alvise lay back and spread out his arms and legs. He shouted. 'Do you think I ever truly wanted your friendship? It was only that you were so gauche that you amused me. You were the monkey pupil at the end of my chain. You, with your strange way of looking out from under your lashes, to the left, to the right, anywhere except to the person with whom you speak, like the sly flirtations of a virgin maid.'

Alvise had taken a flagon of wine from the house. It lay on the ground. Marin bent down and took it. Walking back towards the Rialto, he could still hear Alvise shouting and found himself wondering how long Alvise had to live. Not too long, he supposed. He had only waited for Alvise to give some sign of recognising that, in some things, his, Marin's knowledge might be greater.

Alvise rolled over, felt the knife in his hand and remembered the irresistible urge to use it. Proof that his mind strained still further from its moorings?

Walking through the streets, Marin drank from Alvise's bottle, realising that as the wine took effect his pace had quickened and that now, as he turned in circles, he was laughing. What man, after all, would not give all that he had to be him? He had the power over life and death. It seemed that truly there was nothing he could not do. Was he not a king among men? He shouted his question to the darkness. Receiving no answer to the contrary, he threw away the empty flagon and danced in celebration over the stones.

Reaching the Rialto, he ran to the centre of the bridge, raised his arms and stood shouting at the sky. 'And is it not true that I am free? Is there one who will prove to me otherwise?' Part of him still expected a reply.

As he walked away from the bridge towards the Piazza, the moon slid down behind a cloud, and the night became suddenly darker. A vague idea of what he would do was forming in his mind.

Dawn broke as Marin lay shivering on the ground outside the Procuratie. With the gathering light, out of the mist, scurried the wraith-like figures of porters delivering boxes of produce. And at a slower pace, tardy stall-holders, some struggling with packs on their backs.

A high-pitched call announced the arrival of the soup-seller who wheeled his barrow round the square, ladling the steaming liquid into cups. Stall-holders paused to drink for a moment before returning to their familiar exchange of greetings and cheery insults.

Marin turned onto his stomach and watched, waiting for his audience to grow. Reaching out, he caught a sleepy fly between his fingers, crushed it and then fed it back to life.

At nine o'clock, deciding that the Piazza was now crowded enough, he stood and walked towards the stage that had been set up for the mountebanks. As he passed the butcher's stall, he took from the box there the body of a rabbit.

Pulling his cart, Lelio moved from the shadow of the Torre

dell'Orologio and crept a short distance behind, following him across the square. He had seen him shouting from the bridge the night before and had seen that when he had left there, the ground had become wet behind him as though the canal had broken its banks in pursuit. Now he saw how Death and the youth leapt onto the stage together.

Marin shouted for the people's attention, beckoning as they began moving towards him. 'Come,' he said. 'Good morning to you. I promise you a show the likes of which you will never have seen before. Before I start, may I ask if any of you know who I am? Maybe I will surprise you. Does anybody know who I am?'

Was the question addressed to him? Lelio wondered. Or were there others whom Death wished to call to attention? If he put himself forward now, would it be sufficient proof that he was worthy of favour? Did Death wait for this public recognition?

Holding up the body of the rabbit, Marin waved it at the crowd, swinging it by the leg in demonstration that it was dead. Then with a flourish of his knife, he cut open his finger and pressed blood to the animal's mouth. When it did not move, he tried again, rubbing across its teeth, but it remained hanging limp, lifeless over his arm.

A woman in the crowd shouted. 'Where is the show you promised us? What have you given us that we have not seen before?' An egg splattered at Marin's feet.

Lelio moved closer, then drew back, fighting the urge to leave there. The scene in front of him brought to mind the evening Barnabo Mezzadri was taken, and his own part in those events: the angry people and the man in front of them, helpless.

A pain in Marin's head began. He felt himself perspire and, looking down, he saw a commotion at the front of the crowd.

A man was clutching his throat as he coughed and tried to draw breath. Tearing loose the neck of his tunic, he then fell to his knees, convulsing for some moments on the ground before finally lying still. Others around him began to cough too, swaying as if impelled back and forth by waves. They were choking as their neighbour had. Marin saw that they drowned. How far from the giver of life was the one who took it away?

He wanted to run but the crowd was so dense before him that he could see no escape. Then suddenly he noticed that the people moved, creating a path, covering their mouths and noses as they pulled back from the Collector's approach.

Laying down his cart, Lelio dragged himself up and onto the stage to prostrate himself at Marin's feet. 'I know who you are,' he said, and then looking up for a moment he saw behind the face of Death, intertwined as though they were one, that of Barnabo Mezzadri. Stretching up his hand to touch Marin's, Lelio quietly asked him, 'Barnabo?'

The crowd were silent. Then there was whispering, starting from those nearest the front. Marin heard somebody say the name San Barnabo.

And he felt their love as it struck him, its force of an intensity he had never experienced before. Those next to the stage surged forward, reaching for the one they awaited.

The skin on his back began to stretch, his clothes grew tighter, and jumping from the stage he ran, pushing through the people, feeling as he went the tugging of their love and their insistence that he was theirs.

Agostino leant against a pillar of the Palazzo Ducale and very slowly smiled.

Lelio crouched in despair at the side of the stage. It seemed that he had made yet another mistake, addressing Death in the name of another. A lapse in the expected etiquette which, judging by the speed of His departure, had caused offence of such a degree that it had most probably destroyed any chance of reprieve, condemning him now to wander, mouldering, for eternity. Never to merit early deliverance, even by a day.

A rabbit ran past his feet.

Marin only slowed when the shouts of those pursuing had ceased to echo about the alleys.

Long before he reached Mehmet's tavern, he heard the water's whispered greeting. As he approached the bridge that led there, the tall, dry grasses along the bank swayed and cracked as if something continually walked amongst them. The water began to flow more quickly, curling up in invitation as he passed.

Marin pushed his way through the crowded dining room and ran up the stairs in the corner. Slowly, he opened the door to Mehmet's room.

The smell from the ointment was stifling and, in the waning light from the lamp, he saw that the floorboards were streaked and smeared with blood. Stepping forward too quickly, he slid sideways onto the empty bed. Lying there, running his hand to and fro across the sheet, it was some moments before he realised that the sound of sobbing was from him.

At the end, it seemed there had not been bandages enough, for strips had been torn from the bed sheet, and now he saw on the floor something that filled him with such disbelief and horror that at first he could not bear to look and turned his head away, praying he had been mistaken.

He picked it up. Even though the pale blue silk was heavily stained, it was not so much as to obscure the knotted threads of gold and silver which he had designed himself. Marin held in his hand the handkerchief he had given to Alvise.

Pressing it onto his face so that the blood on the cloth mixed with his tears, he stumbled across the room, slipping on blood that should have been his.

When he reached the bridge, he lay down and felt it creaking beneath his weight. Hanging from the edge, he swung the upper part of his body down far enough for the water to touch his back. Moving closer, as if to give himself completely, he felt the water's agitation in response and, as its caress grew stronger, he suddenly pulled away.

The moon was high. The night screamed out. A desolate keening carried by the wind from the water. A mournful calling for the return of its own.

Marin's intention had been to go home but it occurred to him now that it was because he was running so fast that he had missed the street that led there. But then he saw that the turnings into others had also gone, and he was left with no choice but to continue along the only route that remained open. It brought him to the convent of San Barnabo Redentore.

He passed the church where, many years before, he had left a note telling the nuns where to find Clara's body. He walked through the convent's courtyard and in through an arch to the hallway where he had stood with Sebastiano Finetti.

As he had done that day, Marin read the plaque telling San Barnabo's history, the sacrifice and the procession that he had seen in his dream.

The death of San Barnabo had been portrayed in pale and beautiful colours, and one could see, on looking closely at the faces of the people, how much they had loved him. And Marin could see how, even before everything had started, how similar their two faces were.

Two nuns came through the corridor. They did not remark on his presence.

It was only by his cloak that Agostino knew it was Marin, for he had never seen another like it. A garment as ridiculous as the one who wore it. Of satin cloth with purple braiding on its hem and beading round its neck. Something that would keep out neither the wind nor the rain.

The fabric billowed out in the wind, falling to folds, then rising again as the man it hid collapsed to his hands and knees before continuing to stagger across the Piazza.

As he passed the men drinking and playing with dice next to the booth for the employment of sailors, Agostino saw that the dull gleam of their lamps shone through Marin. The light was scattered, fragmented, less clear than at source, but plain to his eyes still there.

Emerging from the lengthening shadows beyond the Campanile, Marin approached the water and sat, pushing back his cloak so that it slipped from his shoulders to the ground.

Agostino saw his shadow fragmenting, fading, reassembling, wavering in every direction, even though he was perfectly still.

Marin was there and yet not there, only a part of all that was around him, pulled outwards until it seemed he would break.

Marin reached his hands out to the water, and it moved against the wind, stretching to him in return; and when he spoke, Agostino saw that he drew away from whatever had been its reply.

Turning his horse, Agostino rode from the Piazza. Over the years, he had come to learn that everything had its time.

His gold, his beauty, his sight, Mehmet. All gone. Alvise felt his way along the walls of buildings and sank to a crawl over the most slippery bridges. All he could see was darkness, although the heat on his head and his back told him it was day. The smell in the air told him when he had reached his destination.

Only a man of his intelligence would appreciate the exquisite irony in the fact that all the things he had run from had come. Yes, he could even raise a smile and draw some meagre comfort from knowing that even at his last, his sense of humour had not failed him.

Now he imagined the people in the hovels around him, beckoning, smiling with their blackened, rotten gums, their arms held out in welcome, to their world from his, the path of no return.

As he sat down in the mud to wait, the church bells of Santa Maria dell'Orio chimed and struck the hour.

He heard the cart approaching and stood, the more easily to be seen. The footsteps were familiar.

Five horsemen rode into the Campo San Zulian, wheeling together as they spoke in low voices. Too much treachery against the papacy in the past had made them alert to even the slightest suspicion of more. And it seemed that now it came from one of their own.

So it had been decided that they should instead employ an outsider, one who was already known to them. For whom the only gain would be monetary reward and after that some title from Rome if he so wished.

Their purses were deeper and their titles of more weight than anything that could be offered by Venice.

And they knew, as did he and everybody else, that the arms of Rome were longer.

Many years before, a freak show used to perform in the Campo San Zulian. Agostino smiled. Dead things. Only dead things, nothing more, arranged in his mind as steps.

He waited for the men from Rome to come closer, watching them as they rode at a leisurely pace towards the church. Two went in while the other three remained at the porch.

Agostino knew who they were and who it was they looked for. He knew that they would not find the priest who had been warned and left there some minutes before. He also knew where the priest had gone because he himself had urged him to hide.

So when the men came out of the church, Agostino rode forward to speak, ready to prove again that he could be more useful than the one they employed at present.

Domenico Tarabotti sat waiting for his aide to arrive. As his own efforts to date had proved fruitless, he had picked a clever man to help him. Someone whose cleverness could be exchanged for payments, but not so clever that he would be of a mind to object.

It was a matter of urgency now that his endeavours met with success, before Rome began to view his failure as treasonous. For it seemed that there might indeed be a Saviour, albeit one of such poor intelligence that he had not left for Naples. But whether he was the Saviour or not was of far less importance than what the people of Venice believed.

However, on the morning that hundreds had seen this man in the Piazza he himself had taken to his bed with a chill. It had been days before he had learnt of what happened.

From his window now, he saw the rider approach. At first he did not recognise him. Surely the man he had chosen had been of lesser stature.

It was interesting to note, Agostino found, the varying ways in which people went to their deaths. A fearful struggle until the last of life was wrested away, an unexpected calmness in the sliding to oblivion, or those like Domenico who were so surprised at the event or at the manner of its coming, that even as they drew their final breath, they did not believe it happened.

The people waited for San Barnabo to reappear, growing impatient when he did not do so. They cursed their stupidity and lamented that, at the Piazza, they had not been more alert and taken him.

In the evenings they gathered in the squares, lighting candles and chanting his name. Meanwhile, the dying continued. Too many bodies to arrange for proper burial. They lay in open pits.

Marin did not leave his rooms, but the sound of the people's pleas continued to roll in through the windows long after they had ceased to call. He heard their thoughts.

And each night he journeyed to what he had been before, finding it ever harder to make his way back.

He remembered the shouting of the people the last time and how unwilling he had been to be taken.

And he allowed himself the knowledge that something borrowed, lent on goodwill or trust, would sooner or later be due for return to its owner.

Lelio touched the water that came from the mouths of the dead and wiped it onto his face. This was not as the plague of before, and there was much that he could not explain.

The people spoke of Barnabo Mezzadri. It was he that they hailed as their saint. At first, Lelio had not recognised the pictures they prayed to, for the features there were of a more pious cast than those of the Barnabo he remembered.

Thinking back to that evening, he bowed his head in his hands, but all that came forth from his eyes was a sudden scattering of dust.

Constanza arrived in the night, half-dressed, saying that she had walked the streets for days. She did not ask whether it would be possible to stay, and Marin did not say whether she could. He was aware that the event had slid into place as if long ago arranged elsewhere.

She followed him into the bedroom and climbed into his bed. Marin lay down beside her, closing his eyes as he felt her fingers on his back. Turning, he took her into his arms and ran his trembling hand across her shoulders. The woman for whom he had waited. How would it feel? He realised that he did not want to know.

He was gentle with her. He was tender. He made love to her. He tried to forget her presence.

Outside, from the Campo San Luca, he heard the people sing, and as he looked at the new thickness and size of his arms, he imagined himself walking somewhere far away.

A short distance from the gathering in the square, Lelio searched for wood of a suitable width and length. The next day he would start to build his new cart. One with accommodation enough to last him for eternity.

Constanza would have come to Marin even if Pepin had not mentioned his name. It had seemed right that she should be with him.

In the days after she had first met him at dinner, she had gone about her business as usual. All the same yet not so. However, she could not specify what it was that had changed.

Marin's company pleased her, for with him she felt an awakening of things fallen dormant from lack of nourishment. It was the calm that was balm to the senses of others that had so nearly finished her.

She longed for unpredictable storm and excitement. And Marin had about him the irresistible promise of turbulence.

So she told Marin that it was his fault that her husband had cast her out and that now she had nowhere else to go, adding that she knew, under the circumstances, he was too good a man to turn her away.

Agostino felt himself totally at peace. He could feel the substance of his power as a mass between his hands. To be packed in tightly like a diamond, or stretched and laid out to its fullest size so that he could marvel at its immensity.

He rode the streets, seeing things which he chose not to and reporting back falsehoods which he knew would be accepted as true.

A random striking here and there was not what he intended. Rather to take out from the world those who before had considered themselves too firmly fixed to be moved. The silken-haired priest, the four Council members. His whisper. Their punishment. His satisfaction at having been the cause of its arrival – their early, unexpected passage from this world to the next.

He wondered if it were the particular shape of a hypocrite's tongue that made it so easy to remove.

To him, this selective slaughter was an art. As much, if not more so, than the rearranging of colour on a canvas or the erasing of an unnecessary figure on a fresco. The only question was, how long it would take him to finish.

It was Agostino's habit to go about the streets in disguise to gather the knowledge he needed. He had worn the clothes of a banker, a politician, a priest and a beggar so that he could walk freely among them and their kind, unnoticed. He knew who kept company with whom, behind closed doors, and whether they were involved in the latest financial or political intrigue or scandal. He knew the most recent gossip from the salons, and that there were many who missed Marin's presence.

In his new line of work there was much talk of God – a subject which Agostino had often considered. Did He, for instance, order and structure events in the world or did He only watch to see what men would do with the powers He had given them? Did He then judge or make any recording of their actions? Or was His observation of them nothing more than a sport? The loser or the winner something of academic interest alone, and man's free will, if it were so, only an additional source of mirth.

And now, of course, all the talk of one who was sent by God. It was indicative of life's absurdity that the one the people looked to seemed incapable of saving himself.

When he had spoken with his employers about this supposed Messiah, he had shown the amount of concern that he judged was required and agreed that this one should, most certainly, be found and killed.

But while the people and Rome waited, Marin remained in hiding. Of course Agostino knew where he was, but he would not reveal him just yet. For as desperation grew so, in measure, would his reward.

And, very early in the mornings, Agostino saw the debris from the water on the streets and how the officials came hurriedly to clear it so that the people would not see it increased.

He saw the watery slime climbing gradually higher on the insides of buildings and around the doors of churches the tracings of the foam that tipped the waves in the Lagoon. Remants of unseen tides.

He waited.

For two days the Devil had gone but on the third He made His return. Sebastiano Finetti felt His weight settling around his shoulders as he passed the street-girls at the end of the Ponte di Rialto. He felt the Devil shift position as He turned back to them to wave.

His skin came off much more easily than he had expected. He tore it off in strips which he had scored with a knife, laying them onto the table in front of the cross.

Sebastiano hesitated before putting down his knife, unsure how much would suffice. The Flagellants had been condemned by his church. He had spoken against them himself. But he had known, on other occasions before this one, the comfort that pain could bring. And if a penance were sincerely meant, did it matter if its form came as something other than prayer?

Because he was indeed sorry that he had stood there in his satin skirts and velvet mask, waiting with the other girls in the night. For customers. All sorts. And he was sorry that sometimes a man would select him in preference to one of the girls. If this had been done in error, not all minded on discovering the truth.

He had told the girls that the depth of his voice was a defect from his birth, a result of a clumsy midwife and a tangling round his throat with the cord.

He had said that he did not bare his breasts as they did because he only revealed his body for payment.

There was one girl in particular with whom he had become friendly. She was plump, like a pudding, and her dirty skin smelt of fish. They used to talk while they waited for their custom. Of God. He thought that it was interesting that she wanted to talk of God.

He used to look at her soft, hairless skin, the curving and the dimples, and wish that her body was his. But their friendship of sorts, their closeness, the way that she let him hold her when the wind from the water blew cold was, he knew, as near to that as he could ever hope to come.

She used to sit on his knee if the stones were wet and, as she put her arms around him, he had wondered, more than once, if she knew what she did and if there was as much disguising on her part as his.

He used to let her hold the cross he wore on a chain round his neck. Reassurance for him, or for her?

For all of this, he was indeed sorry.

More weed had appeared since the morning, and in among it were small fish that still flipped upwards for breath. It seemed that the tides no longer confined themselves to darkness.

Agostino pushed his way through the crowds who queued outside the yellow tent. The sign on the flap said that the man who sat there sold the finest perfumed oils. However, it was generally known that, in defiance of the laws forbidding the practice of magical arts, he also told fortunes. Matters such as these were not important to Agostino. He would not be the one to report him.

Cracking his whip at the people who blocked his path, he aimed a blow at the tent for good measure. The man was careless for there were too many who knew what he did. And if it were true that he had knowledge of all things, he should have known that he should not be there.

Agostino rode on.

Constanza stood, naked, in front of the mirror, dipping bread into a glass of wine at her side. 'Do you think my figure a little more rounded than yesterday?' She surveyed herself, questioning. 'I do believe it is.'

Marin did not reply. Of course, for him, the dream had always been preferable. He watched her now, soaking her bread and playing with it.

'A little more rounded perhaps?' Constanza persisted. 'Some here and maybe a curving here?' She moved her hand to indicate where the improvements might begin and asked, 'If other men looked at me, would you be jealous?'

Marin replied with a sigh. 'Why should they not look?'

'But if I went with one who looked ...'

'It is for you to do as you please.'

'You would not come to seize me away?'

'If you wanted to be with me, why would you go?'

Constanza retorted, tilting her head in feigned anger. 'I do not believe that you love me at all.' And it occurred to her then that he had not said he did. It was she who had come to him. She did not ask the question and saw that he seemed relieved.

Turning back to the mirror, she enquired, 'And my breasts? Do they please you?'

Marin smiled. He only wanted her gone. He was not even aware of her thoughts, whether she saw another or not. He only felt what came from the people. One thought was as nothing against the desires of so many.

It seemed Constanza had not noticed that nothing of his wardrobe fitted.

Marin pulled his hat down over his eyes. Some attempt at disguise. He could no longer bear to look at her. He had to be away, if only for an afternoon.

And the idea had come to him that to be down among the people might lessen his fear, in some way dispel the horrors of his imaginings. Or at least prepare him for what was to come so that he could approach it with some sense of peace.

He walked towards the singing in the Campo San Luca, intending to stand in a corner and listen. He knew that he should love them.

On entering the square, he saw that the people had gathered around their shrine and were screaming, red-faced, of their love for him, yet with mouths that were twisted and ugly with rage because still he made them wait.

Marin backed away. No, he did not love them.

People queued outside the yellow tent in the Piazza, carrying small tins of burning herbs to ward off contagion from the air.

A scuffle broke out as latecomers tried to push their way in.

As he passed, Marin saw the fortune-teller emerge to settle the dispute, then turn and beckon to him.

The people who had been waiting looked around to see who it was had been invited ahead of them. Marin tried to walk away but found he could not move. Ice-cold beads of perspiration crept down the back of his neck, his legs twitched and trembled but refused to take him forward. What would be the reaction of the people, he wondered, if they learnt that the one they worshipped now stood among them, rigid with fear?

By his side he heard somebody whisper, 'San Barnabo.' Then the voice of another murmuring agreement.

Marin's legs were shaking to such a degree that he now found it difficult to remain upright. Closing his eyes, he waited for hands to seize him but suddenly heard the crowd behind him scatter at the approach of horse's hooves.

'Wait!' The voice was Agostino's.

Having no other option, Marin waited, only to feel the sweep of Agostino's cloak on his cheek as his horse moved swiftly past. Opening his eyes, Marin saw that it was to the five men who rode with him that Agostino had spoken.

'I tell you again that we will not find him here,' Agostino insisted. 'You think he is such a fool as to be out here in the open? There are other more probable places. Here we are wasting our time. They lie. Can you not see that they do not trust us? They do not want us to find him.'

He cracked his whip at the people to silence them, and then again to make them run. As they ran, Marin found himself able to do the same.

Agostino watched him go. Clearly he had not travelled as far as he thought, was still too close to what he had been before – otherwise why would he have shown mercy?

The Devil had been quiet for some while but, as he walked to the bridge that evening, Sebastiano could hear the tip-tap of His feet beside him. And His arm guiding him along, so gently and with such a devious touch that the pressure was too light to feel.

He found the girl, his friend, huddled down among some boxes, sheltering from the wind. But this evening she seemed troubled and did not jump to meet him as she usually did. He saw that she had been crying but had not taken the trouble to wipe her face, and mucous now mixed with the rain drops running over her lips.

When he reached out with his handkerchief, she drew away, and when he asked if she were sick, she simply shook her head. Taking bread from his bag, he suggested they share it, but her only response was, 'No'.

Her manner began to make him uneasy, so he questioned and questioned, pressing, wheedling until at last she told him.

'Somebody gave me a warning today. He warned me to beware of a bad thing.'

'And what manner of thing was this?'

'He told me to be careful. That there was one who would do me harm.'

The night's rain had deterred all but the most hardy and eager custom, and Sebastiano suggested that, as it was quiet, they walk for a while. Taking her by the arm, he led her into a side-street where they would not be observed, and there he resumed his questioning.

'So who was it that told you this?'

'The man in the Piazza. In the yellow tent.'

'And can you tell me what else he said?'

She looked doubtful, creasing her forehead, starting several sentences without finishing them. Sebastiano smiled. He felt her try to pull away from him. When he did not let her go, she swung quickly round to snatch at his mask.

'Why do you never take it off?' she cried. 'Even when we are alone.'

She continued to talk, saying things that he could not hear clearly because, at the same time, the Devil was speaking so loudly into his ear. Pointing out the rights and wrongs of the matter and offering His advice.

And he and the girl had fought and, at some point, he was unsure as to when, he realised that she had ceased to breathe.

Afterwards, the Devil reminded him to wipe clean his hands and his legs, to smooth her clothes, and even to retie her shawl before he finally left her.

He and the Devil walked home.

With the coverlets drawn up over his head, Sebastiano prayed for forgiveness, for God in His wisdom to understand that these had been the acts of another, not his. And that, in all probability, it was only because of his devotion to God that the Devil had chosen him. To drive him, powerless, to do these things which were so opposed to his nature.

For a moment Sebastiano imagined himself as the precious pawn between God and the Devil, each fighting for the privilege of his service.

Before first light he was at the house of Lorenzo Spinelli, a man who worked in the office of the Inquisition. A man of reliability.

Struggling to retain his balance, Sebastiano stood in his gondola and threw stones at the windows until a servant opened the door. Lorenzo appeared in his nightshirt with his hair still curled up in a net.

Sebastiano leapt from his boat and seized Lorenzo's arm. 'I have come to report a practicing of the magical arts.'

Lorenzo nodded. There was no need for words. They both knew that the crime provided sure ground for execution.

Once the yellow tent had been surrounded, three men went inside to pull Ettore out. Sebastiano remained some distance behind them so that he would be hidden from view. Moving pieces of weed with the toe of his boot, he wondered if they were all to die, and whether the time had finally come for him to pledge his loyalty. It occurred to him that it might be refused. The idea that a time of reckoning approached unnerved him.

Ettore fought back, twisting and wriggling when the men tried to carry him. So they beat him with sticks until he was still. They put a sack over his head and bound him with rope into a blanket.

'Can you look into the future, Signor Fortune-teller,' one of them asked, 'and tell us how many rats there will be to keep you company in your cell? And how many days it will be until you burn?'

Despite the blood and the loose teeth in his mouth, Ettore was tempted to laugh out loud. How was it that he could predict the future for others, yet his own remained an impenetrable fog?

Anything of importance entirely shrouded until it had come upon him.

Agostino rode slowly out of the Piazza, looking at the people around him and reminding himself that, with a few words, he could condemn any one of them to death. He paused to decide whose face it was that today displeased him most.

And had Ettore foreseen all this? Had it been written already, the heights to which he, Agostino, would climb? Would there have been more lasting satisfaction from knowing that it had? Recently, something of his peace had diminished.

He passed a group of politicians discussing the price of their votes, but today he did not stop to listen. Across the square, he saw some soldiers of the Inquisition put the fortune-teller onto a cart and take him away. Idly, Agostino wondered who it was that, in the end, had been responsible for the man's betrayal.

Meanwhile the dying continued, and the Administration sealed off one area after another. Yet the barriers they erected to prevent the removal of corpses lasted only for a day at the most before being broken down.

Marin did not leave his rooms.

Still Constanza did not remark on his appearance, the fact that it was changing daily. And when he asked her, casually, if she thought he looked in any way different, he was amused to see that it took her a while to reply.

Eventually, she said that she thought his gain in weight was an improvement and that it had made him more handsome.

Constanza had always agreed with those who said she had no talent for thought and now, much as she tried, explanations did not come easily.

She could not understand how Marin was so changed since the night of the dinner. Yet, if asked to describe in what way, she would not have been able to do so. And the muddle in her head grew worse.

She walked into the dining room and lit the sticks of incense that she had bought from the market. 'The man said that their essence will protect us from sickness.'

Gesturing his approval, Marin smiled in a way that he hoped seemed kind. Did she love him? What did she see? He was not certain but had noticed the confusion in her eyes and guessed that he was its cause.

As they sat down to eat, the voices of the people could be heard, singing, from the squares and from a small gathering somewhere in the street below.

Marin spoke. Not from any desire for advice but to hear the

fact of the matter uttered out loud. That now he had no other choice of listener, only one more thing he was powerless to alter.

Speaking softly, he told Constanza that it was for him the people sang and it was to him they looked to save the city. He said that if he came to them as they wanted, then, well ...

He was interrupted by the clatter of Constanza's fork. 'The Saviour?' she asked. 'You are the Saviour?'

'That is what they say.'

Constanza tried to consider the situation. She imagined herself by the side of the man who had saved the city, riding in triumph through its streets, and searched in her mind for the colour of the dress she would wear. Or if he did not survive how, weeping inconsolably at his grave, she would remove her veil so that the other mourners were better able to see her face.

Did she love him? She was not sure. She only wanted the muddle in her head to stop, and only if he were no longer there would things be any different.

'My darling,' she said, tapping his hand with her fork, 'you must go to the people. Your people.'

Marin placed his hand on hers. 'Tomorrow.'

There had never been any question of choice, only that as to how long it would take him to see this.

Agostino rode into the Piazza as dawn was breaking. Mist rose in sleepy swirls from the water, joining with the gathering light to form shimmering veils of palest pink and lilac that were swept up and dispersed by the wind before drifting back to hang, trembling, as before.

Despite the hour, a crowd had already begun to gather for the trial and the executions, sitting on the ground around the stage at the columns, unpacking the food they had brought.

The prisoners were led into a wooden cage next to the stage and the pyre. The fortune-teller already lay on the floor there, still hooded and wrapped in his blanket. It seemed that none of them thought of escape. No attempts to fight or to run. One, on his knees, turned like a cat in its bed to find the right place to pray. Two others, a man and a woman, held hands and faced the water, so that they could watch their last sunrise together.

Crouched next to the Palazzo Ducale, Lelio watched, envying their imminent returning home and the miraculous laying to rest.

Overcome by his thoughts, he climbed into his cart and pressed himself onto the bodies for comfort.

Walking out to the cage, Sebastiano looked down at the figure of the fortune-teller who would no longer be able to fill the minds of the wretched with his false mumblings and lies.

That same dawn saw Marin walk slowly into the Piazza. Even now there had come no sense of peace or acceptance. Looking across the square to the prisoners' cage, he wondered if they faced the day with better grace than he did.

Stall-holders lit braziers against the November chill and spoke amongst themselves, not noticing that, when their backs were turned, a boy in rags hurtled from stall to stall, stealing his food for the day. Marin recalled a time when he had done the same.

He stretched his legs, surprised that nobody paid him any attention, then first one stall-holder, then another, began to point. Ceasing to speak, they approached him and sat, not daring to come too close.

And although not a word of his arrival was spoken, as the Piazza began to fill, newcomers saw what happened and they too came to sit in silence. The assembly in front of him grew, their faces raised, expectant.

All this was watched by the officials present to organise the executions. Unsure whether the people should be moved on or whether, under current circumstances, this gathering should be encouraged, they muttered among themselves before, in agreement, they too sat down to wait.

Sebastiano remained next to the prisoners' cage, unable to decide if he should go with the others or not. So shaken by recent events, he was incapable of conclusive thought. He did not know whether he was more ashamed of his actions or of the weakness that caused him to feel shame.

Almost five hundred people sat huddled against the cold, the only sound that of their shuffling in surreptitious effort to be as near to the front as they could.

The silence was suddenly broken by the tolling of the Marangona, and as the crowd found voice and rose as one with a roar, they stretched out their arms, reaching forward to Marin.

Leaping to his feet, Marin ran, only vaguely aware that the feet that moved and the body they carried were his, as if he witnessed their passage through the intermittent opening and closing of a door to a distant room.

Agostino watched as the people chased after him. Saw how instead of running to escape, he came towards the water and the stage, bringing the people with him.

They followed, jubilant, singing, chanting, trampling anything that stood in their path.

On arrival at the prisoners' cage, they swept Sebastiano from the ground, held him aloft and turned him around on their arms before throwing him aside. The knowledge that they were to be saved had rendered them drunk, and they fell on each other, embracing with wild shouts and laughter.

So Agostino realised that, in all probability, it was only he who had seen it was Marin who opened the door to the prisoners' cage. Watching the fortune-teller wriggle free from his blanket, Agostino imagined that even now he would rush in the wrong direction, remaining careless to the end.

However, when the fortune-teller jumped from the cage, Agostino could not believe his eyes. Ettore. Could it really have been Ettore? He knew without doubt that it was. But by now all the prisoners had been absorbed into the freedom of the crowd.

The celebrations grew quiet as the people realised that Marin too had disappeared. When they caught sight of him again, he was at the back of their throng, standing on top of a broken vegetable stall. They looked at each other, unable to understand how he had passed through them unseen.

With a cry, they turned and ran, and Marin sank to a crouch as they encircled him.

Narrowing his eyes, Agostino observed the man that Marin had become, the new bulk and size of his body, the sinew that stood out on his neck. But how far beneath the Saviour's skin had Marin concealed himself? Close enough to the surface to make him willing accomplice to the Saviour's actions?

He watched Marin, as Saviour, stretch up his arms, seeming even now as if he had been summoned at short notice to play a role for which he had not prepared. Why did God toss His gifts so carelessly to those too weak to carry them?

Marin stood, seeming to blend with the air rather than breathe it. The outlines of his body blurred still further, as in quick succession it began to take the shape of many others. Men, women, children, all so rapidly that it was impossible for the eye to follow, to perceive where one ended before sliding into the next. Impossible, too, to tell whether Marin's tears were those of laughter. One woman held up a crucifix and screamed.

As Marin stretched up his arms to the sky, mist curled down to embrace him, and a rain started up, the drops of water changing to small beads of light as soon as they touched his skin. The agitation in the wind made a noise reminiscent of singing.

Agostino recognised men from Rome in the crowd, riding slowly forward until they were in front of the stall. He did not bring himself to their notice.

Marin continued to shift and change. Now not one form after another, but the mixing of many at once. The men from Rome drew closer still.

All at once, an acrid smell filled the air. An odour that brought to mind medicines stacked on an apothecary's shelves. It caused the horses of the men from Rome to rear back in fright.

Agostino saw that Marin smelt it too, and that it startled him, woke him, so that for an instant he was still, there only as himself, before jumping down from the stall to run.

Two women reached out, clung to him and would not let him go. The horsemen moved in. People were screaming, hurling themselves forward to touch him.

And in all the confusion it took them a while to realise that Marin was no longer there.

Constanza was waiting when Marin arrived at his rooms. She did not come to kiss him, and she said nothing as he took off his cloak. She did not answer his greeting.

'Did you go to the Piazza today?' he asked.

She nodded.

'You saw?'

She nodded again. 'I saw what you were. What you did. Those things.'

'I tried to explain.'

'You did not. You said you were a Saviour. You did not say you were ...' She moved her hands to make ugly shapes in the air. 'You did not say you were ...'

Marin sat and looked down at the floor. Then he looked up and with his own hands imitated the shapes she had made. 'The changings, yes. It is what I am. It is what happens. I ...'

Constanza motioned for him to be silent. 'Stop. I do not want to hear the lies of a demon.'

Marin stood up. 'A demon? I ...'

She threw a glass at him. 'I said I did not want to hear your lies.'

Holding out his arms, Marin stepped towards her. A wish to comfort her and, just for a moment, a desire to be held himself.

'Do not touch me.' She covered her head with her hands as if she feared he might take flight and swoop at her from above. Edging past him, she left.

Marin heard her feet scrambling on the stairs.

In the district of Dorsoduro, that night, on the two streets behind the church of San Nicolo dei Mendicoli, every single inhabitant died.

Marin dreamt. Pieces of a puzzle assembled out of sight, dropping at random into his head. On hearing Constanza's voice, he tried to push her away.

'No, wake. Wake now. Get up. Before it is too late.'

He opened his eyes to find her there at his bedside, her tears dropping onto his face.

'Go now, before they come.' Crying, pleading, as he did not move, she tried to roll him from the bed. 'Forgive me. Forgive me. I was too frightened ...I told them where you were. They are coming now. They will be here at any minute.' She tugged at his arm, screaming at him. 'Go *now*.'

Half-asleep, Marin stumbled down the stairs in his nightshirt, reaching the street to see a mob approaching with torches. Quickly he pressed himself into the shadows of a doorway, turning his back to them as they passed, wondering how they had not smelt his fear.

They passed, prancing as if demented, their voices cracking as they called out for the one they loved. The one they knew loved them too, so much that he would offer his life and his blood in exchange for theirs, to be given to God in appeasement.

He heard Constanza's screams as they dragged her into the street, her denials that she had warned him. And he heard the voice of Sebastiano Finetti, telling the people to stay back, that it was for him and only him, the Administrator, to find a suitable punishment.

Venturing out only at dawn and at dusk, Marin saw how the shifting shadows and the eddies of the mist, as it rose or fell, conspired together to hide him.

Piles of brine-scented dead littered the streets. When he stopped to touch at their lips with his blood, he noticed that now they did not always open their eyes. Indication that his time was limited. But periods of true lucidity were now rare and mercifully brief.

In the Piazza, a float was being built for the procession which would mark the feast day of San Barnabo. And some women sat weaving a carpet of laurel leaves to cover the throne where San Barnabo would sit and, with those leaves that were spare, they made a wreath for him to wear in his hair.

During the day the people there laboured with hammers and nails and wood and thread, and at night they sat round their work and sang their songs by candlelight. Traditional hymns judged to have a content that might please San Barnabo and new verses composed in his honour, in case that would please him more.

With one breath they sang of how much they loved him and with the next they chanted for the gift of his life.

All of them knew, although none of them said, that if San Barnabo did not offer his life, give himself to the waters of the Lagoon, then they would give it for him.

A celebration had been organised for the eve of the feast day. Fireworks were let off from boats moored at the quayside and the Piazza was filled with clowns, jugglers and acrobats. In the corner nearest the Mercerie, a girl danced. Despite the freezing temperature that January evening, she wore only a flimsy shift, and the sound of the bells on her slippers carried across the square.

Officials from the Administration, present to maintain order and to ensure that no damage was done to the float, paused in their patrol and watched. Nudging each other, they pointed at the person with her, who collected money from the crowd and, when the girl came near, touched her with the familiarity of a lover. This person's figure and face were concealed by a cloak and a hood, but all the same there was something about his stance that reminded them of Sebastiano Finetti.

But, of course, they knew that Finetti was dead. Taken by the sickness the day before.

Years later, people said that at the dawn of San Barnabo's feast day they had seen fish flying through the sky as birds, and that the air had roared and sucked around their ears, flattening their soaked hair to their heads.

They said that when San Barnabo had come from the Pescaria, walking towards the float, they had seen there was already blood on his hands and his feet, spilling in preparation.

Now they stopped their singing and, as silence fell, they watched him come, parting to make a path as he passed and then closing the way behind him.

The men from Rome signalled to each other. Whether Venice was saved or not was of no concern to them.

Marin had not slept for days and found the ascent to the throne almost impossible. Yet no one moved to help.

When the men from Rome rode forward, Agostino was at their head.

Some sat on the shoulders of others. And those with no room to stand nor shoulders to support them hung perilously from the windows and sides of buildings.

As the Contessa watched the man's slow climb onto the float, she caught sight of some Bravi standing close by. Recognising them, she looked round the square for Piero. She saw him speaking to his men, calling them to order. His figure and his face not as she once had wished them but with a perfection of a sweeter kind. That which she had run from.

Piero told his men that he was leaving and handed them their payment, including a portion of his own. Some said their farewell, dispersed into the crowd. When others hesitated and made as if to stay, he shook his head.

The sun rose, its pale rays seeming to wash the air in readiness.

Lelio sat on his cart. He could not breathe and tapped at his chest, causing pieces to break free and fly up. Brushing at what he thought was an insect on his cheek, he found it was a tear.

The signal was given, and the float began to move. Marin saw the Piazza, the people in it, those who danced around his throne, dissolve to mist, fall as dust. He breathed in water with the air and closed his eyes, returning.

The men from Rome were now at the side of the float. Agostino beckoned them on so that the five were tightly on his heels, pushing through the crowd. And when he judged them close enough, he lifted his legs, swung round on his horse and thrust out so quickly with his sword that the first three did not see it move. It must have seemed to them, if it seemed at all, that a shaft of sunlight had cut their throats.

But a sudden sway of excitement from the crowd caused Agostino to lose his balance, and the two men who had been a little way behind the others, in an instant, pressed down flat to their horses. Urging the animals over the crowd, they reached up and caught hold of the float to climb.

Agostino leapt from his own horse onto that of the man nearest, punched him aside, pulled himself up onto the float and flung himself at Marin, carrying him off the throne so that they fell together to the ground. Amid screams of fury and disbelief, Agostino pushed him free.

But the crowd closed in and, baying and yowling, they trapped him. Some wanting to embrace him, hold his flesh next to theirs, were quickly pulled away by others who wished to put him back onto the throne. Marin felt his muscles tear and knew that, within minutes, he would be ripped asunder.

Others turned on Agostino in rage. They hurled themselves at him, beating him with sticks, pinning him against the float.

As the two surviving Romans seized him, Agostino heard Piero's voice, the rallying call of the Bravi and the answering shouts of 'Aye!' from various points in the crowd.

Everywhere confusion as the Bravi moved in to attack. The people could not distinguish between friend and foe. They began to fight with each other.

As the men from Rome held their swords to Agostino's chest, he saw Piero's sword remove their heads which fell spraying the crowd with blood. And he saw Marin break free and run.

Raising his hand in what might have been a greeting or a salute, Piero rode away. He left on the ground behind him the stripe that denoted his rank of Bravi captain.

Lelio was sitting, talking to those in his cart, when he saw Death come running from the Piazza.

Hardly daring to hope that he had been forgiven, he stood to greet Him and this time Death did not run away. Instead He stopped, pulling laurel leaves from His hair as He smiled. Lelio tried to hide his shyness.

Death held out His arms. Lelio trembled, pushing his cart away. And as he pressed himself into the folds of His cloak, he saw in the water, the reflection of Death and himself entwined.

The sun sank. A fiery orb, deep red and glowing, casting its colour in vivid smears, streaming onto the water.

Agostino found Marin floating face down in the Rio delle Colone. There was no pulse at his wrists or his neck.

Removing the dirt from Marin's eyes and his mouth, Agostino wiped his face clean before touching his finger to the blood at Marin's temple to taste. Then pulling at the wound to open it further, he pressed his flask against it.

He wrapped his own cloak around Marin and, as he lowered him back down to the waters, they dipped and parted to receive him.

Agostino rode south towards Umbria and the place of which Ettore had spoken. But before he reached the Campo Rusolo, he heard splashing from the water behind him, followed seconds later by the sound of somebody climbing noisily out. He did not turn back to look.

Marin gazed at his reflection in the water and brushed back his hair. He pulled Agostino's cloak more tightly around him and as he walked towards the Rialto, he saw that the weed on the streets had dried.

Stopping at the bridge, he called out to the street-girls, smiling and staring at each so intently that he could see they thought him mad. They began to throw stones at him, and laughing, he walked on.

The body of a small child had been abandoned in a doorway at the end of the Calle dei Cinque. There was a notice tied round his neck stating he had died from the sickness and should be taken away for burial.

Scraping open one of his fingers with a stone, Marin wiped blood around the child's mouth. He kissed the boy's cheek, holding him close for a moment before the child struggled free and ran away.